Love His Heart

Love His Heart

Jennifer Johnson

LOVE HIS HEART
Copyright © 2018, Jennifer Johnson
Trade Paperback ISBN: 978-1-946608-24-6

Front Cover Image: iStock

Trade Paperback Release, January 2019

Media > Books > Fiction > Romance Novels
Categories:

This print edition is published by author/owner Johnson via El Roi Publishing

LOVE HIS HEART

What happens when your life ended though your heart keeps beating?

Katrina Aaron has never gotten over the death of her husband three years ago. When she accepts an anonymous gift for a two week respite at a beach house, she meets Chef Trey Marshall. Trey's joy of life intrigues Katrina and awakens in her a desire to live and love again.

But their meeting was no chance encounter, and Trey has a secret which could destroy Katrina's newfound faith in life or bring her happiness she never imagined she'd feel again.

Chapter One

Her cell phone rang. Again.

Katrina glared at the number displayed on the screen.

Why didn't Dinah just give up already? Katrina had told her no, and her answer hadn't changed each time Dinah had asked about the Celebration of Life dinner.

No.

Not the first time Dinah asked two years ago. Not last year, and it wasn't going to happen this year either.

Time wasn't going to make Katrina change her mind. She appreciated that some people felt the need to commemorate a significant event in their lives, but as far as Katrina was concerned revisiting the worst episode in her life was not something she would ever do.

So, no, Dinah, I will not talk to you.

The screen morphed into the picture of Jinx, her cat. Tension she hadn't realized was there eased in her chest. Katrina moved her cell phone further away on the desk and turned her attention to her computer screen and the spread sheet open before her.

Back to work.

Her cell phone chirped indicating she had a new voice mail, but Katrina ignored it. She liked Dinah, but she was not going to talk to her.

A knock sounded on the door, and it opened a few inches. Beth, the receptionist, appeared.

"Hi," she smiled. The door opened wider. "There's a visitor here for you. Dinah Windingham."

Katrina shook her head and rose from her chair. "Tell her I'm sorry, but I can't see—"

Dinah stepped into Katrina's line of vision from

behind Beth.

Katrina sighed.

Beth, chagrin apparent on her face, gripped the door. "Umm. I'm sorry. She said you two knew each other."

"We do." Katrina moved around the desk toward the door.

The receptionist backed into the hallway, and Dinah stood at the threshold. She smiled kindly at Beth. "Thank you."

Beth looked at Katrina for affirmation or criticism, some clue about what she should do next.

"It's all right, Beth. Truly."

Beth gave her an apologetic look and left.

"Come in," Katrina said, not really wanting to issue the invitation, but guilt and obligation brought forth the words from her.

Dinah had been extremely compassionate during that—

No. Don't think about it. Don't even think about what happened.

"Hi, Katrina. It's been a long time." Dinah said, her eyes warm.

Katrina turned, folding her arms over her chest. Though the security of putting her desk between them called to her, Katrina perched on its edge instead. She did not want Dinah to think she was welcome here.

Dinah entered the room and sat on the chair in front of Katrina's desk. "Thank you for seeing me. How have you been doing?"

"I've been avoiding you."

"I didn't ask what you've been doing, I asked how have you been doing."

Katrina felt her resolve slip. Dinah had been so good at comfort. It was probably why she was so excellent at her job.

"I know what you asked." And getting into it would only bring up feelings Katrina didn't want to feel or even acknowledge.

"I'm not here to talk about the Celebration of Life or to convince you to go."

"Really?" Katrina didn't quite believe her, though she doubted Dinah had a dishonest bone in her body. The desire to trust her battled with suspicion as to why she was here.

Dinah crossed her ankles. "I know you just want to put everything that happened behind you. I get that."

"Then why do you contact me every year to try to get me to go?"

"What you did saved the lives of five people and benefitted the lives of four others. It's a way to say thank you."

Katrina stood and walked to the window. The two Bradford pear trees in the yard stood sentry at the walkway. Soon the leaves would turn a brilliant scarlet, a testimony of the beauty of autumn.

The season of dying.

"I don't want to be thanked. I don't want to go and be reminded of...." Katrina let the sentence go unfinished.

"Do you like the beach?"

The unexpected question caused her to turn toward Dinah. "What?"

"The beach." She opened the folder she'd tucked next to her in the chair and pulled out a glossy pamphlet from the pocket. "Two weeks at a beach house in Dusky Sands, Florida. It's on the panhandle, and not developed, so it's somewhat remote. You'd enjoy it, I think." She opened the pamphlet, perusing the images there. "It looks lovely."

"I thought the Celebration was always in January," Katrina said.

"It is. The stay at the beach house is an anonymous

gift." The woman paused, and Katrina wondered if she did so for effect, "For you."

Katrina shook her head. "I can't accept something like that. Let someone else have it."

"The gift is designated for you." Dinah shrugged. "The house is reserved in your name a month from today."

"I don't have time to take two weeks off."

Dinah shrugged. "If you don't use the house, it will just be empty for those two weeks."

"That's silly. Someone should use it."

Dinah rose and lay the pamphlet on Katrina's desk. "The gift is nontransferable. The donor...."

Katrina flinched at Dinah's use of the word.

Dinah paused. "The gift-giver specifically stated that the beach house was for your use as a respite to come and go during those two weeks." She moved toward the door.

"Then it's someone I know?" Respite. What was that? Did anyone ever get respite from the ache of losing someone they loved?

Dinah crooked her head in apology. "I'm sorry. It's an anonymous gift. I can't disclose the identity of the source of the gift."

Katrina noticed she was being careful not to say the word donor again.

"I'll have to think about it."

"All right. There's a business card there attached to the pamphlet with the agent who you contact to make the arrangements."

Katrina glanced at the paper, but didn't move to her desk toward it.

"You take care of yourself, all right?" Dinah approached her, and gave her a brief hug, surprising her a bit. The human contact felt good, and Katrina realized it had been a while since she'd given or received a hug.

Shame niggled at her for avoiding this woman. Katrina

raised her arms and returned the embrace. "I'm sorry I haven't returned your phone calls."

Dinah patted her shoulder and stepped back. She gave her a knowing look. "No, you're not, but it's all right. We all move at our own pace." She stepped to the doorway. "Call me some time. I still want to know how you're doing."

With those words, Dinah turned and left.

That evening, Katrina sat at her desk working on the GoPro's audit. What a mess.

A knock sounded on her door, and Brenda, her boss entered, wearing a sequined black top. Her hair and make-up fresh, and a sweet scent of her perfume wafted in the air.

"It was quitting time two and a half hours ago." She tapped her high-heeled shoe, but on the carpet, it was more for effect than annoyance.

"I know. I'm leaving in a little while."

"Hmm-mmm." She approached the desk and picked up the pamphlet still lying where Dinah had set it. "What's this?"

Katrina didn't answer. If she did, she'd have two women nagging her about going.

"Oh, this looks beautiful." Her eyes sparkled in excitement. "Are you going on vacation? When?"

Katrina shook her head. "I don't have time to go on vacation."

"Sure, you do, but you don't. Not since…. So, what is this, then, a business workshop? I haven't seen anything about Dusky Sands, Florida. Where is that?" She flipped the pamphlet over. "Huh. No map. Guess they think the gorgeous house and picturesque white sandy beach is incentive enough to find it without a map provided."

"Someone—an anonymous someone—is giving me a two week respite there next month. It's not you, is it?"

Brenda arched an eyebrow at her. "Seriously? You know I'm not that subtle. I want everyone to know of my generosity, especially when it can be a tax write-off."

"Dinah Windingham from the Foundation came by today with the pamphlet. Their Celebration of Life dinner is coming up, and I thought that's what she wanted to talk to me about. Instead, she tells me someone has rented a house at the beach for me."

"What a wonderful gift. You should go."

"But other than her, I don't know anyone there. Why would this person want to pay for me to have a beach house as a respite? That's how she worded it, a respite to come and go for two weeks. Why would someone I don't even know think I needed a respite?"

Brenda planted her fisted hands at her hips. "Perhaps because your husband died almost three years ago, and you are still grieving. Go to the beach. I'm your boss, so you have to do what I say."

****

Jumping out of an airplane must terrify him. He knew this because of the rapid staccato beat emanating from his chest. Loud enough, he imagined, that the other jumpers would have heard it except for the deafening drone of the Cessna's engine.

Trey didn't feel terrified though. Exhilarated? Yes. Happy? Absolutely. Thankful? Always. But not scared, even at nine thousand feet. The palpitations testified to his excitement.

That's good.

Give that heart muscle a work out so it would last him another seventy or so years.

Trey ran his thumb below his collar bone in a caress, thankful again for a beating heart which meant he was alive and well enough to jump out of a plane.

Scott nudged him and indicated with a hand signal it

was time. He slipped out of the open door and held onto the side. Another jumper, Daniel, exited, but grabbed onto the ledge. Trey, who sat at the threshold, took a deep breath and slid forward into nothingness.

Even with his helmet on, his ears rang as the wind screamed past him at 120 miles per hour. They'd planned a couple of formations after jumping. Daniel grabbed his hand, and he reached for Scott, and they made contact, a trio of men hurtling to the earth with clasped hands. Letting go, Daniel—the showoff—somersaulted. He and Scott each held his feet and held hands. Trey glanced down at the altimeter Velcroed to his arm.

In only a few seconds, the plummeting would end.

He'd pull the cord and his parachute would deploy, then he'd drift downward to the airfield.

5000 feet. It was time. He felt for the handle and pulled, his body jerked as the chute caught the wind, fully open now, and he sighed, a little relieved, if he admitted it. It was the first time he'd folded his parachute without any help or supervision. He congratulated himself that he'd done it right and that he wouldn't die today.

He couldn't see Scott or Daniel above him. They were a lot more experienced and usually opened later, though they'd warned him not to go past 5000 feet.

"Gravity will not forgive you if you miss your window, buddy," Scott had said with a lift of his brow. "We've logged a whole lot more jumps than you, so you pull between five and six, you got me?"

Yeah, Trey got him.

At the more leisurely descent, Trey surveyed the canvas below him—the checkered landscape of fields, trees, and neighborhoods, and the larger expanse that was the airfield. Further out, he saw ribbons he knew to be roads and highways, and small ants moving along them were automobiles.

This time he'd land on his feet, he thought, as the ground approached. He attempted a running landing, but he connected too quickly. He got two steps on terra firma, before his speed tripped him, and he tumbled several times before coming to a heap on the ground, with a mouthful of dirt. Somehow, he came to a stop on his back, and he lay spread eagle and watched the sky and his two friends sail toward the earth.

Both hit the ground with a few sprinting steps, as he had attempted to do, and they both succeeded in a lateral landing. Trey sat up, happy at their skill, and hoping they would have one more go at it before they called it quits.

"You okay?" Scott called as he wound up his chute.

"Yeah." Trey bent his legs and got to his feet. He shrugged out of the shoulder straps.

"You're bleeding," Daniel said. "You land on your feet, not your face, Chef."

"Easier said than done." Trey wiped his sleeve against his cheekbone, and saw the arc of red on the material.

"If you'll pull your chute down with both hands, it should slow you down enough so you land upright. But if you're coming down too quick, just go ahead and roll with it. Less harm that way," Scott said.

"You guys always land on your feet," Trey countered.

"Not when we were green, and especially not landing too fast. You'll break a leg if you keep coming in so quick."

"Can we make another jump?" Trey asked.

Daniel surveyed his friend. "One more. Maybe two if you tell the pilot you'll cook tonight. Seems like you can get what you want when you pull out your apron."

"Carpe diem," Trey said.

"Always." Daniel lifted his hand, and they high-fived.

They walked across the field where a tarp lay with their duffel bags. Scott reached down and picked up a water bottle. Unscrewing the cap, he drank half of the contents.

Loud buzzing signaled the plane would land soon. Trey felt around in his own pack and picked up his cell phone. He unlocked it and saw he had a new text. Scrolling to his message board, he smiled at the news.

Key delivered to client. Confirmed arrival day at beach house.

"Carpe arrival diem."

Seize the arrival day.

Chapter Two

Katrina maneuvered her Subaru Outback into the driveway of the house. Though it was nearly one in the morning, a pole with a lighthouse shaped lantern illuminated the yard. Cute.

Light shone through the white gauze curtains at the windows, a nice gesture as she hadn't relished the thought of entering a dark house so late at night, especially one she'd never been in before.

Well, here I am, anonymous gift giver. Here to grudgingly enjoy my respite.

Brenda had insisted she take her vacation, had encouraged, cajoled, harped, and threatened going so far as to purchase a suitcase and bring it over to the house.

"You're going," she had said holding up the matching make-up bag. "Now, give me instructions on how to take care of this precious cat of yours in your absence, and start packing."

Resigned, Katrina had done as Brenda had commanded. She'd awoken early this morning to drive the sixteen hours to Dusky Sands, thinking two hours ago maybe she should have made it a two-day trip and gotten a hotel room on the way. But it had only been ninety more miles, and by the time she would settle into a hotel room, she probably wouldn't have been able to sleep anyway.

Now she was here, and she could sleep in tomorrow, or rather today, if she wanted. She could sleep the entire two weeks even. Though the 13 days ahead of her loomed, a chasm of empty days and nights with no work to occupy her and only a bag full of books and a digital reader from her to be read pile which had been accumulating for at least five years. She hadn't had her reader on in so long, she wasn't even sure it still worked.

With the key pinched between thumb and index finger, Katrina inserted it in the lock and the front door swung open revealing a spacious wood-floored room with white couches and a white brocade lounger, a blue checked blanket draped neatly across it. Matching pillows on the love seat drew her eye. The sparse neatness soothed her, and she set her suitcase down, toeing off her shoes.

She walked across the room and opened the door thinking it was to a back deck, but it was a sunroom, and Katrina's breath caught at the moonlit beach and ocean displayed by the plate glass windows. Sitting on the cushioned wicker couch, she tucked her feet under her and stared at the view before her. The waves mesmerized her, their foam vanishing then reappearing as crowns on the water.

Leaning against the fluffy cushion, she propped her head on her arm.

Oh, Eric. I wish you were here. You would love this.

A soft cough awoke her. At least, she thought it was a cough. Where was she? She squinted her eyes. Oh, right. The respite beach house, but who had turned on all the lights? When she'd sat down, only a lamp had burned in the corner.

"Excuse me. Hi. Don't be afraid."

A man knelt on the floor near the window. Katrina raised her head peering at him. Was he real? And since he had appeared here in this house, did he think telling her not to be afraid would work if she were afraid?"

"Are you okay?" he asked.

If he was going to hurt her, would he ask if she were okay?

He stood, his hands outstretched in a gesture of trustworthiness. He wore faded jeans, a red T-shirt and sneakers that had seen better days. "The front door was open. I knocked, but no one answered. I thought something must be wrong."

Katrina sat up and rubbed her eyes against the brightness of the room. How long had she slept? It was full day. She looked out the window at the sunlight glinting off the water.

"Have you had breakfast yet?" the stranger asked.

"Umm. No."

The corner of his mouth turned up. "We're in the space of brunch now unless you are one of those early lunch eaters?"

Katrina attempted to smooth down her hair. She'd fallen asleep on the couch with the front door open, and there was a strange man in the room with her who was asking her about breakfast and brunch. What kind of weirdo was he? She placed her feet on the floor and stood.

"Did you want something?" she asked, attempting to mask her wariness.

"I'm the chef. I'm here to cook for you." He stepped forward and offered a hand in greeting.

Katrina glanced at his hand then his face. "No one said anything about a chef."

"Really? Well, how can you have a respite if you have to cook for yourself?" He shrugged and walked toward the door into the living room.

Respite. Huh. There was that word again. He must come with the beach house and Dinah forgot to tell her.

Katrina followed him. "Some people like to cook."

He walked through the room around a counter separating it from the kitchen. A large basket grabbed her attention. Filled with flowers, it was beautiful, but something was off about it. She touched a coral colored rose.

"It's cantaloupe." He had opened the refrigerator, and

he closed it. "Everything is edible except the basket itself. Even the flower stems though they're peanut brittle. You don't have a peanut allergy, do you?"

Katrina drew her hand back. It was gorgeous. "No."

"Go ahead."

She looked at him. He leaned against the counter, as if the kitchen were his. The warmth of his expression radiated throughout the room. "I made it for you." His sincerity and near excitement caused her to watch him. It was as if he really had made it for her, just her.

"You made this?"

"Yep." The spell broke with his answer, and turning, he opened a cabinet. Reaching inside, he brought a canister down and set it on the counter top. "Do you want some coffee?"

"Okay. This is too pretty to eat."

He set about making the coffee. "No, it's not. I made it to be enjoyed with your eyes and your mouth. It's fresh. I brought it in this morning."

"Gee, it must have taken you most of the night." She retrieved her cell phone from her purse and took a couple of pictures of the basket. "What did you say your name was?"

When he didn't answer, Katrina turned to him. He had stopped the coffee preparation and looked at her. "I'm Trey, but you can call me Chef."

She laid her phone on the counter and moved to offer a handshake. "I'm Katrina. I'm sorry I didn't shake hands earlier. You were unexpected."

His grip was warm and firm. Formal, almost, and he drew his hand back then rubbed below his collar bone. With his other hand he spooned the coffee beans in a grinder and sprinkled in some cinnamon before pressing the power button.

"I apologize if I startled you. I usually meet with my

clients early on so I know how best to serve them."

Katrina plucked the cantaloupe rose and bit into it. The fruit was cold and perfectly ripe. "Really, this isn't necessary." She finished it off, and reached for a bud shaped strawberry, nibbling it. "I'm not much of an eater."

Chef's brows drew together in a frown.

"What I mean is, I eat, but, you know, it's just to eat."

He crossed his arms over his chest, studying her.

She slid a leaf made from a grape off the stem and popped it in her mouth. Of course, if she could get fruit this good at the market, maybe she would enjoy it more. She touched a spray of baby's breath. "What's this made out of?"

"Anjou pears and marshmallow cream. You're hungry." He placed a plate and cloth-napkin-wrapped silverware on the counter in front of a barstool. "At the base of the stems is a melon bowl with yogurt cream cheese fruit dip in it. I can cook you a proper brunch, if you would like something more substantial."

Katrina sat on the bar stool. "I appreciate this, but it seems too much." She chose a cluster of frosted cherries and set them on her plate then dipped some of the yogurt beside them with the serving spoon he placed near her.

"Eggs Benedict?"

Katrina grimaced.

"You don't like Eggs Benedict?"

"I'm not really a fan of eggs at all."

"Ah." Chef nodded. "Thank you for telling me. Any other food dislikes or allergies?"

"I'm allergic to shellfish."

"Just shellfish? No other kind of fish?"

"No."

"Okay. No other foods I should avoid?"

"No. I'm easy to please, but, like I said, I don't really need a chef." Was that kiwi disguised as a tulip? Wow. This guy had talent. "How'd you get the kiwi firm enough to mold it into a flower?"

"Gelatin."

He put a small bowl next to her plate.

"What's this?"

"Granola. How do you like your coffee?"

"Just black."

A shadow crossed his face, as if she disappointed him somehow. The coffee maker beeped, and he turned his back to her, working on the cup of coffee, she surmised. She picked a daisy with coconut petals and the face of pineapple. This man was no chef. He was an artist.

In a moment, he placed a steaming mug in front of her.

"Thank you." She raised the coffee to her mouth, but paused detecting a hint of something besides coffee. "This isn't just black coffee." Accusation present in her tone.

"A tad of cinnamon."

She shot him a piercing look knowing cinnamon wasn't the only add-in. He smiled unrepentantly. "Oh, just try it. If you hate it, I'll fix you another cup."

Katrina didn't like surprises, and she didn't like secrets, not even as an ingredient in her coffee.

She held the cup and gave Chef her best audit face. "I just want some plain coffee."

He turned his back again, pouring coffee in another mug. He set it in front of her. She set the first cup down and picked up the second one. She sipped it. Not quite plain black, but no secrets.

Chef pulled a small notebook out of his pocket. He unclipped a pen on the front and opened it. "What time would you like lunch?"

"I'll just fix something for myself. I don't imagine I'll be hungry until supper anyway."

Chef shrugged. "I prepared some turkey club sandwich

fixings. They're in the frig along with a cheese tray. I moved the shelves so you can fit your fruit basket in there. Would you like your supper catered or prepared in-house?"

"Do you see this cup?" Katrina held it for his inspection.

"Yes."

"It is not to the level where I can answer questions politely or even cordially, though so far, I've managed not to be outright rude." She took a sip meeting his gaze over the rim of the cup. "Chef."

He laughed. "I'm sorry. I forget some people don't function well before coffee. Mea Culpa, Katrina." He picked up a sponge and wiped the counter then rinsed it and placed it next to the sink. Reaching into his pocket, he withdrew a business card. "Here's my number. I'm available day or night to cook for you either off site or here. I also offer cooking courses in home, and that's provided as part of your time here. You can get on the website to check out the different meals and menus, but if it's not on there and you want it, I will make it happen." He bowed slightly. "That's a promise."

He placed the card on the front of the refrigerator, and it stayed.

Huh. It must be a magnet. Well, that was nifty.

"K.P. is part of the job, too, so if you want to leave the dishes, I can take care of them when it's convenient for you."

"That won't be necessary." Katrina took another sip of the coffee. It was quite good even with the cinnamon.

Chef strode out of the kitchen to the front door. "See you later, Katrina, and thank you."

He opened the door and walked out, shutting the door behind him.

Had he just thanked her? Why? For being grumpy and refusing to taste his secret coffee? Katrina looked at the cup. She picked it up, sniffing at the still-dark liquid.

She looked at the counter in front of the coffeemaker searching for evidence of what he'd added, but she saw nothing out of place.

He was creative with fruit and efficient. She'd watched him tidy up before leaving. He'd even closed the cabinet door. If it had been Eric every cabinet door he touched would still be standing ajar. In the years they'd been married, she'd never known him to close any cabinet. It had driven her crazy, though she'd resigned herself to living with the quirk, a necessary part of sharing space and her life with him. Picking up another strawberry from the arrangement, Katrina burrowed it in the dip, then touched it in the granola before eating it.

"Mmm." She stood and went over to the cabinet, opening it before leaving the kitchen to find the bathroom.

After showering, Katrina retrieved the rest of her belongings from the car and settled on the porch with a book, but she fell asleep again until the late afternoon shadows colored the room. She stood and stretched, watching the expanse of beach and surf as she did so. Slipping on her shoes, she opened the back door and walked onto the deck and down the three wooden stairs to the sand.

She hadn't been to Florida since she was a child. The few times she and Eric had gone to the beach, they'd opted for the east coast outer banks because it was closer. But she remembered Florida sand—fine white granules making the beach lovely to look at and to walk on. A solitary lounge chair sat on the low rise above the surf, and she rested her hand on top of the vinyl and metal frame back and stood never taking her gaze off the expanse of undulating water and the canvas of sky above it.

This was lovely. Whoever you are—gift giver—thank you.

Turning her attention away from the ocean, she noticed something at the smooth ridge of tide worn sand. Walking toward it, she smiled. Someone had been making sand castles. Well, not sand castles exactly, but a sand village with buildings and a furrowed path winding through them. Bits of debris decorated the sides and roofs—shells, marram grass, and sticks. One building must have been a church because a stick cross, fashioned together with a rubber band, adorned the top and another cross had been pressed in the sand above the engraved door. Another building was, perhaps, a school with a stick playground in the yard and a flag pole crowned with an intricately—but homemade—American flag which looked to be an index card.

There must be children on the beach with a mom and dad who helped them create the display. She checked the landscape for little footprints, but didn't find any.

Further along was a massive turtle with a map of the continents carved on its back and a garland of seaweed atop his head. The turtle's eyes closed as if the big guy slept, but a smile creased his face complete with dimples suggested happy dreams. Nearby was a waist high pyramid, with impressively straight lines on all sides depicting blocks. A doorway carved within the structure faced the ocean. Katrina bent over to peer inside and saw a figure inside, and a burst of surprised laughter came forth. She dropped to her knees for a better look. A fist sized rock with a sharpie-painted face smiled at her.

How cute.

Katrina looked around, but the deserted beach gave no clue of the creator of the whimsical sculptures.

The last work of art was incomplete. But the builder obviously had a plan for sand had been piled in a serpentine form. An upside down bucket sat next to it with a gardener's hand trowel and spike stuck well into the ground testified that whoever had begun the project planned to return. What would it be, a snake?

Katrina scanned the horizon. Dinah hadn't exaggerated. The beach was remote. Other than the house she occupied and the one in the lot next to it, she only saw a few others spaced well away from each other. A gull flew over her squawking. Seeing a pier in the distance, she walked toward it, but after nearly a mile and it still far off, she turned around, going back to sand sculptures and beyond them, the beach house.

She sat on the deck and read a book, and, at times, forgetting the story on the pages as the scene before her kept capturing her attention. The sun dipped lower, and Katrina put the book down. Her stomach twinged, and she decided to check out the turkey club ingredients Chef had left in the refrigerator. She heard the doorbell peal through the open windows of the sunroom giving her another reason to vacate the chair.

It had to be Chef. She hadn't seen anyone else, and as enthusiastic as he was this morning to ply her with food, her guess was he hadn't given up.

She opened the door and found him in a chef shirt and hat.

"Seriously?"

"What?"

"That get-up."

He glanced down at his white shirt and black pants. "You don't like my uniform?"

"I don't like or dislike it, but I don't need a chef, Chef or Trey whatever you want me to call you. I usually eat peanut butter and jelly or something simple. I'm not into food."

He leaned over and picked up the straps of two rectangular duffels Katrina concluded were coolers.

"I was thinking arugula salad and feta cheese with a

blueberry dressing, glazed salmon, rice pilaf, and blackened asparagus."

Katrina's stomach growled. The traitor.

"Do you have peanut butter and jelly? Just give me the jars, and I'll be fine."

Chef grinned. "On white bread?"

She lifted her head haughtily. "Honey wheat if you must know."

He stepped on the threshold causing Katrina to move back. "Creamy or crunchy?"

"Umm." He was supposed to be offended by her choice of sandwich. "Extra crunchy."

He nodded and walked past her, side-stepping so he didn't bump her with the coolers. "Excuse me."

"Hey!" Katrina followed him to the kitchen.

"That's good. Good choice. Very good choice. High texture." He set the coolers on the floor and pulled a cell phone out of his pocket. He pressed the screen rapidly and put the phone to his ear, tucking it in between his shoulder and face, he bent down and unzipped one of the coolers. Removing a cutting board and several other items, he placed them on the counter. "Hello? Got any honey wheat?.... Yesterday or Today? ....Great. Set them aside for me. ....Marshall. Thanks." He pocketed the phone, opened the other bag and lifted a carafe and poured the contents into a glass he'd retrieved earlier.

"Grape spritzer with lemon." He placed it on the bar in front of her then unwrapped a container revealing a square porcelain plate topped with edamame beans and carrot sticks surrounding a smaller bowl with white dressing. "That is artichoke dip. After all the fruit, I thought you'd be in the mood for something less sweet." He moved the bags against the wall. "I'll be back in a few minutes."

Katrina folded her arms over her chest. "I just want a plain peanut butter and jelly sandwich and nothing else."

Chef, who had been striding to the door spoke over his shoulder. "I'm going to prepare a peanut butter and jelly sandwich just for you."

"A plain one. No fancy bread or weird ingredients."

"Fresh isn't fancy." The door closed behind him.

Chapter Three

He signaled his return by ringing the doorbell, but Katrina, settled this time with his vegetable appetizer next to her on the couch and her book in her lap, ignored it. As she surmised, he let himself in.

"It's Chef returning," he called.

Katrina didn't reply. She heard him in the kitchen, various sounds which seemed more involved than PB&J needed. He came into the room, and she glanced behind her, and what she saw snagged her attention. He shook a black table cloth and spread it over the glass topped table on the far side of the room. Then he placed candles and gold china for one facing the window. With deft movements he folded a cloth napkin and placed it beside the plate. Then he left, and returned with a gold tinged plate which he placed on top of the gold plate. Her sandwich sat regally in the middle, the corner of one half touching the middle of the other half. Something else garnished the plate. Katrina rose and approached the table.

She giggled. Chef had crafted a tiny woman with a grape body, a sugar frosted grape pleated grape skirt and a halved grape face. Her hair appeared to be peanut butter fudge in a beehive, and celery stick arm held a pennant with a pretzel rod and a slightly curled sliver of carrot.

Chef put a glass of milk behind the plate and lit the candles. He pulled the chair back in invitation, and touched by the chivalry of the gesture, Katrina sat. She unfolded the napkin and placed it in her lap.

It was so silly to present a peanut butter and jelly sandwich so lavishly. But the pride and humility Chef demonstrated in the meal presentation warmed her. She lifted the half sandwich to her mouth and bit into it, savoring the familiarity of the food, but noting Chef hadn't followed her directive for plain. He'd done something more, and it was the best PB&J she'd ever tasted.

He left the room, and jazzy music began to play from inside the house.

Katrina took small bites and examined the grape woman on her plate. How clever this man was. But what a shame his medium was food, temporal—eaten or discarded after the meal was concluded. She took her time eating in an attempt to enjoy Chef's elaborate efforts for supper.

She heard his footsteps approach. "I've prepared vanilla custard with toasted coconut and candied peanuts for dessert. May I bring it to you?"

Katrina turned in her chair to see him. He stood at the threshold waiting. His white hat contrasted against his dark hair, and the wide band tilted slightly on his forehead. Some women would find him attractive, Katrina supposed. Especially his eyes. When they'd had their coffee standoff this morning, he'd gazed at her, and the green hue of his irises were almost pretty against the dark fringe of his lashes. He watched her now waiting for her answer.

"Okay," she said finally.

He nodded in acknowledgement, pivoting on his heel, he left and returned with a gold serving tray and a crystal cup holding the treat. He began to remove her plate.

"Wait. You're not going to throw out the little grape woman, are you?" she asked.

"You can eat her, if you like." He acted as if it were no big deal, like he hadn't created this cute little thing.

"It seems a shame to."

Chef shrugged. "She's food."

"I think I'll put her on the table so I can enjoy her a little longer."

Chef smiled and looked at the figure affectionately. "She is a cutie, isn't she?"

"Yes, she is."

He placed a spoon on the plate next to the glass, inclined his head to her and left the room. Katrina dug into the sweet and soon the cup was empty.

Yes, some women would be attracted to him. His looks. His enthusiasm. His talent. But not her.

Katrina had loved one man, and he had been taken away from her after only two years. She still loved him, still thought about him often and wished.... She sighed. Well, there was no use in wishing. Eric was gone.

She stood and gathered the dishes. Immediately, Chef appeared next to her. "Please," he said. "Let me."

Katrina backed away. "I'm not used to being pampered."

"No pampering. I prepare your meal, present it to you, then clean up afterward." With the dishes on the tray, he pinched the flames on the candles, and once again headed toward the kitchen.

Katrina trailed him, a habit she realized she did a lot when Chef was in the house.

To her surprise, the kitchen was clean except for the tray he set next to the sink. Immediately, he began to wash the dishes. Katrina sat on the stool across the counter.

"Would you like to talk about tomorrow's menu?" he asked over his shoulder.

"I suppose."

"Breakfast. I was thinking French toast casserole with a pecan maple sauce and bacon cheddar soufflé."

"Or oatmeal," Katrina countered.

"You want oatmeal?"

"You know those little packets of oatmeal that come in the box?"

"Not only does that oatmeal have very little nutritional value, it has very little soul as well," he said.

"Cold cereal then." She felt as if they were negotiating

on real estate. She was trying to sell him on her eating habits, and he wasn't buying, though she had to hand it to him, he was being extremely diplomatic about it.

"You eat cold cereal for breakfast?"

"Sometimes I splurge and put blueberries or bananas on top."

He turned his head and looked at her over his shoulder.

Katrina was sure he was offended, and she felt the need to defend herself. "Not everyone thinks of food as an opportunity to splurge. Sometimes I just have a cup of coffee, and that's it."

Turning off the water, he turned to face her. He picked up the plate he'd just washed and dried it with a cloth from a neatly folded stack on the countertop. "I'd like to treat you while you're here. I'd like for you to sit down at each meal and really enjoy it, to live fully in every bite, as if the consuming of it were an act of beauty in itself."

"Oh, brother. Eating as philosophy." How could she not tease him at this point? "It's a wonder you don't weigh three hundred pounds."

Chef snickered. He dried each dish and placed them in a wicker basket. "Food is the philosophy. Eating is only part of it. How about steel cut oats with a fresh fruit on the side?"

"And plain coffee."

"Okay." That task finished, he opened a lower cabinet and set the basket inside. "What time do you want me to bring it over?"

Katrina dropped her head and groaned. "Do I really have to tell you a time? I'm on vacation."

"Just text me then. Unless you want it earlier, I'll have it ready by seven. When I receive the text, I can deliver it in ten minutes. Or, if you'd rather, I can leave a food case on the porch. That way you don't even have to put up with me, and you can eat in your pajamas, as some people like to do."

"Fair enough."

"Lunch?"

"I'll just eat the bacon club sandwich I didn't eat today."

He clicked his tongue in disapproval.

"Don't be such a snob," she said. "It's all still good."

"I'm committed to cherish preparing your meals because I desire to be at your service with every plated dish. How am I supposed to impress you with my culinary skills when you want to eat leftovers?"

Katrina shook her head. "You take food way too seriously. You need to lighten up. Chef."

Chef blinked at her, then he threw back his head and laughed as if she'd told the funniest joke he'd ever heard. "You might find this hard to believe, but some people think I don't take life seriously enough."

"You're right. I do find it hard to believe. Okay. Fine. Peanut butter and jelly sandwich for lunch."

A mischievous smile crept over his lips.

"Don't think you're getting away with anything. I know what plain peanut butter and jelly tastes like. You didn't fool me. However, it was delicious, so knock yourself out."

"Knock myself out." He nodded in approval. "Text again to signal what time. If you put the food case on the porch after breakfast, I'll use it again for lunch. I'll set the table tonight so tomorrow you'll have an ambient context for your meals."

Katrina rolled her eyes. "I'm at the beach. That's enough ambient context." She'd likely sit on the couch with the plate in her lap, but no sense in telling Chef and depress him.

"So, a beach theme then?"

"No, a plain theme of a plate, silverware, and cup with a napkin to wipe my mouth with."

"It seems rather boring."

"You sneaked secret ingredients into my PB&J and provided a tiny fruit lady as company while I ate. I don't think you could do boring if you tried." She pursed her lips in amusement. "Chef."

"Dinner?" he asked.

"I guess the fish-whatever-you-said-earlier will work."

With his arms crossed over his chest, he laughed again. "Wonderful. We have tomorrow's menu. Do you want a nightcap or late night snack prepared before I leave?"

Milk and cookies. She almost said it as a joke, but figured he'd actually do it.

"Just say it. I'm at your service." His sincerity pulled at her. She'd never met anyone so eager to serve.

To protect and to serve.

The police slogan popped into her mind. Eric had been all about protecting the beat down, the innocent, the young, the vulnerable. But he hadn't been able to protect himself.

Katrina dropped her eyes. With her finger, she traced a pattern on the bar top. "Maybe another night," she said quietly.

"All right." He knelt down, and when he stood again, he held a box. "I'll prepare the table and leave you alone."

The jazz music still played softly, and over the notes, she heard Chef setting the table in the other room. In a few minutes, he walked through not pausing as he spoke. "Good night, Katrina. Thank you so much."

Again with the thanks, like she'd done anything for him other than eat his food and give him a hard time.

****

The season of flying kites occurred any day the wind blew well. The two stores Trey had visited searching for a kite hadn't agreed. The clerk at the dollar store had wrinkled her nose at him and informed him he'd have to wait until March to buy a kite. Trey thanked her and gone to the hardware store where he'd bought string and dowels. In his truck, he'd fashioned the kite itself out of butcher paper in the traditional diamond pattern. He used a black marker to paint a smiley face on it, and positioned it along the shore unrolling the string in preparation of the launching.

With several unsuccessful attempts and a stinging cut on his hand from nearly losing the string after the wind finally caught the kite, Trey braced his bare feet on the ground and watched his creation dance merrily against the vivid blue sky.

He liked Katrina. And he was so happy he'd finally been able to be in the same room with her.

He'd wanted to meet the woman who'd given him a second chance at life ever since they'd gotten the call. He remembered the night well. It had come at ten on the dot, and he and his parents had left within half an hour to go to the hospital.

Through the years, he'd thought of Mrs. E.A. He had only known her by her husband's initials. The program did not disclose identity unless the parties involved agreed, and she never had. What had it been like for her the night her husband died? Perhaps the worst night of her life, but out of the tragedy, she'd decided to donate his organs so someone else could live.

Not just one someone, but nine someones. Trey had met four of the others.

He considered the donation was, perhaps, the only redemption in losing her husband who had only been twenty-seven when he died. Did Katrina feel the same way?

Trey himself was alive because E.A.'s heart beat in his chest. Katrina's husband. She was no longer Mrs. E.A. He knew her name now. At least, her first name.

And he knew other things about her—her appreciation of simple no-nonsense food. Her disregard for showy ostentation. Her pretty smile. The graceful curve of her neck, and how dainty her hands were. How thin she was which worried him a little. Her belief that food was nothing more than a necessary fuel likely explained why she was so thin. Her weariness. Yes, he'd noticed that too. It troubled him that she'd been so tired the night she arrived at the house that she had left the front door open, making herself a target of anyone going by with malicious intentions. Her careless gesture had offered him a precious gift: a glimpse of Mrs. E.A. asleep. He'd witnessed her relaxed form soft in slumber. The moment she'd awoken, the softness had disappeared, as if she'd put on a robe of armor so no one would see her vulnerability, but he'd had another hint of it in the sad, lost look she wore last night when he'd asked her about a nighttime snack.

Had she been thinking of her husband? Had they enjoyed a late snack together as a nighttime ritual? If Trey accidently hit on some dish which reminded her of E.A., would this bring her comfort or pain?

So determined he was to bless her these two weeks, doing anything to hurt her was unacceptable. He owed her his life, and he'd worked a long time to find a way to thank her for saving him.

The vacation at the beach house wouldn't pay the debt he owed her, but perhaps in this small way he could bring her a little happiness.

Trey hoped so.

The kite dipped, and he pulled the stick he'd secured the string with after his injury. Another dip, and thinking it might dive down into the ocean, Trey turned and ran as fast as he could, looking behind him to check the kite's flight.

It caught another current and pulled against him going

higher and higher. He stopped and turning, he collapsed on the sand anchoring the flying object.

He scooted in the sand, making a seat in the ground and feeling the damp seep into his pants. He grinned at the discomfort for it reminded him of the nifty details of being alive.

Thank you, God, for the feel of ocean water against Florida sand though cotton denim jeans. You spared my life so I could enjoy this moment.

Far above him, the kite pivoted, making a straight arrow path downward. Before Trey could get to his feet to run it up again, the butcher paper diamond pitched into the ocean like a cliff-diver.

Cool.

He turned the stick, winding the string up to retrieve the kite to check the damage. Considering it was his first kite ever, it had sailed rather well. He unclipped his cell phone holder and took off his belt and laid them on the sand. Wading in the water, he shivered at the temperature. The salt in the water stung his hand and he stretched out his fingers thinking it was probably good for the wound though it hurt like the dickens. Using his shirt to protect his flesh, he pulled at the string in an attempt to bring the kite in quicker. Finally, with kite in hand, tattered from the crash, he pulled his phone out and looked at the time.

Two good hours before he'd need to prepare lunch and deliver it. Plenty of time to work on another kite. He'd seen a box design and a simple dragon on his tablet when he'd been researching on the Internet yesterday. The box would take more dowels than he had, but if he could reuse the ones from today, he might could create the dragon and have it ready to go tomorrow if the wind cooperated.

Free from the waves, he picked up the items he'd discarded earlier and walked across the beach to the house next to Katrina's. He'd rented both of them—one for her and the one with the bigger kitchen for himself. He didn't really need a house for this endeavor. His catering truck provided a stocked kitchen with an impressive convection oven and gas stove and even space over the cab where he often slept, having a house to stretch out and a real bathroom to shower in was great. His truck had been his home for eighteen months, and in that time he'd been able to pay bills with catering and in-home cooking courses. Living out of the truck had made it easier to go wherever the client was, and he'd cooked in kitchens in fourteen states.

What a great life.

Thank you, Katrina, for your gift which is letting me live my dream.

At eleven, he set the food case on the front porch with her requested peanut butter and jelly sandwich. He'd made the bread himself this time, and had plated two other versions—a grilled sandwich with bacon and cranberry plum jelly as well as a cream cheese cinnamon peanut butter with Nutella. He'd labeled each sandwich and included sweet potato chips he'd deep fried this morning after breakfast and dried to keep them crisp. He'd included to drink fresh squeezed orange juice he'd stored in a carbonated thermos and for dessert two frozen dark chocolate dipped bananas.

After lunch Trey finished his sand train. Then decided he'd dig a six-foot-wide moat and craft a curved bridge through the trench and cover it completely with the sea shells he'd collected since he'd arrived—two buckets full. Choosing a location high on the beach so the high tide wouldn't wash it away, he'd completed the project surprisingly quickly. He'd asked the owners of the property about using their yard tools, and they'd told him where the key was to the storage shed. He'd given them a week's worth of catered meal courses in July for the use of the two houses this month, a sweet deal considering their recommendations had led to jobs with four other clients. It was here in July he'd first begun to think of giving Mrs. E.A. a beach vacation as a way to say thank you since she had never attended the Celebration of Life parties to be appreciated. He understood her reticence, he supposed. Maybe she felt she'd done enough when she'd given up her husband. But the Celebration shouldn't feel like an obligation to her—only an opportunity to receive the gratitude for the decision she'd made that had saved lives, his own included.

She was younger than he expected. Since he knew the age of E.A., he figured his widow would be young, too, but he'd always pictured her as ageless, wise, regal.

He had not pictured her as a PB&J kind of woman who called him on adding butter to her coffee without her consent. Several times she'd picked at him—teasing him he was pretty sure but it was hard to tell in that no nonsense way she had of speaking—she'd paused after the jibe, then called him Chef, as if the term itself amused her.

She was so funny. Even her reluctant acceptance of his efforts to please her in culinary ways was a source of amusement, probably because her acquiescence came with a sarcastic and sometimes bewildered commentary.

On hands and knees, he set the seashells across the bridge, picking out similar colored pieces and designing a few geometric shapes as he went. If he felt ambitious later, he could reset the shells with something more elaborate. Maybe buy some bamboo tiki torches and use them as rails. That would look cool.

His knees were stiff by the time he finished, so he got his shoes and ran a couple of miles down the beach.

Yes. He liked Katrina.

When he'd retrieved the food cases, he'd laughed out loud at a paper tucked into the handle.

No more desserts, with a frowny face over a crudely drawn rotund woman behind the prohibited sign of a circle with a line across it.

He rang the doorbell and waited a moment. He pressed the button again. The door flew open, and her pretty scowling face met his.

"Why didn't you just come in? You did before, twice in fact."

He shifted the box he held and entered. He shut the door with his hip and followed her into the living room. "Sorry. Do you want me to ring the bell and enter?"

"Sure. I know when to expect you." She perched on the barstool.

Her choice to hang out as he cooked made him happy. Was she lonely, or did she genuinely like sparring with him?

"If I don't want to see your goofy white hat, I'll just lock the door."

He laughed. Guess it was the latter.

"Did you get my note?" she asked.

Trey washed his hands and dried them on a towel he'd set aside for that purpose. "About the dessert? Yes."

"Good, because dessert for lunch is just a little ridiculous. And you're cooking for one person. Me. I mean, three sandwiches and two chocolate bananas?"

"Two of those sandwiches were for sampling. I thought you might want to expand your definition of PB&J," he said.

"No, you thought *you* might want to expand my definition of PB&J. I don't want to expand my PB&J repertoire or my waistline, so just stop that nonsense right now."

In the process of running water in the rice cooker, he turned to her. "You didn't sample them?"

"No."

"Did you throw them away?"

"No. I put them in the fridge. I'm hoping I'll spot some hungry homeless guy on the beach to unload all this extra food on."

Trey retrieved the two sandwiches. He should have presented them in a sampling format. The bread of the grilled sandwich was too old to taste good. He'd had reservations about offering it in the first place because of the brief window of flavor with a grilled item. But the bacon would actually be better cold. He deconstructed the sandwich, and making a quick trip out to his truck, he retrieved the items to make a new one. He prepared the food on the counter as she looked on.

"What did you do to your hand?"

He glanced at the water-proof bandage where he'd covered the string cut.

"I cut it."

Chapter Four

"A necessary part of your job, I suppose. Cutting yourself while you cut up vegetables or whatever. I hope you didn't get any blood in my food."

Trey smiled. "I wasn't preparing a meal at the time. I was kite-flying. The wind caught it, and I had the string wrapped around my hand. The string whipped through the skin as it slid out of my grasp. Luckily, I still had the end of it. I secured it to a stick I found preventing further injury."

"You flew a kite today?"

He couldn't tell from her tone whether he detected skepticism or amazement.

"Yeah."

He glanced at her, noting the crease between her brows as she processed this new piece of information.

"Do they sell kites around here?"

"No. I made it."

She stared at him as if he were an exotic h'ordeuvre she'd never tried before.

"Did you ever fly a kite?" he asked.

"No, but I've suggested to a few people they should."

Trey laughed. "It's fun especially with the sea breeze." On a wooden board, he cut the layered food, hoping the smaller pieces would encourage consumption. Arranging them just so, he set the sandwiches in tiny bite sized circles on a cheery red platter in front of her.

She glanced at it critically then at him. "Ha! Recycled leftovers, and, no, I'm not eating bacon with peanut butter. That is disgusting."

"Just try it."

She glared at him indignantly. "It's gross."

"You don't like bacon?"

"Yeah, with tomato and lettuce on mayonaised bread."

Ah. The traditional BLT. He'd do that for tomorrow's lunch. Shrugging her rejection, he arranged the asparagus on a baking sheet and drizzled it with EVOO.

"Mmm. This other one is good. Not as good as the supposed plain peanut butter and jelly sandwich, but good."

Trey let that comment go wondering if she would.

"What kind of peanut butter are you using on my sandwich? I thought you were using the same brand I do, but it tastes a lot richer and the consistency is different. Will you tell me, or are you one of those silly people who keep their recipes secret?"

"I add butter to it."

"What!" She slapped her hands on the counter top. "Why do you want to make me fat?"

She was too thin, but he didn't volunteer that. She already had him in her gun scope. No sense in giving her another reason to pull the trigger.

"Who adds butter to peanut butter, as if it doesn't have enough fat and oil? What is wrong with you?" she asked.

Trey shrugged. "Butter makes everything taste better."

"Then why do you cook with olive oil?"

"Because olive oil is a lot healthier." He tipped his head in concession. "It doesn't taste nearly as good though."

An almost sad expression crossed her face. "I can't add butter to my sandwiches for the rest of my life."

She liked his PB&J. He couldn't keep the smile off his face.

"Want to talk about tomorrow's menu?" he asked.

"As long as there's no dessert, sure."

Trey didn't remark that he had a made a dessert for tonight. If she balked, he'd just say he'd already prepared it before he'd seen her note.

Which was absolutely true.

"I noticed there's a fire pit on the deck. You seem to like traditional fare, how do you feel about roasting hotdogs and popping corn over an open fire?"

Katrina wrinkled her nose, in an endearingly cute gesture. "It sounds a little too Kumbaya-ish to me."

"Okay. Hotdogs, popcorn, but no campfire songs." Trey nodded. He could live with that. The movement of the waves hitting the shore was a perfect soundtrack, he thought. "I even have some wire rack skewers you can toast a PB&J sandwich in, if you like. I usually have them for grilled cheese sandwiches, but—"

Katrina's face lit up. "Grilled cheese?" she asked.

Aha. Trey nodded. "Want grilled cheese instead?"

"As long as it's plain grilled cheese sandwiches." She arched an eyebrow as if daring him to object.

"Plain grilled cheese has butter, you know."

She narrowed her eyes. Yeah, she knew, but she wasn't going to admit it, apparently. Trey let that go too.

"Great. Since we're doing sandwiches tomorrow night, why not a heartier meal at lunch?"

She shook her head. "No. Something light. Yogurt or cereal, if anything. Since I've been here, all I've done is eat. Soon I won't be able to fit into any of my clothes the way you force feed me."

Ideas ran through Trey's head for a solution other than copping out with yogurt or cereal. "I can make a spinach pineapple pear salad with a light vinaigrette."

"Okay."

"Breakfast?" he asked.

"Plain coffee which I will make myself." She declared.

Pancakes did well in the warmer. It was simple, but she seemed to like simple. "I'll leave the warming box on the porch with—"

"No." Her voice was sure, firm. "You've said when I

want my meal, I can text you. If I change my mind about breakfast, I will let you know. Otherwise, I'll see you for lunch."

Trey opened his mouth to argue with her, but she held a finger up in a restrictive gesture.

"Just one comment," he countered.

She lowered her hand. "What?"

"You can text me any time day or night. Any time, and I will cook for you." He hesitated, hoping he wasn't coming across as desperate to please her as he felt. "Happily. Very happily."

She studied him, then pursed her lips. "If you break out into song, Ill kick you out of this kitchen right now. You hear me?"

Trey laughed. "No singing. Not even Kumbaya. Got it."

As requested, he didn't offer dessert though he did put the mango mousse in the fridge in case she wanted some later with his obligatory label so she'd know what it was. He'd set the table in the sunroom as she seemed to like eating in there. He cleaned up while she ate, and after he had given her enough time to finish her meal, he stood inside the doorway.

"Can I do anything else for you?"

She scooted her chair back and rose. "No. It was a great meal."

"Thank you." He took her cue and bussed the table. Her little grape woman still sat near her plate. Trey had placed another person next to it tonight: a celery man with stringed carrot facial features and a cherry tomato for his hat. Trey had crafted the little guy in the likeness of an actual person—Gary Hamlin, a lanky man in his forties. Katrina didn't know it, but she was the grape woman, and tomorrow Trey was going to craft Leslie Buchannan out of a potato to make it a trio.

Katrina must have noticed him looking at the food people. "Is the celery man married to the grape woman?"

Trey shook his head. "No."

"How do you know? They could be."

"They're not married. They just met tonight on the table."

One day, he hoped they'd meet for real.

****

After Chef left, the silence of the house drove her to the back door where she stepped onto the deck, slipped out of her shoes, and walked onto the sand. A street light illuminated the portion of beach beyond the house, and she decided to investigate the sand sculptures. The village still stood, and Katrina didn't notice any changes to it or the castle. The turtle had obtained a rather new-looking baseball hat on his flat head. Meandering over to the unfinished artwork she'd seen yesterday, Katrina discovered it transformed into a choo choo train. Dried seaweed laid in front of it as railroad ties.

Cute.

And, oh my goodness, what was this?

Katrina walked past the train to a sculpture she hadn't seen before—a large square hole with an arching sandbar raised in the middle, hundreds of shells covered the sandbar. She knelt down and ran her hand over the surface, then decided it was smooth enough she could walk over it with her bared feet.

She turned toward the house next to her own. No lights shone from inside, and she hadn't seen anyone on the beach nearby at all. Other than Chef, the area was deserted. But someone had been on this beach from the last time she'd been here. They'd spent a lot of time here building up and decorating the sandbar and the choo choo.

Katrina decided she'd take her book and read outside tomorrow in an attempt to see the artist of the sand sculptures.

****

Katrina looked down at herself in a flowy white dress. She walked across the Wingate Bridge close to the house they'd lived in their entire married life. Why she crossed the bridge in her bare feet instead of driving, she didn't know, nor did it seem to matter. Through the painted rafters, she caught sight of the half-moon high in the nighttime sky.

"Katrina, I'm here," Eric called to her.

She looked around, seeking her husband. There he stood on the other side of the bridge, at the intersection beyond the shore of the water.

She cupped her hands. "Get off the road," she yelled hoping he heard her.

She began to run toward him, making sure to keep her hand on the rail, glancing behind her every few seconds to be sure the way was clear.

"It's all right, honey. It's all right." Though he stood still, the distance between them lengthened.

"Eric, I need you. Please. Come here."

He didn't speak or move.

Katrina let go of the rail and ran faster. A loud rumbling from behind warned her of approaching traffic. She turned and the headlights of a semi-truck blinded her. She stumbled and fell, covering her head as if that meager act could protect her. The horn blasted, deafening her as the truck rolled by, missing her by inches. The whole bridge shook as its massive weight moved forward.

"Eric," she screamed. "Eric!"

The truck barreled across the bridge, but it began to sink as if the pavement beneath were made of sand. Clattering filled the air as thousands of seashells covering the road fell to the river below. The truck dipped, then dropped as the road disappeared beneath the tires and silently the truck fell, plunging into the black water.

47

Katrina's gaze scanned the shore beyond the end of where the bridge had been.

Eric no longer stood there. Only his police jacket remained, lying neatly folded on the road beyond the chasm.

"Eric!"

Katrina awoke with her husband's name on her lips. She sat up disoriented from the intense dream. Stumbling out of bed, she slipped on a pair of pants under her nightshirt. Picking up her cell phone off the nightstand, Katrina left the bedroom and moved through the dark house to the kitchen. Opening the fridge, she perused the contents. Chef had rearranged her fruit flower basket each day, replacing the overripe fruit with fresher alternatives. Though she'd requested he reserve the meal leftovers, he was selective about what he kept stored there.

She looked for the spinach salad, but didn't find it though she knew she'd carefully wrapped it in cellophane. In its place a container of raw spinach sat, with divided compartments of pineapple, pear, and dressing.

Chef had thrown out the leftovers, but had ingredients there for a new salad. His neat black penned scrawl on the gray label with the catering logo emblazoned on it demonstrated he'd placed the separate parts of the salad there in case she decided later she wanted to eat it. His thoughtfulness warmed her.

And she was struck once again of how gifted he was as a chef.

Before he had left tonight, he'd thanked her, a nightly ritual for him, it seemed. Did he need the job so bad that he showed such sincere appreciation to his clients? She wasn't really his client though. Did he know that? Someone else had paid for the house and for his services. An anonymous someone. Perhaps, though, the someone wasn't anonymous to him. Maybe she could ask him who had hired him, then she would know, too.

Obviously, it was someone involved in the Donate Life Foundation, but Dinah had been very tight-lipped about it. Katrina had criticized her saying that the charity ought to use its resources more wisely rather than forking out a large sum of money so she could have a vacation she hadn't wanted in the first place. Dinah finally confessed that, no, the organization had not paid for her respite. It was an individual who wished to remain anonymous. Whether this was a gift every donor family received, Katrina hadn't been able to find out. She was appreciative, however, to the unnamed person. Because of their generosity, Katrina was enjoying two weeks at the beach with incredible food.

If only Eric could have been here, too, to enjoy it. But then again, if he had been, Katrina wouldn't know anything about Donate Life or what they did.

The details of her dream returned to her but she purposely closed her mind to the disturbing images.

Focusing on the shelves in the refrigerator, she decided she wanted something to drink. Chef had brought several kinds of beverages including... she picked up the glass carafe and read the label of the pretty orange liquid.

Mmmm. Dreamsicle almond milk.

That actually sounded pretty good, as Katrina had been a dreamsicle fan from way back. Had she mentioned that to Chef?

She poured some in a glass and sniffed. Immediately, the scent transported her to summers of her childhood. The merry music in the neighborhood announced the ice cream truck was nearby. Mom would give her and her brothers dollar bills, and they'd run outside to the front yard looking frantically up the street for the white truck.

Katrina loved the orange sherbet treat contained in a cylinder with a plastic stick to push it up enough to eat. Had she mentioned that to Chef? How did he know to prepare these things she liked so much?

Bringing the glass to her lips, she drank.

Wow, this is good.

Replacing the pitcher, she closed the door, and her eyes fell on Chef's magnetic business card. She reached forward and pulled it from the slick surface, studying the design and letters then setting it back where it had been on the refrigerator front.

It was two in the morning. Chef had said he'd fix her food day or night. Anytime.

She picked up her phone and scrolled to her texting app. Manipulating the keyboard, she sent Chef a message.

Did you mean it?

In less than a minute, he returned the text.

Yes. What would you like?

Katrina shook her head, bewildered. How did he know what she was even asking?

Her fingers rested above the phone screen. What did she want to eat? It's not like he had left her with a bare refrigerator. If she was really hungry, she had several choices there, including mousse, which sounded suspiciously like dessert.

Where was he anyway? She decided to ask in the text.

Where are you?

Next door.

Katrina stared at her phone in shock. He was staying next door? It made sense, she supposed. If he was going to be at her beck and call, he'd need to be close by at a place with a kitchen, right?

Katrina, are you okay?

She didn't answer.

Do you need something?

She didn't have an answer for his question. Reprieve from a bad dream, actually, but she wasn't comfortable disclosing that to him.

Her phone rang, and it was his number which appeared on the screen.

"Hello, this is Chef," he said before she could say hello. "Are you having trouble sleeping?"

"A little."

"I have some green tea I could bring over with fresh cherries over cottage cheese. They are supposed to promote sleep."

Katrina walked out to the sunroom and opened the back door. The waves brushing against the shore soothed her.

"It's high tide, I think."

For a few seconds he didn't speak, then, "I could start a fire in the pit. Do you like s'mores?"

"Oh, boy, do I."

"I'll meet you on the back porch."

Chapter Five

Katrina sat on the deck chair as Chef nursed the flames in the fire pit. She slid a marshmallow on the skewer he'd given her earlier.

"Is it too early to roast a marshmallow?" she asked.

Chef moved aside, giving her access to the fire. "Not too early." His head was bare, and he wasn't wearing his uniform. Instead he had on blue jeans and a T-shirt under an unzipped jacket. Guess 3am cooking calls meant he didn't have to dress for work. She thought about calling him on it, but figured he—being the good sport that he was—would go retrieve his work duds just to humor her.

On the table next to her, he'd laid out what he called the s'more station—the requisite graham crackers and chocolate bars, but also some interesting add-ons like coconut, caramel, bananas, pineapple, and peanut butter chocolate candy with chocolate and cinnamon flavored graham crackers.

The fire crackled, and she held out her skewer as if it were a sword, and she were knighting the flames.

He picked up a chair and moved it to the edge of the patio. "Do you need anything else?"

"Are you leaving?" She didn't want him to.

He shook his head. "No. I'll stay as long as the fire is going."

"Can't you eat s'mores with me?"

He hesitated.

Oh. "I guess you usually don't eat with people you cook for."

"No. Not usually." He abandoned the chair and came back into the sphere of the fire light. He leaned back against the porch rail.

"I'm sure most of the people you cook for aren't alone." After she said it, she realized how pathetic it sounded. "It's not that I'm lonely. Well, not a lot." She sighed. "I enjoy being by myself, but tonight, I had a dream that was a little upsetting, and... well... I could use a little company."

Chef crossed her arms and watched her. "You can tell me about your dream."

Katrina pulled the marshmallow out from the heat of the fire and touched it experimentally. Deciding it was cool enough to eat, she pinched and slid it off the stick.

"It was about my husband. His name was Eric. He died three years ago. Well, it will be three years on Thursday." She chewed slowly, not even tasting the sweetness.

When Katrina looked at Chef again, he had crouched on bended knees with his arms resting on his thighs.

"I'm sorry," he said simply.

Katrina stood and picking up the marshmallows, she affixed two on the skewer then warmed them next to the fire.

"How did he die?"

"He was a police officer. Killed in the line of duty," she said.

"I didn't know."

"Why would you?"

Katrina rarely talked about him with anyone. Somehow sharing who he was with Chef felt safe.

"I really miss him sometimes. We were only married two years before he died."

"Eric." Chef said the name as if he were experimenting with the sound of it, as if it were some foreign word he'd never known before. Odd. "Eric," he said again. "What was he like?"

"He was a good man. Very outgoing. Loved parties and people. He loved having people over, and as you've noticed I'm not much of a cook. So, we'd usually do something simple like chili or grill out hamburgers. I don't miss all the people. I'm kind of an introvert, but I do miss him." She stepped to the table and fixed the s'more then sat down on the chair she'd vacated earlier holding the s'more in her hand. "I loved him so much, and I think he loved me too though the only time he ever told me was the day we married when he said his vows."

"I'm sure he loved you with all his heart."

Chef's voice held an odd tone to it, as if he had difficulty speaking.

Katrina bit into the treat, ready to break the somber spell she'd woven when she brought up the subject of her dead husband.

"Anyway, I appreciate your willingness to make the fire and the s'more fixings. You're going to eat a few, aren't you?"

Chef didn't move immediately.

"You make me suspicious when you don't eat the food," she said.

He smiled and stood. "You think I'm trying to poison you?"

"No, I think you're trying to fatten me up, like the witch did to Hansel and Gretel, so she could cook them in a stew."

He smiled at her joke. "I have no plans for putting you in a stew."

She finished off the s'more and prepared another one. "Well, there's a relief. If this beach house had been made of candy instead of brick and wood, I would wonder."

He skewered two marshmallows and held them to the fire. "I could probably make a gingerbread house while we're here, or teach you how to make one. It might be fun."

"Have you been out on the beach? Someone has been making houses out there. And lots of other things too." As if a lightbulb suddenly illuminated over her head, Katrina knew. "You're the one making the sand sculptures."

A wide grin shone on his face. "Guilty."

She shook her head in amazement. "They're wonderful."

"Thanks. Want to help me build something later on?"

She shook her head even before she realized she was refusing.

"Why not?" He held up the metal skewer with the burning marshmallows on the end, as if it were an arrow, and he was about to propel it over a castle wall with his bow.

"Your marshmallow's on fire."

"I like it burnt." He held it close to his face and blew out the flames. What was left was a chargrilled mess.

"Yuck."

He grinned at her, then deftly tucked the black gunk in between his sandwich of graham crackers, coconut, and caramel.

Katrina looked at his project critically. "That isn't a s'more."

"Sure it is, if I want s'more of it."

"A s'more is chocolate and marshmallow in between two graham crackers. That extra stuff just complicates the purity of the dessert."

He brought the gooey mess to his mouth and ate. "You sound like a chef. A very snobby one."

"You can't improve the basic s'more. It's perfect."

He finished off the s'more and placed four marshmallows on the skewer. "I certainly can, but you're probably unwilling to sample anything I come up with."

"Ugh. You and your culinary visions."

In a few moments, he had crafted several s'more versions and lined them up on a plate.

"Come on," he urged. "Try them."

Reluctantly, Katrina picked up the coconut caramel melted marshmallow on the chocolate graham cracker. She bit into it, then took another bite. "It's good, but…."

"But what?"

"It's distracting. My tongue is confused. It needs a road map to sort out of the flavors.

He handed her the pineapple marshmallow cinnamon graham cracker.

She sampled it. "That's pretty good, actually. Not as good as the classic, but I wouldn't be opposed to eating another one if there were only one other one to eat." She set the unfinished treat on the plate.

On the next graham cracker, he lined potato chips then small dark chocolate morsels. He placed a lightly toasted marshmallow on top and pressed it down beneath another cracker.

Katrina shook her head in amazement. "Really?"

"Humor me. As much as you love texture, the chips will surprise you."

She made a sound expressing her doubt. When she tasted it though, she discovered he was right. Huh.

"One more." He put the chocolate peanut butter candy next to the melted marshmallow in between the graham crackers he'd swiped a bit of butter on.

Katrina bit into it. "Oh." She ate more of it. "Oh, my, I like this."

"Better than the classic?" Chef grinned triumphantly.

"I'm not admitting anything."

"Want me to make you another one?"

"Yes."

They sat near the fire until it died down, and the sky hinted of the approaching dawn.

"So, what about it? Want to make something in the sand?" Chef asked.

"Oh. I'm not… good at things like that."

"You don't have to be. The point isn't to make it perfect or even good. The point is to have fun."

"It… it's just not me."

"Then come out later with me while I build something."

"Like you need company." Though Katrina felt her reluctance dissipating.

"It's always more fun with a buddy," Chef said.

"Buddies." She rolled her eyes. "We're buddies? Right…. Chef."

Chef laughed. "Peanut butter and jelly buddies. S'more buddies. And we can be sand buddies, too."

His easy manner warmed her. It seemed they'd turned a corner in relating to each other. He was no longer just the chef who prepared food for her. They'd shared time and some of their history with each other in the dark of the morning hours. Well, actually, she had shared some of her history. Chef hadn't disclosed much of anything about himself other than he flew kites and built sand sculptures.

Katrina decided it would be chef's turn to talk the next time. "I'll think about it," she said.

"Great. Let's go build something."

"Not right now. I'm starting to feel sleepy. I think I could go back to sleep before the sun rises, if I try."

"With as much sugar as you've consumed? Good luck."

"I accept your challenge… Chef." Katrina rose and walked across the deck to the back door.

"What time do you want to eat breakfast?" he asked.

She turned, shooting him a saucy look. "I thought we just ate breakfast."

He gave a surprised laugh. "S'mores at three in the

morning, you consider that breakfast?"

"It was nearly four."

"S'mores for breakfast." He shook his head. "No."

"We were breaking our nighttime fast, weren't we?"

He groaned. "S'mores for breakfast? They'll take away my hat if they find out."

"You know, one time when I was in Mexico, we ate mashed black beans and warm tortillas for breakfast. It was delicious."

Chef's eyes glittered with the possibility of fixing her an authentic Mexican breakfast. Too bad. He'd done his duty this morning, and she was happily letting him off the hook.

"What about coffee?" he asked.

"No thanks."

He sighed in defeat. "Will you at least let me do Mexican tomorrow morning?"

"Let's talk about it later."

"Okay. On the beach after lunch. Maybe you can bring some ideas for what I can sculpt next."

"I didn't agree to help."

Chef stood and stepped off the deck into the sand. "It'll be fun."

Katrina watched him stride across the sand to the deck of the other house. When he stepped onto the wooden surface, he stopped, bent his knees and did a somersault. Katrina gasped at the unexpected feat.

Chef was a man of many talents. She'd known of his skill with food. Last night he'd confessed to making and flying kites. This morning she learned he created works of art out of sand and he could somersault with ease. What other hidden talents did he possess?

That afternoon Katrina watched him from the sunroom. Chef.

She'd opted to read instead of helping him with sand

castles. But she caught herself staring at the ocean instead. Movement caught her attention, and she saw Chef digging a hole with a shovel. Soon a mound of sand stood next to him, and he crafted it into a ziggurat. Finished, he disappeared into the house next door, and later she'd seen him running with one arm high over his shoulder. She realized he was kite-flying again. Or at least, attempting it.

She giggled, as the kite refused to take flight, and the man continued to sprint across an expanse of beach, stop, examine and reposition the kite on the ground, and try again. From this distance, she couldn't tell a lot about his kite other than it wasn't the traditional—well, kite shape. He'd made a rectangular box, a kite shape she had seen in an old book once. Perhaps the reason it wasn't still a popular design is it didn't fly as well.

Chef didn't give up easily though. He dashed back and forth until as he watched over his shoulder at the kite's pathetic progress pulled behind him, his foot caught on something and he plunged head first in the sand.

Katrina gasped, and went to the door, her hand on the knob to go out and help. But she paused, not opening the door, seeing what he would do through the window.

Chef rolled over, and rose to his knees. Planting one tennis-shoed foot underneath him, he stood. Walking the few feet to his kite, he scooped it up and jogged over to a chair behind the house he occupied and collapsed in it, dropping the kite next to him.

Katrina watched him a few more minutes, but she couldn't tell what he was doing. Perhaps taking a break after frolicking on the beach like a kid.

He'd told her what his name was when they'd first met, but she couldn't remember what he'd said.

Asking him now seemed an awkward exercise.

In the evening, they sat on the deck roasting grilled cheese sandwiches, sweet potatoes, and plantain.

"You're going to eat with me, right?"

"Sure."

Though she noticed, he sat apart from her, across the expanse of the patio. Why? Did he feel as if they were crossing a line if he sat next to her? Was there a rule against it? If you fixed the food, you couldn't sit at the table and eat it? Though if that were the case, Katrina could argue she'd roasted her own sandwich.

At her request, he'd fixed more of the Dreamsicle drink, and a carafe of it sat on the low table next to her chair. When she'd complained at the suspected calories, he'd told her he'd used low fat ingredients, as if to reassure her that all of the indulging was okay.

"What about the s'mores. Nothing about marshmallows is low calorie."

Chef shrugged. "How often do you eat s'mores?"

Katrina shook her head. "Almost never."

"Before this morning, when was the last time you ate one?"

She didn't answer immediately, as if she were trying hard to remember exactly when. "I'd say twenty years ago."

"All right, so you ate perhaps six this morning?"

"Seven." She clutched her stomach, at the memory. They were so good, and so bad for her.

"Seven then. Seven in twenty years. That is one s'more every 2.8 years."

"When you put it that way, it sounds that I'm very frugal in my s'more consumption."

"It's all about perspective."

She longed to ask him about his failed kite, but didn't want to it to appear she had been spying on him.

"Want to talk about tomorrow's menu?" he asked.

"Sure."

"Any suggestions for breakfast?"

"Plain black coffee I can fix myself," she said, in her

typical I don't want to be bothered early in the morning answer.

"How about I come in and fix brunch for you?" he offered.

"Okay."

Her easy capitulation must have surprised him, but he didn't let it show. Rolling with her wishes meant he was getting what *he* seemed to love to do—cook for her. "Want to eat on the patio again?"

"Sure."

"Great. I'll set it up, and come over about ten. What about supper?"

Katrina shook her head, declining. "I'm getting cabin fever. I think I want to go into town and shop."

"But you have to eat."

"All I've done since I've been here is eat."

Chef ran his fingers through his hair. "So, you don't want me to prepare any evening food for you at all?" His expression was carefully blank, but Katrina wondered if the calm demeanor hid disappointment.

"If I'm hungry when I get home, I'll text you, but I'm sure you're ready for a break. Don't chefs get time away from work?" she asked. It was silly, really, thinking her giving him the night off would hurt his feelings.

"I love my work. I'm living my dream." He inclined his head to her. "Thank you so much for being a part of it."

His humble comment solicited a chuckle. "Yes. I had so much to do with you living your dream."

A small smile lifted his mouth, and some message sparkled in his eyes that she didn't understand. Affection and, if she admitted it, attraction unfurled in her chest. No. No. She couldn't. She couldn't. Katrina stood and collected her dishes. The smile fell as he watched her.

He stood as well, approaching her. "Leave those. I'll get them."

"Okay. Okay. Well, goodnight…. Chef. Thanks."

"Thank you."

Katrina hurried inside the house and shut the door behind her. He'd already tidied the kitchen, so she concluded he wouldn't seek permission to enter again tonight. And that was good.

"It's not okay to like him," she whispered to her image in the bathroom mirror a few minutes later. Running water in the sink, she wet a bath cloth and placed it against her heated face. She recognized the signs of attraction, the first time she'd experienced them since she'd fallen in love with Eric.

And never for another man.

It was okay to like Chef as a friend, to admire his talent as a chef, but not anything else.

She'd loved her husband. She didn't want to ever love and hurt like that again.

Not ever.

Chapter Six

Trey rang the doorbell and waited.

They hadn't made the menu plans for today, so he didn't want to leave her lunch on the porch since he wasn't even sure it's what she wanted to eat. At a little after nine, he thought she was likely awake as he'd seen signs of stirring in the house the last two mornings after eight—lights in the windows, and yesterday she had taken a walk on the beach with her coffee cup in hand. He'd wanted to go out and be with her, but reminded himself of his purpose.

He was Chef. Chef provided meals to nourish body and spirit. Chef did not accompany lovely women to the beach for morning walks.

He'd texted her about half an hour ago, but she hadn't responded back, a first.

Something had happened yesterday that had caused her to withdraw. Had he said something, done something inappropriate? Trey had played the conversation over in his mind a few times wondering, but nothing out of the ordinary surfaced.

He could understand Katrina wanting to explore the area, but eating at a restaurant when he was here at her beckoning seemed odd. Maybe it was just the house closing in on her. Could he provide a different venue? Maybe set up a shelter on the beach to allow her to eat seaside? Or could he rent some place in town, take her there and cook for her?

What would she like? Whatever it was, he'd do it.

She still didn't respond, and he knocked this time. Was something wrong? He pulled out his phone and texted her, asking if she was okay.

In a moment, she returned the text.

Sick. Door's unlocked.

Anxiety filled his chest as he opened the door and entered. "Katrina?" He set the food duffel down and walked further into the house.

"I'm on the couch," a weak voice answered him. "Don't come too close. I might be contagious."

Trey strode forward, finding Katrina's supine form encased in a blanket. An empty bowl sat on the floor in front of the couch. He moved it aside. Kneeling before her, he studied her blanched face visible under the folds tucked over her head.

"Hi," he said.

Her weak eyes gazed at him before she closed them. "Back up. You don't want this. Trust me."

Even her lips were pale.

"Let me take you to a doctor."

"No. It's just a stomach bug. I'll be okay."

"What are your symptoms? Nausea? Vomiting? Diarrhea?"

"Chef, mind your own business. I'm not talking to you about this."

Trey placed a hand on her forehead. She didn't feel feverish, though her skin was clammy.

"When is the last time you ate anything?" he asked.

She groaned and shifted, the blanket undulating. "Don't talk about food."

"When?"

"Last night."

Trey ran through the items he'd left for her in the refrigerator to snack on. "What?"

"Don't be mad. I ate out last night."

"What did you eat? Where?"

The blanket swallowed her face. "You're going to be

mad," she said through the material.

"What did you do?"

She wrenched the cover back. "I ate a salad at a gas station." Then she drew the blanket back over herself. "Go ahead and gloat. Tell me I deserve it for cheating on you."

Cheating on him? She thought he'd gloat because she ate food at a gas station and got sick? Poor thing.

"No one deserves to be sick." He patted what he thought was her shoulder and stood. "Where's the container?"

"What?"

"The salad you bought and ate, where's the container?"

She didn't answer, and he decided she wasn't going to, then, "I hid it in the bottom of the trash can. I didn't want you to see the evidence."

Her obvious misery was endearing, and that she cared enough that she didn't want him to know her infraction, was also endearing.

He dug through the trash, and found the clear plastic container. He opened it and sniffed, but didn't detect anything which smelled rancid. Still. If the lettuce hadn't been washed properly, she easily could have contracted poisoning from the bacteria on it. Some people had even ingested e-coli from unwashed greens.

It could be very serious.

She'd left several lettuce leaves, cucumber, and a tomato slice, with dressing which appeared to be Ranch. The dressing could be the culprit, but if it was from a packet—and they usually were from that venue—unless the dressing packet was already opened, it seemed unlikely. He closed the lid and put it back in the garbage can then washed his hands thoroughly.

Going out to his truck, he retrieved sugar, ginger, and green tea. Once back in her house, he reduced the sugar into a simple syrup with the ginger, then steeped an infuser of tea for a few minutes.

Carrying the tea in a mug across the room, Trey addressed her. "Katrina?"

"Can you just let me die in peace?"

He knelt before her, holding the cup for her inspection. "Take a sip of this."

"No."

"Just a sip. It will help settle your stomach."

"Every time I drink something, I throw up."

"One sip. A tiny one." He gestured with the cup.

She slowly sat up, gracing him with a resigned look. "Have my bowl close and get ready to jump out of the way."

Trey placed the bowl at the edge of the cushion and handed her the cup. "Just a sip."

She placed the mug to her lips, following his direction. He reached forward and took the mug away, placing it on the side table.

"Now, we'll wait for 15 minutes, and if you keep it down, you take another sip. All right?"

Fatigue shown in the dark circles under her eyes and her drawn cheeks. "I'm sorry."

Her sweet sad face moved him, and he resisted the urge to lean forward and kiss her forehead. "You have no reason to apologize to me. None at all."

"But it was dumb to eat gas station food when you were here. You said you'd fix whatever I wanted. The salad looked fresh. It had a sell by sticker on it and everything." Misery poured out with every word. "I was just being stupid and stubborn."

"A lot of food borne illnesses occur from leafy greens."

"Really?"

"Yes."

"I thought I was safe if I stayed away from the beef

and bean burrito."

Trey laughed. "Oh, gee. A beef and bean burrito at a gas station. Really? That tempted you?"

"I was feeling adventurous, but I wasn't brave enough."

"Thank goodness for small favors. Rest, and I'll put your tea in the warmer."

The sip of tea didn't stay down. When Trey moved toward her, she held up her hand. "Please go away," she said after she caught her breath. "I like you and all, but this is humiliating."

She stood up, gripping the arm rest as she did so. She held the bowl to her and stumbled to the bathroom. "I'm used to be being on my own. I can take care of myself." The door closed after that statement.

Ginger snap dough danced around the metal hook in the mixing bowl. Trey glanced at the shut door. Pressing the lever to cease motion, he touched the mixture, judged the consistency perfect, or as near as he could get it, and released the bowl from its mooring. He scraped the dough onto floured parchment paper, balled it, then set it in the fridge to chill.

And glanced at the closed door.

He washed his hands and leaned back against the counter.

Still closed.

Making up his mind, he strode across the large living room and knocked on the bathroom door. "Are you okay?"

"No. Go away." Her voice sounded weak, weary.

He'd heard her retching, but not for a while now.

He knocked again. "Can I come in?"

Silence. Trying the knob experimentally, Trey found it turned beneath his hand. He opened the door a fraction.

Katrina sat on the tiled floor with her head face down on folded arms on the edge of the bathtub. His chest ached at the sight, and not for the first time he wondered if the organ somehow retained recognition of Eric's wife or was it Trey's own feelings causing the heart to react?

"Katrina?"

"What?" The word echoed off the enamel tub, so forlorn in the clean, almost antiseptic room.

"Come on. Let me help you off the floor."

"Just leave me. It's more convenient this way."

Trey sighed, not wanting to leave her there, but also wanting to respect her wishes.

"Can I get you a blanket so you'll be a little more comfortable?"

She didn't answer. Trey waited, and was about to get one anyway. Finally, "Okay."

Immediately he sought the offered object, finding it in the linen closest next to the bathroom. He placed it on the floor next to her. She raised her head and looked at him with gratitude in her sick-dulled eyes.

She turned her face toward him. "Thanks," with her oft-used pause, "Chef."

Her response encouraged him, and he hurried to the kitchen to retry the elixir. In a few minutes he returned with a tray. Kneeling beside her, he set the tray in the spot where the blanket had been, now gracing her shoulders. She looked at the tray with the small ceramic dish on it.

"What is that?"

"I cooled the ginger tea mixture. I think the cold temperature will help you keep it down."

"I am not eating or drinking anything ever again."

Trey didn't believe her. On his knees now, he picked up the bowl. She gazed at it warily.

"It's just a tablespoon's worth. This way, we can be sure you don't overdo."

She lifted a hand and he placed the ridged bowl in her reluctant fingers.

"If it doesn't stay down this time, will you give up?"

"This will pass. You will feel better," he said softly.

"Chef," she grumbled, then placing the cup to her lips, she drank.

He sat back and waited.

Handing the cup to him, she said, "Stop staring at me. If I get sick again, I do not want a witness."

She was grumpy when she felt bad.

And cute.

He stood, taking the tray with him. Leaving the room, he opened the door wider, pushing it all the way back against the wall. Before he made it to the kitchen, she'd shut it again.

The cold tea stayed down, and he offered more, a tablespoon at a time at 15 minute intervals. After several hours, he prepared a small bowl of chicken broth and brought it to her where she'd made a nest of sorts on the couch in the sun room. She wrinkled her nose at the bowl. "I don't want that. I want a cookie."

He'd baked ginger snaps thinking the aroma would promote healing.

"They're really just to smell. The ginger fragrance discourages nausea."

"You're kidding. You baked cookies, didn't you? I mean that is all the noise I've been hearing, right?"

Trey nodded.

Her mouth hung open. "You baked cookies, and I can't have one?"

"They contain butter. The fat is harsh on your stomach."

"Just one."

He'd relented, and she ate the cookie without any ill effects. He considered it a victory because she didn't throw up, and she considered it a victory because he was wrong about her getting sick from eating the sweet.

With only cherry gelatin for supper, she called it a night, and demanded he leave.

He agreed only after soliciting a promise from her that she'd text if she got sick again.

****

The door opened, and there she stood in yoga pants and an open cardigan over a T-shirt with a panda bear on it. Somehow, she looked elegant. He'd never seen a woman who could pull off the look like Katrina could. Her shoulder length honey colored hair hung loose. He'd wondered if her hair was as soft as it looked. Of course, he hadn't touched it to find out.

"Hello," he greeted her.

"Hi."

"Feeling better?"

"Yes. I'm going to live. What's up?"

"Lunch."

She opened the door further and stood back. "I was thinking a hamburger would taste really good." She shivered. "I'm done with gas station food, but I figure a fast food chain restaurant has more rules about food preparation. And, seriously, Chef, you've gone way beyond the call of duty. I'm sure this job was the first time you've had to play nurse because your client had a moment of weakness while filling up her car with fuel."

Trey, in the act of shouldering his food duffel, paused. "Any commercial enterprise is subject to the same rigors of the health inspector. Including me and the gas station. Do you want a hamburger for lunch?"

She laughed. "You can make a fast food hamburger?"

"I can make you a hamburger that will make you never want to eat fast food again."

She touched her finger to her chin as if she were considering his offer. "Huh. My close call with death makes me never want to eat out again, but a hamburger just sounds so good right now." She gestured for him to enter, and he did so walking through the foyer toward the kitchen.

"You will break my heart if you eat fast food or go back to that gas station while I'm here to serve you."

"Is your heart so easily broken?"

He laughed. He couldn't help it. The irony of her statement was too much. "Oh, Katrina. This heart, it is amazingly resilient."

In the kitchen now, he put away the items he could still use for lunch. He loved that she threw him these curve balls, and he considered it a challenge to serve her the meal she requested even with very little prep time.

He'd have to go to the grocery store for beef, but he had some Kaiser rolls he could use as buns. Good.

"I need to run to the store. I'll be back in ten minutes."

Katrina shook her head. "No. Please, Chef. Don't go to so much trouble. Whatever you had in mind for lunch will be fine."

"If you want a hamburger, then I am going to make you a hamburger."

"We can eat burgers tonight."

He caught her pronoun, as if she were going to eat with her. He set out English cucumber and zucchini around the bowl of dip he made for her aperitif. Then poured passion fruit infused tea in a goblet. "This should tide you over until I can get back."

Katrina sighed. "I wish you wouldn't go to so much trouble. You're spoiling me." She arched an eyebrow, then added, "Chef," in that wonderfully provocative way she had of stating his title, as if she didn't really believe he was a chef, and she just said the word to tease him.

He left and returned within the ten promised minutes, though he used the grill in his truck to cook the patties. He prepared three, one for himself for later, and two for her though he knew there was little chance she would eat two dressed hamburgers. Still. He always cooked for the remote possibility that his client would want seconds. It was a wonderful compliment when they did, especially someone like Katrina who seemed rarely inspired by food.

With the food plated, he rang the bell again and waited.

She materialized in a moment. "I thought we had an agreement you would just come in."

He entered the house and went straight back to the sunroom to set the table.

"I think I want to eat at the bar tonight."

Her words halted his progress.

Her request confused him. "You don't want to eat in the sunroom?"

She stood near the counter with her hand on its surface. "That's okay, isn't it?"

He retraced his steps. "Of course, it's okay." He'd have to wait until she was finished to clean up, but there wasn't that much to do since he'd prepared the burger in his truck. She settled on the high chair as he worked.

"I thought you'd give me a hard time about eating such a heavy meal after being sick."

"Your appetite has returned. If you think a hamburger would taste good, maybe it's your body craving the calories and protein after two days of fasting."

"So, you think a hamburger is okay?" The dubious expression on her face informed him she didn't trust her body yet.

"Sure. Listen to your body."

"What about fries?"

"Fries?"

"Fast food fries. Can you make those?"

"Shoestring, or homefries?"

"Mmmm. Hard choice."

Chapter Seven

Trey rested on his knees in the pit he'd dug days ago surveying the sand and making a plan for what he'd do next. Katrina sat on a chair on her deck. He'd invited her outside several times, but she'd declined each time. Seeing her outside he felt was progress. Though she still hadn't joined him. Maybe she would.

"Hey," she called to him.

"Hey," he echoed.

"What are you doing?"

"What?" Okay. It was a lie. He heard her loud and clear, but thought if he acted like he hadn't she might join him.

"I said, 'What are you doing?'"

He shook his head and put his hand to his ear, in a mime of can't-hear-ya. She stood up, her hands on her hips.

"Yes, you can," she accused.

"What?"

"Chef, I know you can hear every single word I'm saying."

He bent his head down to hide his grin digging in the sand and chuckling. "No, I can't." He peeked up and saw her rounding the rail and stepping down to the beach. He put the wet sand in a mold, then turned it over, gave it a small twist, then revealed a perfect fish. To make a school of them, he was thinking 30 total.

"Why are you acting like you can't hear me?"

"Because I want you to come supervise."

She stepped down into the shallow pit. "Oh. I get it. It's underwater, and that's the sandbar."

Trey looked up at her. She had on capri pants, a long

fisherman's sweater, and house shoes. Cute.

He tore his eyes from her to the sandbar. "That's not a sandbar. It's a bridge."

"A bridge?"

She stepped on the cement block he'd placed there as a step, then back up on beach level. She walked across the pathway and bent down examining the shells.

"You've rearranged some of these."

"Yeah. I put them down the first day just to make sure I could cover it. Then I thought it would be fun to do some designs."

She crawled across the bridge. He climbed onto the end of the bridge, watching her near the far end.

"What do you think?" he asked.

She looked behind her, spotting him and turning fully, she fell backward, watching him with a fearful look on her face.

"Katrina? What's wrong?"

She shook her head. "I didn't think it was a bridge. I thought it was a sandbar, but...." She closed her eyes tightly, then sat up. "I must have known on some level because I dreamed about a sand bridge." Her eyes opened, and her pained gaze found his. "I was walking on it. Eric, my husband, was calling to me. I tried to get to him, but a truck came across the bridge and almost ran over me. The bridge was made of sand though I didn't realize it at first. But when the truck reached a certain point, the weight of it caused the bridge to collapse. The truck fell, and when I looked to where Eric was, he had disappeared."

She stood up.

"He was standing about where you are now."

Trey quickly sprinted halfway toward her. "I'll just tear down the bridge. That way it won't remind you of the dream."

"No. No! That's silly. You've worked so hard on it."

Trey shrugged. "It was just for fun. It if upsets you, I'll get rid of it."

"No. I'll know it was here even if you destroy it. I'll know it was in this spot."

Trey crouched down. "Well, what could we do, then, so it doesn't upset you?"

"This is dumb. It was just a dream. Why am I letting it bother me?"

"What if I make a net in the pit. That way it would catch the truck and Eric, too, if he fell."

"I didn't see him fall. He just wasn't there anymore. Just his jacket. It was...." She shook her head. "It was folded neatly, like he'd made the time to make sure it was taken care of." Katrina walked across the bridge, her head down as if she were examining the shells, making sense of the pattern. "Do you think the dream means anything?"

Maybe her subconscious knew there was a part of Eric close by. Was that even possible?

Trey jumped down from the bridge and studied the sand. He could engrave a net on either side of the bridge, but he like the idea of another medium, a bolder statement of the safety net.

"I don't know. Do you dream about him very much?"

"Not lately. Maybe it's because the anniversary of his death is coming up."

"That's possible." He'd seen a net at the hardware store downtown. Until he could get there, he'd draw one in the sand. Perhaps it would ease her spirit a bit, and seeing the sand bridge wouldn't upset her. He retrieved a dowel and yardstick from the box of tools he'd gathered to use when he sculpted.

"What are you doing?" she asked.

"Creating peace of mind, I hope." He glanced up at her, and saw her bite her lip. What? Had he made it worse or better by what he'd said? He didn't know. Food, he knew. Offering comfort and elegance with traditional or elegant meals, he could do. But providing comfort to a grieving widow through sand sculpture, this was all new.

****

After lunch, Katrina stood on the sand bridge and gazed at the recessed sand below her. A net made of thick rope rested on the ground on either side of the bridge, lifted on the outer four edges by short thick posts anchored in the ground. How Trey had placed the net under the already existing ridge, she had no idea, and she'd examined it not believing he'd done so, thinking instead he had used two separate nets, but, no, it went about a third of the way up the column of sand which constructed the bridge.

Knowing he'd accomplished such a feat, impressed her, and it moved her deeply that he would go to so much trouble on her behalf.

His kindness and gentle manner touched her.

She liked Chef.

Katrina decided to walk on the road in front of the house instead of the beach. Heading out the door, she walked in front of the house where Chef was staying, and stopped. Tucked on the other side of the house was a large black vehicle, similar to a mid-sized moving van. She approached it, and realized what it was and whose it was. Elegant silver script on the side proclaimed Chef@Home with an insignia Katrina recognized from the double breasted shirt Chef wore.

Of course, he'd have a company truck with all of his supplies in it. She just hadn't seen it until now.

That night, she sat on the high chair and watched him prepare supper.

"What did you do today?"

Stalks of celery lay in front of him. In lightning quick movements, he transformed them to fine cross-cut slivers. How he didn't butcher his own fingers was a mystery she had yet to solve.

"Went sailing."

"On a boat?"

The knife paused. Katrina's gaze moved from his hands to his face. He gave her one of his you're-so-silly-but-I'm-too-nice-to-tell-you looks.

"Well, you don't own a boat, do you?"

"No." He slid the celery aside and washed the knife. Picking up a peeled carrot, he began to sculpt it using an odd shaped blade. "There's a rental place about a mile from here."

Katrina watched him work, fascinated by the intricate lace pattern he inscribed on the carrot flesh. "Why do you waste so much time designing food that's just going to be eaten or thrown away?"

"Because eating shouldn't just be about consuming calories."

"But the carrot will be gone tomorrow."

With a small curved pick, he detailed the top. "Who says there will be a tomorrow?"

"Oh, brother. You're going to get philosophical with me about a carrot?" Katrina had the urge to take the vegetable out of his hand, bite it and hand it back to him.

"Enjoy today. Be in the beautiful moment. The meals I prepare are about taking complete pleasure in the space and time at the table." He studied the carrot then set it upright on the cutting board. He'd carved flowers and lacework in it.

The intricate art testified his commitment to his work and probably his life as well. The transitory nature of it created a wave of sadness in Katrina. So much work in that small vegetable, and for what? She wasn't going to eat it.

"Katrina?" Chef said quietly.

Once again, her attention moved to his face, and she found there compassion. "I do this so you can enjoy it right now. It's not meant to go beyond the meal, except the memory and the good feelings of partaking of the dish and setting."

She didn't understand. She didn't like things that didn't last. She liked permanence and things that you could hold and preserve and keep.

"You should do wood carving."

"Wood doesn't taste good."

"You know what I mean, don't you?"

He nodded. But obviously, he wasn't going to argue with her. Katrina decided to change the subject. "I saw your food van. Very nice."

"Thanks."

"Do you cook in it when you're not here?"

"Depends on what I'm doing. I like my oven because I know it. But if I need a lot of space, I use the kitchen at the other house. The refrigerator over there is pretty much full."

"You ever challenge yourself by making something you have never made before?"

"Sure, though when I'm cooking for other people, it's important they like what I prepare, so I have a repertoire I draw from."

"I imagine working for yourself and by yourself it could get easy to get in a rut."

He shook his head. "Several times a year, I get together with some friends I went to culinary school with. We have cook-offs. It's a lot of fun."

Glee bounced in Katrina's chest. It was the first piece of personal history Chef had shared.

"A cook-off? Like a cooking competition?"

He nodded. "Someone picks ingredients, and each of us prepare a dish with the ingredients. The best tasting dish wins."

"Where do you go to do it? Does everyone have their

own food truck?"

"No. We retreat at a culinary arts school or a 2 year college with a culinary program. Sometimes we do it as a fundraising event either for a community or challenge each other and the winner gets the kitty to donate it to their favorite charity."

"That does sound like fun."

"Do you want to have one?" He had begun carving another carrot.

"One what?"

"A cook-off."

"I don't cook. I told you that."

"No, the challenge would be for me to cook, and you to come up with ingredients you think I couldn't use to make an enticing dish."

"Who would judge?"

"You. If you like it, I win. If you don't, you win."

The idea intrigued Katrina. "It seems unfair to you. I can give you really disgusting ingredients, and even if I like it, I could lie and say I didn't."

"Except, you wouldn't." He studied the carrot, rubbed its surface, and cut again.

"Well, maybe I wouldn't lie, but choosing bad-tasting ingredients is what would make it challenging."

"Exactly."

Katrina turned the idea over in her mind. "Huh."

She hadn't been further away from the beach house except walks on the beach or road, other than the unfortunate gas station incident. "I could go grocery shopping and find some really challenging food. Where's the closest grocery store, and do they carry macaroni and cheese out of a box?" She crooked her head as she watched him. "Or maybe some Oreo cookies and shrimp."

Chef graced her with a handsome smile which made her heart skip a few times. "You're allergic to shellfish, or did you forget?"

Obviously, *he* hadn't forgotten.

****

It was the first time she'd been in his food truck, and the efficiency of the space was inspiring—a fully equipped kitchen in the back of the truck with a driver's chair and a passenger seat which could convert to a small table if needed. Chef had told her the loft over the cab held sleeping quarters. At her request, he'd lifted the panel he'd installed to prevent lint or dust from falling into the food preparation area and secured it to hooks on the ceiling, pushed aside the curtain and shown her the neatly made mattress in the small space.

Katrina studied the area. "You can't even sit up."

Chef shrugged. "I don't sit up to sleep."

"How do you manage to get out without banging your head?"

His mouth turned up at the corner, and he looked upward as if seeking the answer. "Just sort of fall out and hope my feet is the first thing that hits the floor."

There was no bathroom, though the kitchen area sported a sink with a flat tank of distilled water on a shelf at ceiling level for times when the truck did not have access to potable water.

"Can't believe you don't have a bathroom."

"I wasn't willing to sacrifice the kitchen space for it."

"But you live here."

"I stay here, and oftentimes I park at a campground that has a bathhouse."

What an odd existence. Having no permanent place, traveling around cooking for strangers. "You're homeless."

"Home is where the heart is." Rubbing his chest, he laughed as if he'd made a joke. "I have a kitchen I designed and built. I'm living my dream." The smile fell, and a thoughtful expression settled on his face. "I am so blessed, so thankful to be alive."

The fullness of his sincerity filled the truck, so strong was it that Katrina swore there was a palpable vibration in the air. She stepped back away from it. Him. Ducking her head, she grasped the back of the headrest and sat on the driver's seat. Katrina moved her legs to the side so she could watch.

She'd challenged Chef to a cook-off in which he had to prepare an edible meal using the ingredients she'd put in a basket. He could have as much time as he needed to obtain additional ingredients and prepare the dish. But he only had five minutes to work up a menu, and the dish had to be tasty enough that, Katrina, picky person that she was, would enjoy it.

She'd purposely picked food she didn't like, and that did not go together well.

She leaned forward to see his face when he opened the basket.

Black licorice, chicken livers, boiled eggs, and beets.

Aiming her cell phone at his face, she waited. He snickered and shook his head in amusement. "Can I open the basket now?"

"Yes." She looked at him through the small screen.

He lifted the split top, his attention inside the wicker box. Reaching into it, he picked up the package of meat.

"Chicken livers." Katrina informed him unnecessarily.

"I see."

He set it on the work station beside him and lifted the candy and the bowl of eggs. Putting the bowl aside, he palmed a single egg and set it on the counter spinning it in a deft movement. His gaze met hers. "These are boiled eggs."

"Yes, they are. Have I told you how I feel about eggs?"

"Not a fan, I think you said."

"That's exactly what I said." His memory impressed Katrina. But if you made your living cooking for others, remembering their food likes and dislikes was important.

"And...." He opened the package and brought it to his nose and sniffed. "Black licorice." Tearing off a piece, he ate it.

"As per our rules," Katrina stated, "You have five minutes to come up with a menu using all of the ingredients in the basket. You will write down your dishes and put it in the envelope. Then after you've prepared the food, you will announce the menu, I will eat and judge."

He wrote on the paper she'd provided, and in less than a minute, he folded the paper and placed it in the envelope.

He folded his arms and looked at her.

"What?" she said. "Are you giving up?"

He smiled. "No. I'm done."

She balked. "You already came up with an idea?"

"Yes."

"Oh." She was almost disappointed. Hadn't she made the ingredients challenging enough? "Okay. Well, let's go to the grocery store then."

"Nope," he said.

"What do you mean?"

"I have everything I need to fulfill the menu." He stepped to the sink and washed his hands.

"Oh, dern. I was hoping you'd let me drive your van to the store."

"Do you have a special license? You'll need one to drive this truck."

He was chopping something now, but she couldn't tell what.

"I would? Or are you just saying that so I won't bug you about driving it?"

"A commercial driver's license."

He was so quick. How did he not lose a finger?

A knock sounded at the window. Katrina turned and saw a man standing outside of the driver's door.

"Hi," he said.

"Chef, there's someone out here."

Wiping his hands on the apron he wore, Chef approached the cab and leaned in next to her. He switched on the ignition and rolled down the window.

"Hi there," the man said. "You Chef at Home?"

"Yes," Chef said.

"I'm Mike van Kirk. I wanted to thank you for Saturday. That was a really nice thing you did."

"You're welcome."

What was he talking about? What had Chef done?

He reached into his pocket and pulled out his wallet. Withdrawing a card, he handed it into the window. Katrina took it then handed it to Chef.

"I run the shelter at 40th and Vine. If you're interested in helping out again, call me."

"I can be there between four and five on Saturday evening, if that suits." He offered one of his own cards to the Mike van Kirk.

"Would love it. Thanks."

After he left, Katrina shifted in her seat, facing again the mobile kitchen. "What was that about?"

"I took the truck downtown and made sandwiches for anyone who wanted them."

"Wow. That was nice. I wouldn't think downtown would be real busy on a Saturday afternoon though."

"It's getting to be cooler weather which means a lot of homeless people are migrating down this way. They tend to stay close to the downtown area because most of the helping agencies are located there. But Saturdays are hard because not many places offer food on the weekend, so if I'm in town, I usually take my truck and help out."

"Don't you need a permit to sell food though?"

"I need a permit to sell it or give it away. But I have one, so it's all legitimate."

Admiration rose in her chest as she watched him return to his food preparation. "Do you need me to be quiet so you can concentrate?"

"No. You talk to me when I'm in the house preparing a meal. The only difference is we're in the truck."

"And it's a test to see how good you are."

He measured flour then poured it in his big mixer.

"What are you doing?"

"Am I allowed to tell you?"

"Oh." She sighed. "I guess you could. They are our made up rules after all."

"So, you want me to tell you?"

"What do you and your chef friends do? Do you keep it a secret or tell ahead of time?"

"We usually wait. Otherwise, some smart aleck will chime in and suggest a better way to prepare whatever the dish is."

He turned on the mixer, then opened the refrigerator, poured a pale pink liquid into a glass and handed it to her. "Here. I made you something."

"What is it?"

Chapter Eight

"I call it Katrina's delight."

She sniffed and detected strawberry. Taking a sip, she fell in love.

"What is this?" she asked him, before drinking again. It tasted remarkably like the PB&J breakfast tarts she splurged on once a month.

"It's a peanut butter and strawberry jam smoothie."

"I knew it! PB&J, my favorite. My absolute delight. I love it."

For the big reveal, Chef had fixed two place settings at the counter at the kitchen.

"Oh. You're going to eat with me. Big deal," she teased.

"It's a cook off. I get to eat what I fixed too, and either delight in it or suffer through it. We're in this together."

"You're just trying to be sure I don't cheat."

"No. Totally your call whether you like it or not."

He lit two candles sitting side by side in crystal holders. "Ready?"

"Yes."

He opened the envelope. "I have prepared for you today liver and egg paté´ with sweet pita crisps for the appetizer. The entrée is chicken cacciatore over hand cranked fettuccini with bacon seared asparagus, and for dessert beet custard with caramel and dark chocolate swirled vanilla bean ice cream.

"It sounds really good, but the ingredients were supposed to be in the same dish. It's cheating to make three different things."

Chef pursed his lips. "You didn't specify one dish."

"Yes, I did."

He uncovered the dishes and set the rectangular platter of the pate and pita crisps in between their two plates. Then served the entrée at each of their places. Katrina waited until he was seated before she ate. The appetizer tasted decent, but not something she'd probably choose to eat again. The chicken cacciatore, however, was delicious. She ate what he'd served her, then scraped the plate with her fork.

"I have to admit, this is really good. Of course, when you put the liver, eggs, and beets in everything else, this shouldn't even be part of the completion."

Chef rose and retrieved the ice cream—already scooped—and place them in silver dishes with the beet custard he'd spooned from a chafing dish. Though she'd watched him put the ingredients for the ice cream in a maker in his truck and she was excited to try it, the beet custard sounded gross, though she had to admit, it was a pretty scarlet color.

She dug into the ice cream and passed the spoon through the custard. Bringing it to her mouth, she tasted it.

"Are you sure this has beets in it? It is surprisingly tasty."

Chef placed his own spoon in his mouth. "So, is that a win, then?"

Katrina shrugged. "The appetizer wasn't great. I could taste the eggs and livers which I didn't like. I loved the ice cream, but it didn't have any of the challenge ingredients in it. I did like the beet custard, surprising since I have never liked custard before, so good job there."

"And the chicken cacciatore on fettuccini?"

"I loved it. Definitely want to eat it again, but it didn't have any of the challenge ingredients in it."

Chef grinned. Looking down at his ice cream, he buried his spoon in it. "It had all of the ingredients in it."

Shock caused Katrina's mouth to drop open. "What?"

"Chicken cacciatore including the chicken livers with sauce containing black licorice, bits of egg yolk, beets and tomatoes."

"Are you serious?"

"Yes. I win."

Katrina stuck her finger in the custard then placed it in her mouth. "Yes, you win."

"And there's beet juice in Katrina's delight as well."

"I don't even like beets. Why'd you put it in my special drink?"

"Because I could."

"All right. You're the chef, gifted in the talent of disguising disgusting food in delectable dishes. I'm delighted."

"You made my night. Thank you."

****

Katrina wished she had binoculars.

She leaned toward the window watching the crazy cook. He'd been standing at the shore casting out to sea with a fishing pole which she thought had a tennis ball on the end. For almost half an hour he'd done this. Then she'd set the pole down and stood with legs apart staring at the ocean. He lifted his arms up to the sky, arched his back, then without any warning ran full speed into the water.

She gasped. Was he trying to kill himself? If he didn't drown, he'd catch pneumonia. Opening the door, she ran toward the water, wondering how she was going to save him. Pivoting, she grabbed a tiki pole from the corner of the deck.

"Chef! Chef! What are you doing? Get out of the water?"

He didn't hear her at first. His head disappeared.

Oh, no! She was too late.

"Chef!" The soft sand made it difficult to run fast, and

it seemed to take forever to reach the waves breaking onto the packed terrain at water's edge.

Chef's head emerged, and he stood. He spotted her, and his mouth curved up in surprise.

"Hey, what are—" he began.

"What are you doing? Are you insane?" she yelled.

"Huh?" He looked down at himself. "Oh. Just having some fun."

She was up to her knees at this point. "Are you kidding?" Turning around, she trudged out of the surf, then facing him again on dry land, she speared the tiki torch. "You're going to kill yourself. You don't go swimming in the ocean in October."

"Why not?"

"Because it's cold."

Chef walked toward her, then fell backward, then sat as a wave washed over him at chest level. He laughed. "It certainly is cold. Feels fantastic." He raised a fisted hand, then opened his fingers and let clumps of wet sand fall through them.

"How have you survived to this point in your life?"

"I was sick as a kid. Didn't I tell you? When I got better, I had a lot of making up to do. I made a list of all the things I wanted to do in my life. Crazy, wonderful fun things and the dream of owning my own food truck so I could eat whatever I wanted wherever I wanted, and I could do the same thing for other people."

"You have a list?"

"Yep."

"Is catching pneumonia on it? Your lips are blue."

Chef's blue lips opened, revealing a charming and joyful smile. "It's wonderful to be alive, isn't it?"

****

Katrina had requested breakfast with an ulterior motive in mind. She sat at the counter over French Toast pecan casserole and coffee while he squeezed juice from oranges one at a time using a levered juicer.

"What are you going to do today?" she asked.

"Cook for you."

"I mean other than that."

With the innards mashed within an inch of their dehydrated lives, Chef placed the peels on a cutting board and chopped them. She wondered what he was going to do with them, but left that topic for another time.

"There's a parasail place over in Gulf Shores. It's closed for the season, but I got a hold of the owner, and he said if the wind isn't too high, he'd let me go up."

"That sounds fun."

"It is fun. Want to go with me?"

Katrina speared a piece of the breakfast with her fork and brought it to her mouth. It was the best version of French toast she'd ever eaten. "Have you done it before?"

"Well, not exactly, but I've been skydiving, and it's similar."

Katrina stopped chewing as she stared at his back, as he was washing something in the sink. "Skydiving? You've been skydiving?"

"Yes. Quite a few times. My goal is to jump in every state."

"Jump as in skydive?"

He cast her a glance over his shoulder. "Yes. I've jumped in eleven states so far."

"Is there anything you won't do, Mr. Adventure?"

He shut off the water and dried his hands. "That's Chef Adventure to you."

She laughed.

"Carpe diem. Do you know what it means?"

"Yes. Seize the day."

"Exactly, I try to seize every day and to do it joyfully and thankfully."

"Carpe diem. That's your motto."

"Absolutely."

"I was wondering about that man—Mike van Kirk who runs the shelter."

Chef leaned back against the sink, listening.

"What about him?"

"Are you going to fix a meal for the homeless people there?"

He nodded.

Nervously, Katrina fidgeted with her fork. "Do you need any help? I mean, I'm sure you don't need any help, but would you mind if I came along and helped? Maybe I could help you seize that part of your day."

"I'd love for you to seize that part of my day. It's just sandwiches, apple chips, and some vegetables, but sure, if you want to help, it will go a lot quicker."

Relief that he'd agreed to let her help warmed her. She smiled, and noticed he ran his hand over his collar bone, as she'd seen him do a few times since she'd met him.

"Can I ask you a personal question?"

"Yes."

"Do you have some problem with your collar bone? I see you rub it sometimes."

He inclined his head and lifted his hand and touched the spot again. "I didn't realize I did it." He smiled as if he remembered a private joke. "When I was...." He took a deep breath. "I used to have a problem with my heart. When it would go out of rhythm, I could feel it. I used to keep my hand there on my heart, trying to control the beats, by staying calm, breathing deep. I guess I never lost the habit of feeling my heart even after...."

"After what?"

He took a deep breath in and chuckled. "After I was healed."

"Like a medical healing?"

"It's a story I would love to tell you, but it's probably something to share another time."

"How come?" Disappointment flitted at her.

"It's....involved. I'll leave it at that for now."

"Maybe before the two weeks are up, you will tell me."

"I'd like to. You were asking about preparing dinner for Harmony House."

"Is that the name of the homeless shelter?"

Chef nodded. "I was thinking turkey club sandwiches, deep fried apple chips, and carrot and celery sticks."

"Can we do peanut butter and jelly sandwiches too, like how you make them? They're so good and PB&J keeps for a long time."

"That's a good point. I can label the wrapping with the kind of sandwich so anyone with allergies will have a choice."

Chef accepted her offer to help, so Katrina found herself wearing an apron and plastic gloves spreading his special peanut butter on homemade bread with a batter knife.

"You don't wear gloves when you fix my food," she observed.

"I can start, if you like. It's a private home, so the guidelines aren't as stringent." He lowered a mesh basket of fresh apple rings into a fryer. The sizzling filled the air, and a sweet oily aroma assailed Katrina. "Especially when preparing food in this venue, it's important to follow the established rules. Otherwise, they could take away the privilege they have granted me to be here. Gloves are to be worn for food preparation as well as hair covering." He gave a meaningful glance to the net he handed her before they began. Self-consciously, Katrina had placed it carefully on her head then tucked her hair inside.

He came up next to her, and in seconds had slapped the slices together until a stack of sandwiches stood ten high. With square sheets of waxed paper, he showed her how to place the sandwiches in the middle and fold the paper neatly then secure it with a black sticker with his logo on it. Then they placed them in small white paper lunch sacks. It was simple and elegant, and Katrina loved being a part of it.

Together they made fifty sacked meals and placed them in boxes to make it more convenient to carry into the shelter. Mike van Kirk stood outside of the building when they arrived. Chef rolled down the window and greeted him as they pulled up to the curb.

"Hi. You made it." He smiled and waved.

Chef parked and shut off the engine. "We've got fifty meals. I know you said twenty-five, but Katrina and I figured we'd double the order just in case."

"I like the way you think."

Chef and Katrina exited the vehicle through the back door carrying the boxes. "Where do you want them?"

Two men materialized to help carry the rest.

Mike indicated with his hand. "Right this way."

Katrina followed Chef into the modest brick building. The furnishings were dated, but everything was clean. Mike led them through a large dining room into a kitchen.

They set the boxes on the counter. Chef looked around. "Not bad," he said.

"We got a grant about six years ago to update the kitchen. During the week we feed around a hundred people for lunch, but on the weekends, it's just the residents living here who eat."

"What do the other people do on the weekend?" Katrina asked.

"They get by, and we usually send to go packs with them after the Friday meal." Mike indicated the boxes. "Your extra meals will help. I can send a few guys out with meals to distribute them."

"Whatever you think is best."

Mike held out his arm, and the two men shook hands. The other men, also, shared the gesture of thanks with Chef and Katrina.

On their way back to the house, Katrina sat next to him in the truck. He handled the vehicle well, without taking any risks. In fact, he seemed overly cautious. It didn't seem to fit her picture of him as a man who had gone parasailing earlier in the day or who had admitted to jumping out of airplanes in 11 states with only a parachute on his back.

"Chef?"

He was watching the traffic, waiting to pull out onto the highway from a side street. Once he maneuvered the truck successfully, he glanced over at her.

"Yes?"

"That was a very good thing you did."

He smiled. "I had help. Thank you."

"You're always thanking me."

"I have a lot to be thankful for."

"Not from me. I'm just some goofy woman who loves peanut butter and jelly."

Chef didn't reply.

"This is where you say, 'You're not goofy.'"

Chef chuckled. "I need to read my script. Sorry."

And he still didn't say it.

"Do you think I'm goofy?"

"No."

"I guess you cater to a lot of people." Who was Katrina among all of his clients? Just a woman alone at a beach house. She was probably not anyone special to him. The insight brought a sadness to her.

Chapter Nine

Trey resisted the urge to pull the truck over, invite her to stand on the side of the road so he could kneel at her feet, paying homage to her. If he'd lived in Scotland a few centuries ago, he would have offered her his sword in deference to her, a sign of his trust and his adoration.

But Katrina wouldn't understand his behavior. If she had any clue of the depth of his gratitude and affection for her, she'd probably go back to the beach house, pack, and leave as quickly as she could.

So, Trey didn't say anything. He hoped he had blessed her with his cooking and hospitality while they'd been together. That had been his goal. He'd achieved it, he was pretty sure. He'd expected the overwhelming sense of gratitude and good feelings at being able to serve her. He had not expected the yearning he felt, a literal ache in his heart at times when she spoke. It was eerie and amazing.

And not something to share with her unless he wanted to scare her.

Anyway, if they were living in ancient Scotland, he wouldn't be driving her around in his food truck talking of peanut butter and jelly sandwiches. He imagined himself kneeling before her with his 8 inch full tang high carbon Wusthof palm up in his hands in a humble offering of his devotion.

She'd laugh at him, maybe.

Make fun of him, probably.

He could just hear her: What are you doing, giving me your knife, she'd pause then add, Chef.

"What's so funny?" Katrina's question pulled him out of his reverie.

"I was thinking about ancient Scottish traditions."

"Yeah? Which one, hiding your Tartan blessed by the priest or playing your bagpipes to intimidate your foes?"

"Wedding ceremonies, actually. The husband presents his sword to his wife who will one day pass it down to their son."

"What's funny about that?"

"I suppose it's not really that funny."

"Only that you could make a mental leap of me being goofy to ancient Scottish wedding sword exchange."

"Quite a leap."

"Are you Scottish?"

"On my mother's side, yes."

She didn't speak for a few minutes. "Have you ever cooked Haggis?"

He glanced sidelong at her and saw her grin. "You're kidding."

"Yes, I am. I'll stick to PB&J, thanks."

"Want to talk about tomorrow's menu?" He stopped at a traffic light which had turned red.

"Sure."

"Do you want breakfast?"

"Why not? I haven't had it since we arrived."

"Traditional?"

"No eggs."

"Right. Want to go south of the border? You said you had a Latino breakfast once and really liked it."

"All right. You ought to be able to do authentic since we're in Florida."

"I'll do the best I can. Lunch?"

"Surprise me."

"Dinner?"

"It's hard to come up with ideas when I'm not that hungry."

"Is there anything in particular that you really like that

I haven't fixed yet?"

"Well." She sighed. "There's this restaurant Eric and I used to eat at. They made really good fish tacos. I've not been back there since he died."

"How come?"

"It's hard to go to the places we went together. It makes me miss him more than I should."

"Who says how much you should miss him?"

She sighed. He looked at her and she was staring at her hands folded in her lap. "I should be over missing him by now. It's been three years."

He resisted the urge to reach over and take her hand. Let her be. These two weeks were about thanking her—however that needed to happen, even letting her talk about the man whose heart beat in Trey's chest.

Especially that.

"Don't you think it's been long enough?" she asked.

"Maybe some people never get over losing someone they love."

"Well, I don't want to be like that." She shifted in her seat. "But I think I am. I think I've become that person."

"Tell me about that person you've become."

"Never going out. Doing anything. Just staying home alone. My friend Brenda gives me a hard time about it, but her husband is still alive. She doesn't know what it's like."

"Do you like never going out and staying home alone?"

"Most of the time, I do. Sometimes though…."

He waited for her to finish her sentence, almost prompting her, but he didn't. She'd say what she wanted to say if she wanted to.

"Sometimes, it gets lonely."

That last word amplified itself in the cab of the truck. *Lonely. Lonely. Sometimes, it gets lonely.*

He felt her look at him then. He counseled himself to

keep calm without jumping in and offering to cook for her every day for the rest of her life. He was the chef. He was not here to save her. But he could help her. He absolutely could do that.

"Well, next time you feel that way, just call me. I'll come to your house and do a cooking class."

"Oh, that's silly. I live 10 hours away."

"I live six hours from here in Athens."

They arrived at the beach houses, and he turned the steering wheel of the truck into the driveway between the two structures. He shifted it into park and would have exited, but instead….

"You drove six hours just to cook for me?"

"I'm the Chef@Home. That's what I do. It's why I have my truck."

"How did they find you?"

Uneasiness wrapped tendrils around him. He absolutely did not want to lie to her, but what could he say? That he was the they she'd just asked him about?

He opened the door, hoping her question was rhetorical.

"Who was it that hired you anyway?"

"Who hired me?" Of course, she wanted to know. She'd just asked him, but his question bought him some time to think of a clever answer, a clever non-answer. And then to kick himself for not coming clean. If she wanted to know, shouldn't he tell her?

"Yes. I'd like to know. Did they tell you not to tell me?"

He searched for words. She studied him as he groped for something to say. "They did." She concluded by his silence. "They asked you not to tell me who they were."

He tucked his chin down and returned her stare. "Why is it, do you think, that they wouldn't want you to know who they are?"

She bit her lip in thought. "Maybe they didn't want me to know because if I knew then I wouldn't have accepted the gift."

"Is it true?"

"Well." She cut her eyes to him, as if checking to see if he knew more than he was admitting to. Or maybe that was just Trey's guilty conscience. He should tell her. If she wanted to know, he should.

"I don't think it's a friend of mine who has given me these two weeks here. Brenda is the only one who would do something like that. And she said herself she wouldn't do it anonymously. It has to do with my husband's death. I'm afraid it does." She shook her head. "But... this is a very generous gift they've given me. I do appreciate it, but it's all I can do for now. I can just appreciate the gift without doing something in return. That probably doesn't make sense to you, but...."

"Please. Don't feel like you have to explain. The house and me, there are no expectations for you to do anything, but show up here. You've done that. I'm glad you did. Really glad."

She looked at him with pained eyes. "There's something more they want."

He shook his head. "No. This is a gift with no strings attached. Otherwise, it wouldn't be anonymous."

"How do you know?"

"Because I've been anonymous, and I did it because I didn't want someone to feel they owed me for the gift I gave." He fisted his hands so he wouldn't take her by the shoulders to show how important this was to him that she understand. "Giving the gift was the only thing I wanted."

She searched his eyes, then dropped her gaze. "That's all I wanted, too. Just to...." She sighed. "Never mind. It doesn't matter."

"What? What doesn't matter?"

"When my husband died, I did something, and I did it anonymously. I just wanted his death and all of the nightmare that went with it to be over. But there's this woman I know, and she's very nice, but she doesn't understand that I don't ever want to think about it again."

Oh. I've been so selfish. So selfish. I was so determined to thank her I didn't realize doing so would open up a wound Katrina has tried so hard to heal.

She shook her head. "I'm sorry to put all this on you, Chef. I shouldn't put you in the position where you would disclose the giver's identity against their wishes. I'm sorry." She held up her hands in a gesture of throwing it away. "You know," she said opening her own door and jumping down from the truck. "My grandmother was a country girl. She made the best biscuits and red eyed gravy I've ever eaten. I've never been able to make that dish like she did. Do you think that's something you could teach me to make?"

Oh, fair maiden. Here is my life. Here is my sword. Take it.

Before Trey could fall on his knees in front of her, he gave himself a mental reality check. *You're Chef. Act like it.* "I'll come by around eight in the morning with your breakfast. Want me to fix it in house, or bring it prepared?"

"Umm. Maybe just bring it ready to eat."

"Okay. Good."

"Why? Do you have some place to be?"

"It's Sunday, so I'll go to church if at all possible."

"You go to church?"

"I always go to church."

"But you don't know anyone here."

"I know you." He grinned. "I like to worship with people. It keeps me honest."

Katrina shook her head, confused. "What do you mean?"

"I travel around a lot; love to do things I've never

done before. I actually get lonely at times, too, so I look for communities I can be involved in. Plus, I have a lot to be thankful for, and going to church keeps me grounded. I show my gratitude appropriately instead of painting water towers or sculpting public property, things like that."

"Flying kites on beaches."

He snickered. So, she'd seen him.

"I'll have your lunch on the porch at 12:30. Is that too late?"

"No."

"I used to go to church, but I haven't been in a long time."

Her unexpected comment made him pause.

"Because going there reminds you of your husband?"

"Actually, he never went with me. I thought it important to go, but he worked nights, and Sunday mornings was one of two mornings we had together. I gave up church to be with him." She paused. "That's just an excuse, I guess. But I'm not sorry now I chose to spend that time with him. I'm glad now I did. I didn't realize then how precious our time was together."

"I'm glad you had that time with him." Trey had often wondered what E.A. was like, who he was, who he loved even. That person stood before him now, and he felt the pull of desire for her. Not physical desire—more than that, like when you desired happiness, contentment, peace, love.

Yes, love.

I can't have her. It's wrong to even think it.

"Do you need anything else right now?" This heart, but I'm realizing it has belonged to you all along.

"No."

"All right. See you later then." Trey opened the back door of the truck to clean up after their meal preparation.

"What are you doing?" She asked after he had stepped inside.

He looked at her. She was framed in the doorway. "K.P." He reached into his pocked, pulled out his cell and snapped a picture of her.

"What did you do that for?"

"A woman at the door of my food truck. I think it makes a nice picture." He looked at the screen. "I was right. Want to see?"

She blinked at him a few times. "How about this?" She crossed her eyes and stuck out her tongue.

Trey snapped another picture.

"Hey, I was kidding."

He looked at it and grinned.

She stepped into the truck with a determined gleam in her eyes. "Delete that."

"Please don't ask me to. I like it."

"It better not show up on social media."

"Cross my heart." He made an X on his chest, and the words and gesture brought to his mind how sadly ironic all of this was.

He was in love with Katrina.

Trey pocketed his phone and cleaned his hands with sanitizer.

"I can help, if you like."

He shook his head. "I couldn't ask you to do that."

"You didn't. I offered. Clean up is part of making the meal, isn't it? And I did help you with the sandwiches."

He nodded and gestured for her to take the sanitizer. He quickly placed the dirty dishes in a bin to take inside the house. He gave her a new sponge to disinfect the surfaces in the kitchen, then he wiped them down with a low lint towel.

"You are serious about having this space clean," she remarked.

"It's too small to have clutter or germs."

"This has been really fun. Thanks, Chef, for letting me

help today. I really appreciate it."

Guilt nagged at him. She thought he was so nice. What would she when she found out he'd been deceiving her? It was wrong. He had to tell her.

Chapter Ten

She was awake. He'd seen her on the beach when he'd gone out to bring over her breakfast. Good. It would make things easier. He'd done some soul searching last night and decided he owed it to her to be honest about who he was and who the anonymous donor was. She'd be hurt, but more so if she found out without him being the one to say it. Today was a significant day for him. Perhaps it was fitting that he'd tell her on the anniversary of his new heart.

He hefted the strap on his shoulder and headed down the stone path leading to the sand. She must have taken a walk toward the pier because she came from that direction. She waved when she spotted him, and as she came closer he noticed her hat and that cardigan she seemed to like to wear.

"Good morning," he called to her.

"Hi."

"You're up early."

She shrugged. "Woke up and couldn't go back to sleep."

"Want to eat breakfast out here?"

"The sunroom, I think. I've walked three miles at least. I have had enough fresh air."

They fell in step together to her deck. Once inside the house, he set the table with her breakfast. "I'd like to invite you to dinner," he said when she came back from the bathroom.

Katrina arched her eyebrow at him. "Haven't you been doing that every day since I got here?"

Cool. Keep it cool, he told himself. If she figured out how badly he wanted this, how important it was to him to fix a special meal for her on the anniversary of his new heart, and somehow ease the pain she'd probably feel when she knew the man she'd spent her time with these last ten days had had a secret agenda. He hoped she'd forgive him.

"I'd like you to come to dinner next door. I've fixed up the sunroom for a special dinner."

"Nah."

"Nah?" His heart, their heart, felt as if it turned in his chest in disappointment.

"You've a gifted cook...errr... chef, Chef. But eating by myself, especially when you go to so much trouble, well, it feels pathetic."

Oh. "Pathetic?" he echoed. She thinks I'm pathetic?

"Not you." She play punched him in a suspiciously affectionate gesture. "Me. Eating a fancy meal by myself feels spinster-ish. Awkward. I don't want to do it."

"You could invite someone to eat with you. Don't you have a friend or something?"

He'd rather not have someone here when he disclosed who he was, but if it would make it easier for her. He'd absolutely do it.

"Why don't you eat with me? You're already here, and it's convenient. I know there must be some kind of chef-code or something against it with the way you act, but I'm not going to ask a friend to fly down here or drive ten hours just to have a nice meal with me. So, make peace with it, and sit at the table."

Trey was torn. But he owed her, and probably after tonight she wouldn't want to see him anymore.

Setting the table family style, Trey made fish tacos and the platter sat between them along with handcut cole slaw, guacamole, and homemade corn chips.

He waited until she had filled her plate before he served himself.

"You never really told me if you know who hired you."

He was in the middle of bringing the soft taco to his mouth when she'd spoken. Her question came out of the blue. He thought they'd put it to rest until he was ready after supper to tell her.

He put the food back down on his plate and looked at her.

She pinned him with her stare. "Do you know who hired you to cook my meals and answer every culinary whim I can imagine?"

Trey wasn't ready yet. He took a deep breath to confess, but before he could, she went on.

"A couple of times you've used the word respite, which is what Dinah Windingham said when she told me about it. Dinah works at a foundation I dealt with after my husband's death. I think whoever hired you is the same person who rented the house, and I can't figure out who it could be. It has to be someone I know. Otherwise, how would they know I needed a respite?"

"Maybe they figured you needed a relaxing vacation apart from a life without your husband."

Katrina's lips turned up in a sad smile, and the urge arose in Trey to lean over and kiss her.

Whoa. Where did that come from? His heart thumped hard in his chest. Sorry, Eric, he thought. I know she's your girl, or at least she used to be.

If Katrina knew he was talking to her dead husband's heart in his chest, she'd freak out, for sure. And rightly so.

"It doesn't fix anything. Even as nice as this is, it is still a life without my husband. So, do you know?"

Here it was. Did he tell her the truth or not? He reached forward and picked up the recreated grape lady: the third one he'd made. "This is you," he said.

"Really?"

"Yes. The flag is a banner of virtue."

Katrina laughed. "Virtue?"

"Yes. 'Who can find a virtuous woman? For her price is far above rubies." He paused, not wanting to continue quoting the Bible verse. If he did, she'd know. She'd see it in his eyes, his face, everything about him who he really was.

"The heart of her husband doth safely trust in her, so that he shall have no need of spoil, yes, I know that verse. My grandmother was big on Proverbs and hoped I would be a virtuous woman. She used to quote it to me when I was in college and not settling down with a husband." Katrina laughed at the memory. "I'm flattered that you think so well of me. Grandma would be proud."

He picked up the celery man. "This is Gary Hamlin."

"Friend of yours?"

"Not exactly, though we have something in common, and this is Leslie Buchanan. This is me. Do you remember when I told you I had some heart problems when I was younger?"

"Yes."

"Three years ago, I had surgery to correct my heart problem. I would have died otherwise, but because of the miracle of modern medicine and science, the surgery saved my life." He watched her wanting her to make the connection and not wanting her to. "Three years ago today I received a new heart."

"A new heart? That's great."

"Three years ago, Katrina."

He counted the seconds as he waited. One. Two. Three. Four. Her eyes widened, but otherwise, she didn't move.

"Why is three years significant?" she whispered.

"You know why."

She shook her head.

"I received a new heart."

"No."

"I wasn't going to tell you. I only wanted to do something to thank you, but it seemed to bother you that you didn't know who gave you the beach house and the chef service. I don't want anything from you other than to do everything I can to make sure you enjoy yourself here."

"You have Eric's heart?" she asked brokenly.

The heart hitched, as if it had a mind of its own. As if his heart knew finally his first owner's wife had found him again.

He nodded, and she pressed her hand over her mouth.

"I hope you don't see this as deceptive. It wasn't meant to be. If you had known who the gift was from and that your chef was your husband's recipient, I didn't think you would have come. And I wanted so much to give you something, to be a little part of doing something for you because of what you and Eric did for me."

She stood up, knocking the table as she did so. He reached out and steadied it.

"I can't... I can't stay here." She turned and hurried away.

Trey sighed. He didn't think it could have gone better. There was no easy way to tell her. And not telling her who he was would be wrong. He had to tell her before she found out some other way. Yes, he did do the right thing. Absolutely, he did.

But he'd risked the tenuous friendship he had begun with Katrina, and that made him sad. He liked her, and he wanted to spend more time with her. He'd told her, and she'd run away. He kind of expected that. He'd, in effect, dropped a bomb on her. She was in shock. Hopefully, after she had some time to absorb the news, process who he was, she'd talk to him again. The next move was hers.

Please, God, let her make that move. He had two more days to be with her. He didn't want to spend those days wringing his hands wondering if she'd ever speak to him again, ever see him, or want to.

****

Katrina had come into the house, run to the bathroom, and thrown up every bit of the dinner she'd just eaten. Afterward, she lay on the couch and stared out of the window at the ocean. She hadn't turned on any lights when she'd entered and made the dash for the bathroom. Later she'd clicked on the outside electricity so it would illuminate the beach beyond the house and the water.

God, why? Why won't you let me put this behind me? Why did you bring Chef into my life, to care about him, then have him to be the one....

Her throat closed up with emotion, but she didn't cry. As a matter of fact, she had not cried at all over Eric's death. It had all seemed surreal as it was happening, as if she were living in a horrible dream. The doorbell ringing in the middle of the night. The squad car taking her to the hospital. ICU and life support. The meeting in the conference room when the doctor had told her Eric was dead. The ventilator continued to move oxygen in and out of his lungs, but they'd done a test on his brain. Two of them, actually, and there had been no activity.

Eric was dead.

She'd met Dinah then. Dinah worked for KODA, the Kentucky Organ Donation Association. It was law that every time a person died, their death was reported to KODA. Because of the circumstances of Eric's death, he was eligible to be an organ and tissue donor. They had never discussed anything about it, but when Dinah asked Katrina if she would consider donating his organs, she said yes. No agonizing about it. No ethical navel gazing. Not to donate didn't make sense. Eric was dead. He no longer had use for his organs. Of course, if they could be salvaged, she'd want someone else to have them.

She'd signed papers. She'd stayed with Eric until they

took him to surgery two days later, then she'd gone to her empty house and slept for thirty straight hours until Brenda, worried because she hadn't been able to get in touch with her, had called the police who had broken into her house.

She hadn't cried. She'd gone through days and nights. The police escort to and from the funeral. The salute to their brother in blue that was meant as a way to honor their comrade who had fallen in the line of duty, but it had just twisted her gut so that she had vomited every time she'd eaten for over a month.

Then one day, she'd woken up, and it didn't hurt to breathe or look at his picture or even say his name. After that, she found she could visit his grave without getting sick. And then one day she'd gotten an invitation in the mail with the words Celebration of Life engraved on the cover. Katrina realized when she'd open the card that it was a celebration of other people's lives. Not her husband. If anything it celebrated his death and that horrible decision she made to preserve his organs in the bodies of other people.

She did not regret the decision. She regretted that she'd had to make it in the first place. And, no, she did not want to hear the thank yous of people who had pieces of Eric in them. She didn't want to hear about what a good person she was because she'd agreed for her dead husband's organs to be donated. She didn't want to see it, hear it, know it, feel it.

Eric was dead.

That was the only truth she knew.

He was dead.

Nothing else was real to her about him or his death.

Until tonight when Chef had told her that he had Eric's heart. His heart! Chef was alive because of Eric's heart.

It was a horrible twisted irony that the first—the only—man she'd noticed and spent time with since her husband's death was the very one who was intimately connected with him. Katrina couldn't see him again. She couldn't sit at a table and eat the food he cooked knowing that he'd received Eric's heart. Even now she understood why he hadn't told her who he was. He was right, she wouldn't have come here if she'd known.

She didn't blame him for that, but there was no way she could continue on as if it was okay or normal. Nothing was normal about this situation.

Surely, Chef understood that.

Some time later, she put on her cardigan and went outside. The sky, normally clear, had clouds occluding the moon, but enough light shone through that she could see her way to the pier. With her phone on her which tracked her progress, she found the pier was not quite four miles from the house. By the time she made it back, grey streaks shone on the horizon. Dawn. As the sky lightened, she arrived at the back door of the house and fell into a fitful sleep.

She awoke and found Chef had texted her around eight informing her a carafe of coffee and cinnamon rolls waited on the front porch. She retrieved the coffee, but stared at a roll as she picked at it, wondering if she would ever be able to eat again.

She would have to talk to Chef, if for no other reason than to tell him her respite was over and she was going home.

He couldn't expect that she'd want to stay, not after what he told her.

****

Trey knelt in the recessed area next to the bridge, putting shells on the sides of it. He wasn't aware that

Katrina had approached him until she stood on the bridge, hugging her cardigan to her.

"Who is Gary Hamlin?" she asked.

Trey looked up at her noting the circles under her eyes and knowing he was responsible. "He received one of Eric's kidneys, and Leslie got the other one."

She crouched then sat cross-legged on the bridge. "How do you know them?"

"There's a dinner called Celebration of Life."

She sighed. "Oh. Yes."

Obviously, she knew of it. Of course, she did. She had been invited every year. And had declined every year. "We met at the dinner. They're there every year. So am I." He paused wondering if he should say what came to mind. But he wanted to give her his honesty from now on. "We had hoped to meet you."

She shook her head. "I didn't want to."

"I know, and I hope what I've done here isn't a mistake." He sat back in the sand, settling in to the talk. "I'd never want to hurt you. I only want to give back to you, show you how much I appreciate the decision you made so I could live."

She nodded, watching her clinched hands in her lap. "Okay. Okay, but I don't want to talk about it anymore."

"All right."

"I wish we could go back to how we were before, to me not knowing."

"I don't want to keep secrets from you. You said you hated surprises."

She made a sound that could have been a sob or a laugh. She turned her head away from him so he didn't know which.

"I want to be honest with you, to let you know you can trust me."

"You deceived me. I understand why. It bothers me

though."

"I'm sorry. When you asked me about the one who'd given you the time here, I decided I should tell you. I was planning on a nice dinner anyway because it's my heart anniversary."

Katrina's whole body flinched. She looked at him then, the sadness in her eyes tearing at him.

"It seemed fitting to tell you then. If you hadn't asked who hired me, I was prepared to finish up the two weeks, thank you one last time, and never see you again."

She leaned forward, placing her face in her hands. "I'm so stupid."

"No, you're not."

"I was going to ask if we could meet again after we left."

"Of course, we can. What kind of meeting?"

Raising her head, she shook it. "I have been so stupid."

"Katrina, as in hiring me as your caterer?"

"No. As in let's go out and let someone else do the cooking. You could just be you without the apron or the hat, and I could...." She looked down, and her skin turned a lovely shade of pink. "I could find out what your first name is because I forgot."

He smiled. She liked him.

"Trey. My name is actually William Marshall, but everyone calls me Trey."

"Well, it can't happen now."

"What can't happen now?"

"Us meeting up again. Me calling you Trey or Chef or anything." She shook her head in disapproval.

"Why not?" He asked, trying to follow her logic.

"I don't know. This is weird, awkward, sad, creepy. Tragic. I mean, it isn't just me thinking so, is it?" Her downcast face made his chest ache. This was hard, so hard, on both of them. But he was thankful, finally, it was out.

The truth was out, and he felt liberated because of it. No more secrets between them now.

"It's…." He stopped trying to figure out a phrase to fit their situation. "It's a unique place for us to be, yes."

"Unique." Finally, she made eye contact with him, and the fire in her gaze worried him a bit. Was she angry? "Haven't you broken just about every HIPAA violation there is by finding out who I am?"

He shook his head willing himself to stay calm. If he stayed calm, she was more likely to stay calm, too. He'd delivered quite a shock just now. "I didn't even know your name until you told me. I tried to get Dinah to tell me who you were, but she wouldn't. She couldn't without breaking HIPAA. But all I wanted to do, all I want to do is to thank you. To somehow perform a very small gesture to demonstrate my gratitude."

"This is your small gesture of gratitude? Just tell Dinah you wanted to give me an all-expense paid vacation in Florida?"

"Basically, yes," he said.

"And she fell for it?"

"She doesn't know the house came with a chef. I worked with two rental agencies to rent both houses separately. That way, if you did find out, you would know it is all on me. Dinah did not disclose any private patient information." Trey opened his hands in an appeal. "She doesn't know, and if she did know, she'd be very upset."

Katrina pursed her lips. "I don't think Dinah gets upset."

Trey had to concede to that remark. "Well, if ever she was going to, it would probably be because of what I've done."

Chapter Eleven

The overcast day promised rain which began to fall late afternoon. At the table with a light fruit, cheese, and chicken salad plate, Katrina checked her phone to look at the forecast. Uh oh. A tropical storm had moved into the bay.

"I'm worried about the storm." Katrina had been reading her book as she ate, and without conscious thought the words spilled out of her mouth. Trey stood inside the door as he sometimes did after he'd cleaned from preparing her meal. He kept a pad of paper with him and wrote out menu ideas while she ate. Katrina knew this because she'd asked him one time.

"They're predicting it won't come inland. But if it looks like it will, we'll leave early."

Marking her place in the book with a card, Katrina closed it and turned around to face him. "If I leave, will you leave too?"

He put down the leather notepad he was writing on. "Probably not."

"But we're right on the beach. It feels vulnerable. You should leave."

"I didn't count on hurricane season," he said.

"What do you mean?"

"Oh. When I made the plan to come here. I wasn't thinking about the weather."

"You decided this time of year because it was your heart anniversary."

"Yes."

Lightning flashed, lighting the room brighter than usual. Katrina stood and went to the window. Sheets of rain beat against the window.

"Oh, no." She opened the door. "What do we do about the bridge, the village, the turtle?" Rain pelted her face, but she didn't care. He followed her outside. She looked back at him, and he shrugged.

"We do nothing. They're sand sculptures. They're not meant to last forever."

The wind whipped her hair, and in a moment she was drenched.

"But you worked so hard on them." The injustice of it clenched her fists.

"It doesn't matter." He blinked against the water running down his face.

"Yes, it does." It absolutely mattered. It wasn't fair. "I'm going to find something to cover them. The bridge might be okay because of the shells, but the turtle and your beautiful little city."

"Katrina, let's get out of the rain. I don't care about them. I can always build more."

"It won't be the same. They won't ever be."

"No, but we enjoyed them while they were here. It's all right. Let it go." He took her hand to lead her back to the house. But she pulled out of his grasp.

"I can't. I'm tired of letting it go, letting things go."

Trey pulled his hat down closer to his eyes. "Sometimes we don't have a choice. We have to make peace with what we don't have control over."

"That's easy for you to say. You have it all together." Katrina raised her arms in frustration. "Your list, your dream of your cooking truck. Going after everything you've ever wanted and getting it. When have you ever had to let something go?" She hadn't done any of those things. In fact, when Eric died, she had just stopped risking anything. It was too hard anymore.

"Every day of my life before Eric's heart, I had to let

go knowing that my heart might give out before I could get a new one. For three years. That's a lot of letting go."

"But you've got everything you've ever wanted now. You don't have to let go anymore."

"I don't have everything I've ever wanted, but I do have a good life. This is a good life because of you...."

"No! No!" She put her hands over her ears as if to ward off what he was saying.

"Yes. Yes, Katrina." He took a step toward her, but stopped, as if he were afraid she'd push away from him again.

"I don't want to hear this," she whispered fervently.

He didn't move for a moment. Finally, he placed his hands on her shoulders. With a calm and sure voice, and gratitude in his gaze, he watched her as he spoke. "Please, sweet Katrina. Please listen to me. I don't have everything I've ever wanted because I would never have wanted someone to die so I could live. Never, but that's how it happened. I think about that every day. Eric died. He didn't die so I could live. He died, and out of the horrible event, God twisted it into a second chance at life for me and Gary Hamlin and Leslie Buchannan and Leila and James who got his corneas and veins. We all have a chance to live because you made a decision to not let Eric's death mean the death of Eric. He lives through all of us, don't you see? So, I have to live this life to the very hilt, to the fullest extent. Every moment. Every single one because now I can. You can."

"I can't." She shook her head in denial.

"You can. Your heart is good. Your life is good if you decide that it is. You've given so much, given up so much. Let this life give back to you."

Tremors shook her body as she looked at him. As if the whole world was coming apart. Again. Trey stepped forward. Something flashed in his gaze, almost as if he.... No. Not Chef. She had to be mistaking the attraction there.

It would be wrong to kiss him, for him to kiss her. Katrina lifted her face. He wouldn't, and she wouldn't.

He lowered his head and touched her lips with his, a gentle chaste kiss, the sweetest she'd ever received.

When he lifted his head, a sad expression shone on his face, probably matching the one on hers.

"I'm leaving tomorrow." And even as the words left her lips, she realized they were true.

****

Katrina sat in her office staring at her computer screen and running numbers trying to find $2,100 more dollars her client could write off. It wasn't a big deal if she couldn't. It would just mean Jillian Saunders would have to pay state and federal tax this quarter. A knock sounded on her door, and Brenda entered.

"Hi," she said leaning on the side of the desk. "How are you?"

"Fine and dandy. Even more so, if I can unearth another couple of business expenses for Jillian."

Brenda peered at the computer screen. "Charities?"

Katrina shook her head. "I've got them all."

"Is she in any business organizations? Take any trips?"

"Done."

Brenda picked up the folder and leafed through it. "I don't see where she listed the Little Lamb DayCare in her charities."

Katrina looked at her friend. "She didn't report that she gave them any money."

"Well, she didn't give them money, but she sure as shootin' donated goods and services to them. Saunders Heating and Cooling put in new central air for the building back in June. I know that because I volunteer there, and the bookkeeper told me they would have had to close the doors if they hadn't had help with it."

"Did she say it was Saunders Heating and Cooling?"

"No, but I saw the vans there that week. It had to be them, unless they were giving an estimate."

"Wonder why she didn't report it?"

Brenda shrugged. "Call her and ask."

Katrina did as she suggested. "Hi, Jillian? It's Katrina."

"Oh, hello," the woman said. "Are you ready for me to come by and sign off on my taxes?"

"Not yet. I had a question about some work you may have done pro bono for Little Lamb."

"How do you know about that?"

"How come I didn't hear it from you? I'm trying to make sure you don't have to pay any more than you already have this quarter."

"No one is supposed to know about that. I don't want to claim it."

"How come?"

"It's… an agreement I have with a friend."

"Are you getting any goods or services in exchange for the work you did and the equipment you donated?"

"I'm not, no. But as a favor to me, they are providing discounted daycare for two kids there. I really don't want the mother to find out I'm involved. It's just less messy that way, plus if I report it, then the daycare has to report it as a gift."

Katrina's gaze cut to Brenda's. "It's not a gift if it's a quid pro quo agreement. But what I'm wondering is if you have paid more in gift and services than the tuition of the children?"

They continued the conversation, and though it did not completely cover the difference, Jillian's tax would be less. That was a good thing.

That finished, Katrina closed out the file and shut off her computer.

"Are you going home?"

"I think so."

"You look different. What happened in Florida? Did you meet someone?"

"I only talked to one person down there. The chef who cooked for me."

"You didn't tell me catered meals were provided. How nice."

"Yeah, well, I didn't know when I got there. I must have been really tired when I got in because I fell asleep with the front door open. The chef came in the house and woke me up. He cooked most of my meals. He is... was very kind. Very…." She sighed.

Brenda's eyebrows arched upward. "Very?"

Katrina shrugged her shoulders. "Very sweet and funny and talented. He could cook anything. He even showed me how to make the perfect peanut butter and jelly sandwich."

"Wow. Is he single?"

Katrina's eyes widened. "I… I don't know. I think so. But we never talked about it."

"You should always ask. Especially, when you start sighing over him. Ask first, then sigh if he's available."

Katrina held her hand up. "Now don't get any ideas, Bren. Of all the men I might think about getting involved with—"

Brenda clapped her hands. "Oh, gracious. Gracious. Gracious. Gracious. Katrina is talking about getting involved with a man."

"No, I wasn't."

"Oh, yes, you were, and it's about time."

"No, it isn't about time, and you can quit jumping to conclusions. He is absolutely not a good choice."

"If he's married, then no. But if he's not, then kind and funny and sweet and he cooks? You should call him or go visit him again. Does he live in Florida?"

"Please stop."

"Well, think about it at least, will you?"

And Katrina had thought about it for a couple of weeks. Maybe it would be nice to see him again, to talk to him knowing now that a part of Eric was with him, had helped him. Katrina dialed Dinah's telephone number.

"Hello."

"Hi, Dinah, it's Katrina Aaron."

"Oh, hi, Katrina. How are you?"

"I'm okay."

"I haven't talked to you since you took your respite at the beach. How was it?"

"It was really, really nice. Would you pass on my thanks to the person who gave me such a nice gift?"

"Of course, I will."

Katrina had already decided Dinah would not find out from her what Trey had done, and she'd devised a plan to smooth it over.

"I have a question for you."

"All right."

"The person who received Eric's heart, I was wondering if I could meet him."

There was a long pause, a very long pause on the phone. Was Dinah putting it together that Katrina had received the beach house from the same person she now was asking to meet?

"You remember it was a man, then?"

"Yes, I kept the letter with a general description of each recipient. The man who received Eric's heart has the initials W.M. He was single and 23 at the time, and he was a senior in college in Ohio."

"If you come to the Celebration of Life dinner, you—"

"I know I could meet him there if I came and if he came. I could meet all of the recipients if they were there, but, Dinah, this is a big step for me, and if I could just meet one person at my house, then I think it wouldn't feel so overwhelming. I could handle it in a good way."

"Why do you think you could handle it in a good way? What does that mean?"

Katrina put her head in her hand. "I haven't been able to move on. I never even thought that I hadn't, but something shifted when I was at the beach. If I could meet the recipient, a recipient, the heart recipient. Meeting the person who lives because of Eric's heart, I think I'd like to know him. Maybe I could be okay." She took a shuddering breath. "I'm not okay, Dinah. I haven't been okay since I got the news he'd been shot."

"And you think meeting the heart recipient would help you?"

"I don't know. I hope so. I want to be okay. If he's willing to meet with me. Do you think he would?"

"Let me call him and see, and I'll get back to you. All right?"

"Thank you, Dinah."

****

She had dialed his number a thousand times. Well, not all of the numbers. She'd get the area code and about three or four of the rest of the numbers, but she would disconnect. It was odd to see the word Chef pop up on her screen. Her heart beat hard and fast. Dinah had called him, and now he was calling her.

She let it go to voice mail. She just couldn't talk to him yet.

If he agreed to meet with her, then she'd talk to him then. She'd see him with Dinah there. Maybe it would be safer with her there.

Not that she was afraid of Chef…Trey….even thinking his name felt odd. She'd come to know him by his title. Thinking of him as Trey was foreign, as if it were someone else.

Her phone dinged signaling she had a voice mail. She

opened the app and stared at the small number one next to the icon. He'd left her a message. Her heart thundered in her ears. She reached her finger forward to touch it, and the screen opened—a long line indicating the message was ten seconds long.

The phone shook in her nervous hand. This was stupid! Why was this freaking her out so much? She knew Chef. She didn't have to be afraid of him. She's spent nearly two weeks with him staying next door to her and cooking her meals. He was safe.

At least, he had been before she realized he had Eric's heart.

Closing the app, she promised herself she would listen to his message. But not now.

Her phone rang again. This time the screen showed it was Dinah. Katrina slid her shaking finger across the screen and held the phone to her ear.

"Hi, Katrina."

"Hello."

"I talked to Trey Marshall, the man who received your husband's heart. He's willing to come over with me for a visit."

"When?"

"He and I are available Monday. Would that suit you?"

"I can meet you after four. I'd rather meet at my house." Good grief. She knew she didn't want to meet in a public place. The potential for—what—something was too much. All of this made her feel vulnerable, like she was going to have heart surgery. Yes, it did feel remarkably like she was agreeing to have someone come in and rip her heart out of her chest. This...this...revisiting of past actions however noble they were, this rendering of emotions and grief.

"Agreed."

"Do you want to come for dinner?" What a joke.

Preparing a meal for Chef? Of course, he'd graciously eat whatever she cooked. But all the while he'd probably be cringing inside. Poor Katrina gets by on sandwiches and coffee.

"It might be best—initially, if we plan to keep the visit short. This time."

The weight on her chest eased just a little. Yes. A short visit was a good idea.

Monday. Two days away. Okay. That would give her time to prepare. To be an emotional wreck until it was over.

Forget it. I changed my mind.

Katrina almost said it. No. She needed to do this. Just do it and get it over with. She felt that she had unfinished business with Chef. She'd left before dawn the next morning without saying goodbye. It was cowardly. She knew it even as she packed her bags the night before. Even as she formulated the plan to be gone.

She was so afraid he'd meet her at her car that morning. But he hadn't.

And after she drove away, with the beach house in the rear view mirror, she'd still been edgy, as if he'd follow her. As if she'd catch a glimpse of his food truck behind her at the traffic light on her way out of town.

But she hadn't seen it or him.

Ten miles she'd still felt the discomfort that he'd follow her. When a half hour had passed, she'd sighed in relief. He was still at the house. Still asleep probably. She'd gotten away, and she hadn't had to say goodbye.

She'd expected him to call or text her, but he hadn't. Maybe he meant what he'd told her. He was prepared to give her the gift of the beach house with catered meals then never see her again.

But there had been more than catered meals.

He'd given her companionship. He'd shown her a whimsical side of himself that intrigued her.

He'd made little fruit people representative of her and three of the people who had received a second chance of life because of Eric.

He'd provided the respite he'd invited her to. But respite wasn't exactly the right word. It had been an invitation of sorts.

To let go. To open up. To move on.

And the kiss he'd given her was the culmination of that invitation.

She knew it, and that's why she'd run away.

Did he know it too?

What did the kiss mean to him?

Was he just being friendly? A kiss between a man and a woman—non-sexual though it was, there was a physical connection there which was all man and all woman. Had he been carried away by the intensity of their conversation in the rain about the transitory nature of all things, including sand sculptures and people?

Was he encouraging her to live in the moment?

Or was the kiss an invitation for something not imagined, not expected, something new that had budded in their time together?

What did it mean to him?

She didn't know, wouldn't know unless she did see him again, unless she could find the courage to ask him and hope he would tell her the truth. Could she trust him?

What had the kiss meant to her?

Not what she was afraid of it meaning, but what it actually did mean?

She'd known he was going to kiss her. She hadn't turned away, she hadn't stepped out of his space. She'd lifted her face, thinking he's going to kiss me.

She'd allowed it to happen.

Why?

A response to his kindness and attention, or something

more?

Dread for the upcoming visit washed over her like a tsunami. No, she didn't want to see him again.

She didn't want to examine her feelings; afraid she'd discover a path leading to heartache.

Heartache.

She shook her head at the expression.

If she ever became involved with another man, Chef shouldn't be the one. Even if he wanted to. It was inappropriate. Was she just feeling this way because a part of the man she'd loved and pledged to love the rest of her life was now in Chef?

She wished she knew. She wished there was someone she could talk to who could tell her the answer. But the fact was no one could tell her what was in her own mind and soul. Only she could do that.

That night, Katrina lay in her bed. Her cell phone lay on the night stead plugged into the charger.

She turned to her side and propped herself up on her elbow, staring at the phone. Torn. Not knowing what to do. Knowing what she wanted to do, but so afraid to do it.

Chef's message was there waiting on her to listen.

What had he said?

Was she brave enough to listen? Even if he asked her to call him or to leave him alone, or whatever, she wasn't obligated to do anything. He'd said the beach respite was a gift with no strings attached.

He said he was prepared to give her that gift, walk away, and never make contact again.

But that was before she'd asked him who the anonymous donor was, and it was before he'd told her who he was. And it was before he'd put his arms around her and touched his lips to hers.

Did he still feel the same way, did he still mean it, that he was really prepared never to see her again?

Was her call to Dinah a mistake?

Resolutely, she picked it up, disconnected the cord, and opened the voice mail app. There it was. There he was. His voice waiting for her to listen.

She pressed the speaker icon and the triangle to start the message.

"Katrina, this is Chef. I just got off the phone with Dinah. She says you want to meet me. You know we've already met, right? That guy who cooked you all that delicious food? Same one who has Eric's heart, so I'm guessing you're just trying to protect me so I don't suffer the wrath of Dinah. Thanks for that. I'm sure if she ever decided to get mad, look out, and... I'm rambling. I'm going to hang up before I break out in song. Something both of us would regret, I'm sure. See you soon."

She listened to it two more times, smiling.

"Chef, you goofball," she whispered before plugging her phone back in and settling down to sleep.

Sunday night found Katrina sleepless. She went to bed, but felt the frustration of attempting every posture and position in order to claim sleep which was so reclusive.

It proved hopeless.

Around two, she gave up and went downstairs to read. But couldn't keep her mind on the book. She tried the computer next, and surfed through some of her networking sites. On a whim, she called up Chef's website and read through his menus and specialties. A few pictures showed him in different people's homes obviously teaching cooking classes, and one of him through the back window of his food truck serving breakfast burritos in downtown Louiston.

Around five, she lay down on the couch and fell asleep until her phone woke her up at six. She dressed and went to work, wondering if she would be able to keep her mind on her tasks. With a full day of audits, five arrived more quickly than she imagined, and when she walked in the house, she just had time to freshen up before their expected arrival.

Chapter Twelve

The doorbell rang promptly at 6 in the evening.

Katrina's heart hammered in her chest. This was so silly. She'd already met the man. Why was she so nervous? She closed her eyes and breathed in and out several times in an attempt to calm down before walking to the front door and opening it.

Dinah stood in front of her with Trey beyond.

"Hello," Dinah said. She stepped aside and gestured to the man behind her wearing a black overcoat with a white button down shirt and gray pants. "Katrina, this is Trey Marshall. Trey, Katrina Aaron."

He moved forward and grasped her hand in a shake.

"Nice to meet you, Ms. Aaron," he said with a twinkle in his gaze Katrina was sure Dinah had to have noticed except she was looking at Katrina instead.

She didn't speak as they shook hands, mostly because it was taking all of her concentration to remember to breathe.

When Dinah stepped inside the foyer and Trey followed. She noticed he carried a black bag with handles with his catering logo on the side. He winked at her as he walked by, and Katrina resisted the urge to giggle at this game. Pretend we don't know each other, that she hadn't spent days watching him run the beach dragging a kite behind him or sculpting net markings in the sand next to his bridge, or eating the food he'd prepared every night.

Dinah and Trey stood inside the room. Katrina closed the door then led them to the living room.

"Can I take your coats?"

Each of them took off their jackets and she hung them

in the closet in the hallway. Vanilla, apples, and cinnamon wafted from Chef's coat, and she shook her head when she caught herself sniffing the wool. She realized she recognized the aroma. Chef smelled like apple dumplings. How odd as he hadn't even baked any the whole time in Florida. But the coat smelled like him.

She closed the door and walked back into the room, attempting to forget she'd been sniffing the man's clothes.

"Have a…." she croaked, cleared her throat then tried again. "Have a seat, please. May I offer you something to drink?"

"Sure," Dinah said.

"I have tea or water or soft drinks."

"Water is fine."

"Me too," Trey said.

Katrina nodded and went into the kitchen to retrieve the beverages. Jinx, her kitty appeared and rubbed on her leg. Jinx wasn't very friendly with strangers, so Katrina didn't need to worry about her making a pest of herself.

Still.

"I have a cat," she called. "If anyone is allergic, I can put her away."

In a moment, Dinah spoke. "No issues with either of us, Katrina. Do you need some help?"

"No." She poured water into two glasses.

She returned and found Dinah and Trey had sat down on the couch, leaving the matching chair available.

She set the glasses on the coffee table in front of them. Awkward.

That would be the word she'd use to describe this situation. Why had she thought this was a good idea? They should have met at a restaurant. That way if it got too intense for her, she could just stand up and walk out. What would she do now? Invite them to leave?

Dinah leaned forward.

"Katrina, I'm so happy you wanted to meet Trey. He's been wanting to meet you for a while now."

Katrina's attention moved to him, and he smiled as he watched her.

"Would you like to know more about him?"

"Sure."

"All right...." The name Chef came to her, but she remembered to call him by the name Dinah told her. "Trey, isn't it?"

He nodded. "What would you like to know....Ms. Aaron?"

"Call me Katrina."

The fake. He'd only called her Katrina the whole time they'd been in Florida. Was he being so formal now for Dinah's sake?"

"What's in the bag?" she asked.

He reached forward and picked it up. Standing he walked to her and presented her with it. "I own a catering company. This is something I made for you. I hope you like it."

Katrina opened the sack and looked inside. She pulled out a large jar with his signature black label on it. In gold lettering it said, Butter Infused Peanut Butter.

A delighted laugh escaped her. "My favorite. Thank you."

"You're welcome." Trey moved to sit back down, and as Katrina tracked his progress she saw a look of confusion on Dinah's face.

"What is it?" she asked.

"It's a special blend of peanut butter. I thought Katrina might like it."

The woman studied him for a moment perhaps trying to figure out how he could have known Katrina liked peanut butter.

"So, Chef...." Katrina said. "You own a catering

company called…." She looked at the label on the jar. "Chef@Home. How long have you had your business?

"A little over a year."

"And do you share recipes?"

"Yes. I also do in home cooking courses and demonstrations, and I have a food truck." He glanced at Dinah, then back at her. "You should see it some time."

"Maybe I could even drive it. I've never driven a food truck before. I'm sure I'd have to have a special license or something."

Chef laughed, for they'd had a similar conversation at the beach.

"Where's your home?" Katrina asked.

"My home base is probably in Louiston where my parents still live. I travel around a lot with my business, so if I'm not on the road, I live in a garage apartment attached to their house."

This bit of news intrigued Katrina. She hadn't thought about him having parents. How proud they must be of him.

"What was wrong with your heart?"

"I had a congenital heart defect which didn't show up until I was about sixteen when I had my first heart attack."

"How old are you now?"

"Twenty-six."

"What difference has it made in your life, having my husband's heart?"

"My life, Katrina. I owe my life to him and to you. Thank you."

When he said those last two words, Katrina recognized the same tone, the same genuine sincerity every single time he'd uttered them in Florida. He hadn't been thanking her for allowing him to serve her meals. He had been thanking her for his heart. For Eric's heart.

All of the nerve endings in Katrina's body fired at once at the realization. She stared at him, and he returned her look calmly.

"You've already thanked me," she whispered clutching the peanut butter jar to her chest as if it were a baby.

"Every day I'm thankful."

Breathe. Breathe. Breathe.

Katrina attempted to rein in her riotous emotions. All the while she'd thought he was so goofy, so job-needy, and that had been why he'd taken special care to express his gratitude. But it hadn't been about the job at all.

"Trey, do you have any questions for Katrina?" Dinah asked.

"Do you like to cook?"

"I...used to when Eric was alive," she replied.

"Do you remember the last thing you two said to each other before he died?"

"He worked the night shift. He was a policeman, and he was walking out the door. He said, 'Do you want me to pick anything up from the store on my way home in the morning?' I said, 'We're almost out of milk. Can you get two gallons, and I love you.' And." Katrina bit her lip. "And he said, 'I'll get the milk, but I don't think they sell I love you at the store.' Then he closed the door, and that was the last time I saw him alive."

Katrina stared at the carpeted floor lost in thought.

"Eric wasn't one to talk about his feelings ever," she said. "When we got married, he repeated the vows the preacher said—to love me until death do us part, but the only time I ever heard him say that phrase, I love you was that morning." She blinked and looked at Dinah whose eyes shone red with unshed tears. "Weird, huh? As if maybe he knew it would be the last thing he'd ever say to me."

"What a sad and wonderful gift he left you with," Dinah said.

Katrina sighed. "He couldn't have known we wouldn't see each other again, but it was such a strange thing, the way he said it, like he was telling me but he was embarrassed so he made a joke out of it." She shook her head, "Or maybe that's just what I want to think. Like I'm assigning meaning to something dumb to make me feel better."

"Or maybe," Chef said, "He wanted to tell you, and so he did."

So, he did.

No one spoke for several minutes. Finally, Katrina felt the need to play hostess. "I can order a pizza if anyone is hungry." She set the jar of peanut butter back in the bag and put it on the coffee table.

Dinah shook her head. "I'm sorry. We can't stay long. If you all want to meet again, we can schedule a dinner together, if you like." She shifted and unzipped her purse. Reaching inside, she pulled out a stethoscope. "Katrina, I brought this in case you want to hear Eric's heart."

Katrina's attention caught and held on the device in the woman's hands.

Eric's heart. Eric's heart.

A lump formed in Katrina's throat, and she gasped feeling as if she were choking.

You want to hear Eric's heart.

The room grew dim, then in bright sharp relief, and somehow Eric knelt in front of her, an expression of kindness shining in his eyes.

"You don't have to," he was saying. "Katrina, really."

She felt something, and realized he'd placed his hands on her upper arms. She blinked again, and it wasn't Eric, but Trey.

"What?" she said, wondering what she'd missed, what had happened. She'd thought it was Eric, but, no, it had been Trey. Why was she freaking out?

Oh. Because Dinah had just invited to let her listen to Eric's heart in Trey's chest.

"Dinah was just offering to let you listen to Eric's heart," Trey said.

Katrina swallowed, attempting to get a hold of herself. "It's your heart."

Trey leaned back and grinned. "Well, yeah, it's mine now, but it was his first. Want to hear? You don't have to, but you have to admit, it would be kind of cool. Don't you think?"

Fear and excitement bounced around inside of her. "I'm not sure I can."

"What's the worst that can happen?" Trey shrugged as if it were no big deal.

What was the worst that could happen? She'd get to hear Eric's heart again.

"Okay," she whispered.

Trey reached behind him, and Dinah gave him the stethoscope. Picking up Katrina's tightly fisted hand, he tapped her knuckles. When she opened her fingers, he placed it on her palm. Then unfastening three buttons on his shirt, he moved the metal circle over his skin. In shocked silence, Katrina glimpsed the riddled scar over his breastbone. She held the stethoscope, affixed the earpieces, and waited through the static-y placement.

Lub-dub. Lub-dub. Lub-dub. Lub-dub.

Eric's heart beat strong and loud in her ears. Tears welled up in Katrina's eyes and spilled down her cheeks. She gripped Trey's shirt and moving forward, she pressed her forehead into his chest, listening to the vibrant rhythm of Eric's heart.

For the first time in three years, she wept the long suppressed tears of a grieving widow. For the agony of losing her husband. For the lost chance to say goodbye. For the loneliness of days and night without him. For the children they'd never have. For the years and life time they had been unable to share.

And now for the wonder of his heart providing a second chance to another person.

And gratitude to listen and weep against the warmth of Eric's recipient.

Chef.

He wasn't just another person or a recipient. He was Chef, the man who had figured out a way to gift her with a coastal respite, meet the elusive wife of his donor, then introduce her to whimsical pastimes like kite running, sand sculpting, and cooking contests, and cause her to gain six pounds all within the span of two weeks.

She wept until spent, and realized she was sandwiched on the floor between Chef and the chair she'd been sitting in. She lifted her head, embarrassment flooding her.

Trey shook his head, "Don't you say it," he murmured.

"Say what?"

"That you're sorry for crying."

"But I—"

"Better not." He graced her with a mock scowl. "Crying is good for you."

"If crying is so good for you, why don't you do it?"

"I do. I have. I cried the morning I woke up with Eric's heart in my chest. I was so relieved and thankful and sad, and I felt really guilty because of what having his heart meant to the people who loved him."

A knot formed in the back of her mouth, making it hard to swallow or breathe even. A new wave of tears poured from her eyes. Was she ever going to get a hold of herself? She reached up and wiped the skin under her eyes with her index finger hoping her mascara wasn't as smeared as she suspected. Tissues appeared in front of her, and Katrina looked up. Dinah held them out to her in one hand, and with the other she wiped her own face.

"Well, thanks for permission not to be sorry, Trey," Dinah said. "I haven't cried like that in at least a year."

Trey took the proffered tissues and dabbed Katrina's cheeks in a gesture so tender, that another tear leaked out of the corner of her eye.

"Tell me to stop it," she said, grasping the tissue and wiping the side of her face.

His eyes widened. "Why would I do that?"

"Because I need to."

"Why?"

"Because."

"Because why?"

"Move…. Chef."

He smiled and moving back, he placed a foot underneath his body and stood. He held a hand out, and she took his offer to help her up.

"Are you going to be okay now?"

Faking confidence, she dropped his hand. Lifting her chin, she answered him. "Yes." Something caught her attention, and her gaze focused on the black smudges on his shirt. "Excuse me." Turning quickly, she strode from the room.

****

Trey watched her go, the urge to go after her so strong, he actually took a step in her direction. Dinah blew her nose, and it jolted him. Right. He and Katrina had just met, as far as the other woman was concerned.

"Should you go check on her?"

Dinah shook her head. She pulled another tissue out of the box on the side table. "We'll give her a few minutes. Grieving is a tough job, you know."

"I would have thought most of her grieving had passed."

"She confronted a big part of it tonight that she hadn't recognized before now." Dinah wiped her nose. "I think her vacation down south must have been cathartic, Chef." She arched an eyebrow at him.

Trey looked at with what he hoped was an innocent expression.

She studied him and waited.

"What?" he asked when the continued appraisal made him want to squirm.

"I'm wondering if there's something you haven't told me."

"Like what?"

"Like any connection between the respite and Katrina wanting to meet you."

"I didn't write her a letter and leave it in the house, if that's what you mean."

"I'm sure you wouldn't write a letter and leave it in the house because you've just told me you didn't." The woman continued to watch him. "It's obvious there is something between you two. Whatever else you've done, I hope it was only in the same gracious spirit as the gift of respite for a grieving woman. Don't make me regret that I agreed to the vacation house, okay?

"I promise, Dinah." He drew an X across his chest. "Cross my heart."

"Very funny."

"Will you go check on her?"

Dinah's gaze softened. "All right." She walked out of the room and through the door Katrina had disappeared into a few minutes before. Trey heard voices as the women engaged in conversation. When Dinah emerged, she shouldered her purse.

"She's shaken up, but she'll be okay. It's best if we leave now."

Disappointment blanketed him. "I want to tell her goodbye." He probably sounded like a little kid, but he didn't care.

Dinah shrugged. "Okay."

Trey walked into the darkened hallway. "Katrina?" A

light shone under a closed door. He knocked. "Are you in here?"

"Yes." He heard the word muffled through the door.

He searched his mind for what he should say next. *Are you okay? Do you want me to stay? Can I stay?*

None of them sounded good.

He put his hand on the wood, as if somehow it would connect them. "I wish…" He sighed. "I wish this were easier for you."

The door opened a few inches. Her face, scrubbed cleaned, appeared with her hair pulled back from her face. "Thanks."

"I wish there was something I could say or do to make it easier. But I know there are gaps that will never be filled."

The door opened wider. Katrina stepped into the hallway. She reached up and kissed his cheek. "You've already done something for me. We're even now." She turned him toward the living room and pushed him gently. "Now go away. I'm tired, and the most I want to do is get a spoon, my butter peanut butter, and go to bed."

"You don't need a spoon. Just scoop it with your hand."

"I have standards. Don't forget your coat. It's hanging in the hall closet."

With a big goofy grin on his face, he stumbled toward Dinah.

Katrina had kissed him. Well, on the cheek, but it counted. She liked him. As Dinah said, they had a connection, and it was more than Eric's heart.

Tonight had been one of the most difficult and painful episodes he'd ever experienced. Never had he witnessed someone fall completely apart. He had certainly never been the one to comfort such a soul, to pat her back, feel her tears soak his shirt front. He'd felt it was a sacred moment, a holy one, and the fact that Katrina had allowed him to be a part of it filled him up.

Every day he sought opportunities to live his life to the fullest. Tonight, he hadn't sought out that opportunity. Katrina had offered it to him. She'd given him a glimpse of the gut-wrenching grief a widow feels at the loss of her beloved. She'd allowed Trey to comfort her as she wept for Eric. What a privilege that was.

Every hoop he'd had to jump through. Every penny he'd spent. The time and finagling he'd done to make the beach vacation happen. It had all been worth it every moment of their time in Florida.

And tonight, though, he'd hit the jackpot.

"Trey." Dinah laughed and shook her head. "Let's go. We've accomplished what we came here to do. Come on down to earth, will you?"

Perhaps Dinah had accomplished what she wanted to do here, but had he?

He remembered the last time he'd seen Katrina walking away from him as it poured down rain on both of them. He didn't realize he wouldn't see her again. He thought he'd be able to smooth things over, ply her with good food, tell her he was sorry or he was thankful, anything, whatever it took to get that horribly sad shadow darkening her face to leave. He'd awoken that morning and gone over to the house. Her car had been gone. He thought maybe she'd just run into town for something, well, that's what he'd wanted to believe, but a part of him knew. The door was unlocked so at noon he let himself in and saw evidence of her departure. No suitcase in the bedroom. No book on the coffee table. No sweater lying on the back of the loveseat.

She'd gone.

She'd left without saying goodbye. Without saying anything.

But that was her prerogative. He hadn't asked anything

from her, didn't have the right to expect anything. She'd given him a gift just by showing up.

He had told himself the ball was in her court. He'd even made up a little poem to remind himself how he needed to handle the respite.

He'd let her set the pace.
Allow her to have her space.
Back up so she could run her own race.
Provide respite, comfort, food, and grace.

There was something here. Between them—more than just the history of their time together at the beach house. Dinah had noticed it. A potential for something more. And he wanted it. Really wanted it. But it wasn't his call. Even before she met him, Katrina had given him everything. Yet, he found himself wanting more from her.

She'd given him his life.

But now, he knew he wanted her love as well.

Though he had no right to ask it.

And he'd never ask her. It would have to be her idea, her next step.

Chapter Thirteen

Now what?

Katrina awoke the next morning strangely rested. She'd anticipated another night of no sleep, but the cry-fest on the floor in front of Trey and Dinah must have exhausted her.

Thank goodness she wouldn't have to face either one of them again if she didn't want to.

If she didn't want to.

Did she want to?

Face Chef…or Trey again, that is.

Not very soon, but some time. Why though? Because he made her feel closer to Eric? Did he?

Katrina rolled to her side and looked out the window. She pulled the comforter over her shoulder.

Even before she knew who Chef was, or his connection to Eric, she liked him. He was nice and funny and so generous. She'd enjoyed spending time with him.

That was okay, wasn't it?

They could be friends, right?

Is that what Katrina wanted? To be friends? Or had she been subconsciously working up to something more in those 13 days together? This was silly. Only 13 days. What could you know about another person in less than two weeks?

He'd told her he'd given her the respite as a thank you.

That was all he'd expected back from her—to enjoy the gift, and then, as he had said, he'd leave prepared never to see her again.

Except she'd requested this meeting.

What was she to him? Only the widow of his heart donor, or more?

What had the kiss meant? Not the one in the hallway when she'd kissed him on the cheek, but the one on the beach when it had been raining and she'd wanted to save his sand art, and he'd been totally unconcerned about it, as if his enjoyment of building them was all that mattered. How did he find so much joy in living in the present moment? Was it because he'd been born with a faulty heart?

Dinah called her a few days later. Thinking perhaps Chef wanted to meet again, Katrina answered the call hopefully.

"Hi, I'm checking to see how you're doing," Dinah said.

"I'm okay."

"You are?"

"What do you want me to say?"

"Whatever you want to say. I called because I care about you, and I'm concerned. Are you still crying a lot?"

Katrina sighed. Dinah cared, and she had called. But what about Chef? "I've cried more in the last few days then I have my entire life, I think."

"Have you thought about grief counseling? I can recommend someone, if you like."

"I...." The familiar throat clog, and the burning in her eyes alerted her that more tears were immanent. "It's okay to cry." Chef had told her so.

"It is okay to cry." She paused for a few seconds. "You wanted to meet Trey because you told me you didn't think you were okay. You said you realized you hadn't moved on and meeting Trey might help you do that. You've had a few days to process what happened the other night. Do you think it was a setback, or a step forward?"

"I think... I needed that night with Chef and you.

Something broke in me, but something lifted too. I'd like to…." She blew a breath out. "Did he say anything about getting together again?"

"No. I haven't talked to him again, but if you want to, I can call him."

"Do you think it's wrong to want to? Like it's weird?"

"It could be part of the healing process for you, and for him. And if you come to the Celebrate Life dinner, I think you'll find more healing there. Because so many people got a new lease on life because of your husband. It's such a sad and beautiful thing. I'm glad you met Trey."

Katrina let go of another dinner with Dinah and Trey. After all, she wasn't quite sure of her own motivations where he was concerned. She liked Trey, but the liking him wasn't all about him being the heart recipient. If she'd never found out he had Eric's heart, she was pretty sure she would have called him again after they'd left Florida.

She wanted to see him again, and that was a problem.

It felt inappropriate.

Was it?

As the days wore on and Thanksgiving approached, she drove the two hours to her parents' house for the expected family gathering and requisite turkey and dressing. Keith, her oldest brother, and his wife Mary-Kate had already arrived with their two daughters, four-year-old Olivia and six week old Ava. This would be Katrina's first time meeting her baby niece. Her other brother, Kyler, was expected any minute with his girlfriend of a year, Melody.

Mom had asked for an expected time of arrival, so when she pulled into the driveway, the door opened, and her parents walked out and were beside the car before she turned off the engine. Greeting her with hugs, they were joined by Olivia who grabbed Katrina around the legs squealing.

So happy to see her family, Katrina reached down,

extracted the little girl to encase her in her arms. "Hello, Miss Livie. How is Aunt Kat's favorite sweetie pie?" She kissed the fat cheeks of the little girl.

"I am your favorite, aren't I?" she asked. "Not Ava?"

Katrina blinked at the little girl. "Who is Ava?"

"A baby who cries and poops, and that's about it."

The throng moved toward the house as Olivia informed her aunt how awful things had been since Ava arrived on scene, and Katrina made appropriate sympathetic noises.

Mary-Kate met them at the door, holding her tiny daughter.

"Oh, my gosh, Livie, is this the baby you were telling me about?" Katrina asked.

"Yeah, that's her." She scowled at her sister. "I don't see what the big deal is."

Ava slept snugly wrapped in the yellow blanket with embroidered angels on it that Katrina had given during Mary-Kate's baby shower a few months ago.

"She looks a lot like you did when you were a baby," Katrina remarked.

"Oh, come on," the little girl said.

"Come here, you little munchkin." Dad took Olivia from Katrina, snuggling her.

"Do you want to hold her?" Mary-Kate asked.

"Of course, I do, if for no other reason than to give you a break. Livie says all she does is cry and poop. Since she's not crying, I guess I know what she is doing."

Mary-Kate placed the baby in Katrina's outstretched arms. Bringing the bundle close to her body, love filled her heart as she gazed down at the sweet face of Ava.

She was so beautiful and perfect. Finding a place to sit, she carefully settled in the recliner and cuddled the baby to her. Her older brother came out of the kitchen.

"Hey, Sis." He leaned down and kissed the top of her

head. "Don't let her sleeping angelic form fool you. She's mean when she's hungry."

She looked up at him. "I'm so happy for you, Keith."

His gaze went from her to Ava, and his mouth turned up. "Yeah. Great life here. I'm blessed. I know it." He moved his hand to his mouth and began chewing.

"I thought we weren't eating until one."

"I'm starving," he said around a mouthful of food. "Snagged a roll. Don't tell Mom."

"I know what you're into," she called from across the room. "Luckily, I made enough so we'll have some left for the actual Thanksgiving meal."

Katrina knew when Kyler and Melody arrived, because Mom announced it. Between her requested ETA texts and watching from the front window, Mom made sure everyone had a welcoming committee.

Olivia climbed into the chair and tucked herself in between Katrina and the armrest. She stuck her pacifier in her mouth and nudged her head against Katrina who settled Ava on the other side of her.

"I'm not eating any turkey, just so you know."

"Is that so? What are you going to eat?" Katrina asked.

"I told Granny Nan I would only eat corndogs and French fries. She said no problem." The little girl nodded, confident of her grandmother's love and willingness to bow to a four-year old's wishes.

"No problem." Katrina chuckled. "Wow. Wonder if I can put my order in too. I like corndogs."

"And ketchup. If you don't have ketchup, there's no reason to eat the corndog, I don't think."

Excited voices from the foyer signaled Kyler and Melody. Mom squealed. Olivia looked at Katrina, then slid down from the chair. "BRB, Aunt Kat." She ran into the other room, and in a few minutes, she returned with the adults behind her. "Uncle Ky's getting married," she yelled.

Katrina attention rose to Melody, her face alight with happiness and Kyler behind her who looked more nervous than happy.

Mary Kate and Mom followed next already discussing wedding plans. "When in December?" Mom was asking.

"The sixteenth, we thought," Melody said over her shoulder.

"December?" Keith laughed. "Are you insane?"

"The insanity will end after the wedding," Ky stated which made Keith laugh harder. He slapped his younger brother on the back. "You know you have to live with her after the wedding, right? The insanity is life-long, bro."

Mary-Kate reached over and popped Keith on the ear without even looking at him, eliciting an *oww* from her husband. She peered at her phone. "That's a Friday. You want to get married on a Friday?" she asked, the expression of disbelief on her face showing she expected a negative response.

"Friday night. Yes. Everything will be decorated for Christmas, and we'll have two weeks off before school starts back."

"You mean in three weeks? Three weeks from now?" Katrina asked in shock.

"Why not? We only want close family, and there's no reason to wait," Kyler said. "Right, Mel?"

"I've got three older sisters who have all been bridezillas. I am not putting myself or my family through that. I wanted to elope, but Ky said we needed to at least pretend it's respectable."

"It is respectable. Good heavens," Mom said. "We can do something really nice in three weeks, if you want."

"Where do you want to get married, here?" Mary-Kate asked.

"Well, the church if it's available. If not, we can look somewhere else."

Kyler and Melody both lived in town. They taught in the public school system. Melody was a special ed teacher in the middle school, and Kyler taught science and chemistry in the high school. The wedding plan discussion continued over the holiday meal. Later as Katrina played with Olivia in the floor with a puzzle she'd bought her, Olivia looked up at her aunt.

"Do you got someone special, Aunt Kat?"

"I've got you."

"I mean like a dad like mine or Uncle Ky."

"Well, they're special to me, too."

"Yeah, but Dad's got Mom, and they're one, two. Now Uncle Ky has Melody, and they'll be one, two. How come you aren't a one, two?"

Olivia was too young to remember Eric. Trying to explain to the little girl that Katrina used to be a one, two seemed more than she wanted to go into.

"Not everyone is a one, two, sweetie."

The trusting eyes studied her. "How come?"

"You're not a one, two, are you?"

"Not yet, but there's this boy at school named Aiden. And he's my best friend." She looked up at her aunt. "He could be my one, two, but Daddy says I'm too young." She leaned toward Katrina and whispered in her ear. "But I'll be five in February."

Katrina hugged her. "It's nice to be a one, two with your best friend. But I'm not sure your daddy will think five is old enough."

"I'm not sure he'll think twenty-five is old enough," Mary-Kate said from where she sat on the couch nursing the baby. "He's mighty protective of his girls."

Olivia scowled. "Twenty-five? It takes me forever to count that high."

That evening, Katrina lay in the bed in what was now a guest bedroom, but it had been her room before she'd gone to college. The house was quiet, and she scrolled through the galley of pictures she'd taken. Of course, most of them were of Ava and Olivia.

One poignant one Mom had taken with Katrina's own phone. Katrina was gazing down at Ava, with such naked yearning it was almost painful to look at. She tagged the photo to delete it, but stopped when her phone asked was she sure she wanted to erase the photo.

She sighed.

No, she wasn't sure she wanted to delete it. It was a sweet picture, but so sad. Disturbing even.

She'd wanted children—always assumed she and Eric would have some one day. But one day had never happened. They'd waited too long. If she had known he'd be killed after only two years of marriage, would she have insisted they try right away? Or would that have been wrong? It wasn't really fair, was it, for a baby not to know her daddy?

Still. If Katrina had gotten pregnant before Eric had died, he could have left a legacy through a child.

But he had left a legacy anyway through the people whose lives he'd saved in his police work and after his death with the organ donation.

Katrina opened her contacts list and found Chef's number. She listened to the voice mail he'd left her before he and Dinah had visited. After they'd left, Katrina hadn't talked to him again. She wondered if he wanted to.

If so, why didn't he call her?

Was it because she'd told him to go away the night he and Dinah had come over?

She set her phone face down and shifted in the bed. It was late. She'd told Mom and Dad she was leaving shortly after breakfast. She wasn't going to feel like driving if she didn't get any sleep.

Her phone dinged, and reaching for it, she peered at

the screen and saw she had a text.

From Chef.

Whoa. She was thinking about him, and he texts her?

Is there something you want to tell me?

Katrina blinked at his comment balloon. What did he mean?

She opened the dialogue box and gasped.

She'd inadvertently sent him the picture of her and Ava.

Pict of me and my niece Ava, she texted him. *Didn't mean to send it to you. Sorry.*

He replied in a few seconds.

I'm not sorry. Lovely picture of you both.

"Flatterer," she whispered with a smile on her face.

****

The next morning Katrina sat at the table with Ava on her shoulder rubbing her back as she had done years ago with Olivia. Mary-Kate had just finished feeding her, and Katrina was hoping to encourage a burp. So far, nothing.

"How in the world do they plan to pull together a wedding in less than three weeks?" the young mother asked.

"Maybe Melody is expecting her family to make all the arrangements," Katrina said. She leaned in and put her cheek next to the baby's and listened to her soft breaths.

Nancy sipped from her coffee cup. "No. Her family goes overboard. She's determined not to get them involved. She doesn't even want bridesmaids because she doesn't want her sisters fighting over who it will be."

Mary-Kate put her hands out in a helpless gesture. "Does she want anything?"

"She wants to get married, but Ky is wanting a church wedding. I think it's going to fall to us."

"She has no idea what she's getting into. There is no way we can pull this off in less than a month, and that close to Christmas?" Mary-Kate said.

Ava belched, and Katrina moved her, then wiped her mouth and chin with the bib around her neck.

"We can if we keep it simple," Mom said. "They both agreed last night no more than forty people including family and the wedding party."

"Forty people? If they stick to that, then it won't be a problem."

"The problem is going to be the party afterward," Mom said.

"The reception?"

"No," Mom answered. "They want to have light refreshments after the wedding. Cake, punch, nuts, mints, but on Saturday night, Kyler wants to have an all-out party."

"Where?"

"They've already asked about using the middle school gym. That way all of their teacher friends can come."

"If they get married the Friday night after school is out, when are we going to have time to decorate for the party?"

Mary-Kate sighed. "They have no idea what they're doing."

"No problem," Nancy said. "We'll figure it out. Katrina?"

She looked up from the baby to her mom.

"Is there any way possible you could take the week off to help us get ready?"

"Yeah, I should be able to."

"Great. That would really help, I think."

****

Katrina stared open-mouthed at her computer screen and the video she'd just watched on Chef's website. A local news story had run a story about him fixing sandwiches and passing them out in downtown Louiston.

Patricia Garrison, the reporter introduced the story with a shot of Chef's food truck as he, in his signature hat and shirt, handed out wrapped sandwiches from the serving window.

The camera focused in on Patricia and Chef in a small kitchen. Katrina recognized it as the inside of his truck.

"Why are you doing this?" she asked, as he prepared sandwiches at the counter.

"I love to cook, and I found out there were some people here who were hungry." He smiled at the camera, his sincerity she'd seen at the beach showing through.

"The homeless population is a real problem. What makes you think you can make a difference, Chef Marshall?"

"Today, I made a difference, and today is the only day that matters."

The camera panned from him to her, and Katrina clicked the button on her mouse. She looked closely at a photograph taped to the wall next to the serving window. The photo was of Katrina smiling framed in the doorway of his food truck. It couldn't be. Was she mistaken?

She backed it up and looked again. Yes. It was the picture he'd taken with his cell phone.

Why did he have a picture of her in his food truck?

Chapter Fourteen

With shaking fingers, she found him in her contacts. Hitting the green icon and holding the phone to her ear, she tried to speak, but her throat closed up.

"Katrina?" he said. "Are you there?"

Katrina opened her mouth to respond, but nothing came out.

"Hello, is this the peanut butter and jelly fan I met at the beach?" he asked.

"Hi," was all she finally managed, then silence as he waited for her to speak, and she waited for something intelligible to utter. So many emotions churned inside. Her mind. Her stomach. Her heart. Her throat closed, and she reached her hand up, clutching at her neck.

This was silly. Crazy. It was just a picture. It didn't mean anything. And this was Chef. She could talk to him without freaking out. Why was she freaking out?

"Want to do something fun?" Trey asked.

"Why do you have a picture of me," she whispered.

"What? Oh. So, you saw the news story, huh?"

"Yes."

"It's a great picture of you. I keep it in the truck to remind me of our time."

"Chef, I don't...." She shook her head. "I don't understand."

"How about I come over and we'll figure it out," he said. "I've missed cooking for you. Have you missed my cooking?"

Breathe. Breathe. Breathe.

Katrina nodded.

"I can be there by three. Is that okay? Is that what you

want to do?"

"Yes," she managed to say through the emotions clogging up her throat.

"I'm glad you called and that you want to see me, or at least that you want to see my cooking. I'm going to cook, right?"

"I'd like that."

"Do me a favor?"

She swallowed, finally getting air enough in her throat to speak. "What?"

"Get a blanket and go outside. Spread the blanket on the grass and lie down. Are you with me?"

"No."

"The clouds."

The clouds?

"The clouds are so pretty. The sky is clear and gorgeous. Go look at the clouds. See what you see."

"You want me to lie down in the yard and look for clouds?"

"Yes, I'm giving you an assignment."

"What if someone sees me?"

"Who cares? Just do it. All right?"

In a few minutes, Katrina was obediently following Trey's directive. She saw the white clouds. She saw the blue sky. This was hard.

"Hi, Miss Katrina."

Bobby, her six-year-old neighbor stood next to the blanket. He wrinkled his nose. Katrina resisted the urge to sit up. She'd promised Trey—hadn't she—that she'd find three cloud pictures in the sky—animal, vegetable, or mineral, plus another category for whimsical creatures like unicorns or dragons. Apparently, there were a lot of whimsical category creatures in the sky.

Go figure.

She hadn't seen anything but clouds. No horses. No

castles. No unicorns. Not even any mounds of whipped cream. They just looked like clouds. Cirrus. Cumulus. And... what was the other kind of cloud?

"Whatcha doing?" Bobby asked. He turned and looked up at the sky, craning his head so far back, Katrina considered he might fall over.

"Be careful now, Bobby."

"What are you looking at?" he asked.

"I'm looking at clouds." And feeling like an idiot.

"How come?" he asked.

Good question, she thought.

"My friend is coming to visit. He asked me to find three clouds that look like something else. But I'm not very good at it."

Bobby flopped down on the blanket. "Can I help?" he asked.

Katrina smiled, that the question had only come after he had settled himself next to her.

"I sure could use some help. Have you ever played this game?"

His big blue eyes stared at her. "What game?"

"You know. Looking at the clouds to see if they look like something else."

His attention left her and moved skyward. "It's not a game. It's what you do."

"Why?"

He made an I-don't-know kind of sound. "Just something you do. For fun."

For fun. Is that why Trey had requested she do it? How could he possibly know the turmoil she was feeling, finding out who he was, and that a part of her husband was inside of him.

God, why? Why? Why did you take Eric away from me?

Katrina resisted the urge to curl up in a pitiable ball

and cry. She watched the puffy clouds move at a steady, though leisurely pace.

"There's one," Bobby said, lifting an arm and pointing straight up.

"Where?"

"Lion. See it? He's crouching like he's about to jump on something."

Katrina crooked her head. Yeah, that could be a lion, she supposed.

By the time Chef's food truck pulled into her driveway, Katrina had found a chair shaped cloud and a cluster of grapes. Not very exciting, but she was new at this anyway.

She sat up and so did Bobby. The door opened, and there was Chef wearing jeans and a sweat shirt and looking so wonderful that Katrina lost her breath for a few seconds.

"Hey," he called as he approached. "Who's your buddy?"

"This is my next door neighbor Bobby. He's had some experience with clouds, so he was helping me. Bobby, this is my friend Chef."

Chef held out his hand, and Bobby gave him a high five. "I found a lion and two dragons, but all Miss Katrina found was a chair and some grapes. Can you believe it?"

Chef laughed and plopped down on the other side of the little boy. "Well, I tell you, on my way over here, I saw a bull with horns. Let's see, where did it go? Right there." He pointed, his arm at an 80-degree angle.

"Naw, that's not a bull. It's a donkey. Those are its ears."

Katrina opened her eyes wide attempting to see what they were seeing. "Where? I really don't see it."

"You see the big cloud and it looks kind of like a staircase?"

Huh. It did look like a staircase, and he wasn't even counting that one as something interesting.

"Look up and to the left. He's got his front leg up, and uh-oh, one of his ears just separated from his head."

"That's the thing with clouds, Miss Katrina. You got to pay attention because they change all the time."

"It's a great exercise in enjoying it right in that moment," Chef agreed.

Katrina realized how relaxed she felt and how happy she was to see Chef again. She turned her head to look at him and watched his profile as he sky-gazed. He'd known how nervous she was so he'd come up with an activity that would calm her down until he arrived. His head shifted, and he turned his face toward her.

"Are you okay?"

She nodded. "Better. Thank you."

"I wasn't sure I'd get to see you again."

"Other than that picture you promised me would not show up on social media?"

"I didn't think you meant a glimpse of a photograph in a news story on my website. Since that aired, my business has increased 23 percent."

Happiness filled her. Chef was here. Really here. "That's great news, but promise me before you do any more truck tours, you'll put my picture away."

"All right."

"It's getting a little chilly. Want to come inside?" she asked as she knelt on the blanket, then rose.

"I've got to go home, Miss Katrina." Bobby sat up then stood brushing off his pants.

"I was just getting started. We haven't even seen a dragon yet," Chef said.

"If you want to stay out here, okay, but let me get you a jacket or something to cover up with."

He faked a disappointed expression. "Okay. Fine. Let's go inside then out of the cold." He jumped up and began to fold up the blanket. "Have you eaten yet?"

"It's three in the afternoon. What meal are you referring to?"

He studied her. "You didn't eat lunch, did you?"

Katrina huffed. How could he possibly know that?

"Why don't you let me cook something? It's been a long time since I've cooked for you, and it'll be fun."

They walked toward the house. "I gained six pounds in less than two weeks at the beach," Katrina said.

"Good. Let's try for six more." He stood aside as she opened the door.

She glared at him as she paused at the door waiting for him to enter. "What are you saying, I'm too skinny?"

He shook his head adamantly. "No way, I'm not saying that. I'd still like you no matter what you weighed. But you telling me that you gained weight demonstrates you ate well at the beach. I'm a chef, so that means I did my job well." He lifted his arm, crooked his elbow, and patted himself on the back.

Shutting the door, she led him to the kitchen. "No, it means I ate like a pig."

"Pigs will eat anything." Chef followed her. He paused before he spoke again. "You are more finicky."

"Finicky. Huh. Well, Okay." She crossed her arms over her chest and shot him a challenging look. "Want to play what can Chef find to cook in Katrina's bare pantry?"

He grinned. "You know, I love a challenge."

"This will be a huge one."

He saw her cat stride by. The cat paused, saw Chef, approached him cautiously, then continued to walk on out of the room. "I do draw the line at cooking or eating cat food."

Katrina rolled back on her heels. "Ever tried it?"

His eyes narrowed, as if he were accessing whether she was serious or not. "The very fact that you just asked me that causes me concern."

"Really? Chef Adventure is too chicken to make a gourmet meal out of canned cat food? What a snob."

"Are we really having this conversation?" He walked to her refrigerator and opened the door. Perusing its contents, his shoulders relaxed. "You had me scared." He looked in the freezer and arched an eyebrow, probably at the impressive selection of ice cream. Wisely, he made no comment.

"I'm impressed. I thought I was going to have to make something peanut based."

He opened the crisper, and removed a package of celery. He lifted it to his face and sniffed, then broke a stalk which made a loud crunch, testifying to its freshness. "Are you always so well stocked, or is this for my benefit?"

"My benefit, actually."

He bit the stalk and grabbed the bag of carrots. Setting them on the counter, he clapped his hands. "Let me get my knife. I'll be right back."

"What's wrong with my knives?"

He laughed. "No offense, but I use my own knives."

"Afraid you'll cut yourself on one of mine?"

He crossed his arms over his chest. "When have you sharpened them?"

She tapped her finger on her chin as if in thought. "Well, the last time the guy came through with his water stone, I was getting my teeth cleaned, so...." She let the sentence trail off with a dismissive shrug of her shoulders.

"So, never."

"It's not like I cut on glass or something horrible like that."

"Where are your knives?"

She pointed to a drawer, and he opened it. Studying the contents, he scowled. "Well, this is downright dangerous. Not only are you at risk for cutting yourself whenever you reach for a cutting utensil, but all of your blades are dull because they're constantly in contact with each other."

He carefully set them out on the counter, separating them from each other. Then opened another drawer and clicked his tongue in disapproval.

"What are you doing?"

"Creating order."

"Stop right there, mister. I did not give you permission to rifle through my drawers.

He stopped and looked at her. His stern expression collapsing in laughter.

"That's not what I meant," she said joining in with his chuckles.

"I know. And sorry. You're right. Your house." He gestured to her and the knives. "Your drawers. If you want, I can sharpen them for you while I'm here, and I've got a drawer organizer in the truck you can have."

She accepted his offer, and later they stood side by side in front of a stock pot of boiling water. In an enamel skillet, he'd begun with olive oil from a fancy bottle he'd brought in with him along with his fancy knives and a black canvas case he'd called his mobile kitchen. He showed her how to sauté carrots, onions, and celery.

"This is what we call the culinary trinity. You can make stock from this as a base for so many dishes. Gives a fullness of flavor, and much lighter than chicken or beef stock."

"I thought we were making spaghetti."

"We are."

"You're putting carrots in spaghetti sauce?"

"If you weren't in here, you wouldn't even know, and like I said it will give the sauce a much richer flavor and also add texture. You like texture, so you should appreciate that."

"You've said that before. What makes you think so?"

"Because you like super chunky peanut butter and you thought extra butter improved the taste of it. Butter adds creaminess which is a texture character. Also, some of the dishes you complimented me on were high texture foods, like the potato chip s'mores and the French toast casserole." He shook his head. "As much as you enjoy it, I'm surprised you eat as much yogurt as you seem to. There's no texture fun in that food at all."

"Yes, but I don't eat for fun. At least, not unless you're around."

"Yeah? How long did it take you to finish up the butter peanut butter?"

"I refuse to answer that." She left the kitchen and entered the front room which she used as an office though it had a formal dining table there and a cabinet where she kept her fine china, dishes she'd only used four times since she'd gotten married.

"What are you doing?" he called.

She poked her head out the door where she could see his hands working pasta dough on the wooden island in her kitchen. "My house. I get to set the table." He leaned forward to catch a glimpse of her, and she shot him a challenging look. "I'm setting two places because you are going to be sitting at the table with me eating while I eat."

"Is this where I say 'Yes, ma'am'?"

"Yes, Katrina is also acceptable."

"Yes, Katrina."

She opened the drawer on the sidebar and pulled out a neatly folded table cloth, hoping the creases wouldn't show too much once she covered the table with it. Inside the cabinet, she found crystal candle holders and set them in the middle of the table. Standing back, she decided they needed to be further apart and adjusted them. Then she laid out the dinner plates.

"Eric," she whispered. "I think you'd be okay with

this. Me using our china. I mean, part of you is here. Your heart will be sitting at your table in front of the plates we picked out the pattern for."

With the table set, she went back into the kitchen. Chef had attached a metal contraption to the edge of the counter.

"What's that?"

"Pasta maker."

"I thought you were the pasta maker," Katrina quipped.

"Pasta cutter, then."

His floured hands held the flattened dough and he fed it through the cutter while he cranked it. "Will you look in my bag and get me that container of flour? I thought I was done with it, but I think I'll need more."

Katrina retrieved the item and noticed a small leather book. "What's this book? Recipes?"

She opened the container and sprinkled some into his outstretched hand. "Thanks. No, that isn't a recipe book. It's my life book." In a graceful motion, he draped the noodles over his fingers and lay them aside, then fed another batch into the pasta maker.

"I've never heard of a life book. Is it like a diary?"

"No." With the pasta cut, he picked up a hand towel and removing the lid from the pot of boiling water, he dropped the pasta inside, then stirred it with a long handled spoon. "It's my list of things I want to do in my life."

"Like a bucket list?"

He shook his head. "It's not a bucket list."

"It sure sounds like one to me."

"What's on a bucket list?" He stirred the spaghetti sauce with another spoon, tasted it, washed the spoon, rifled through several small jars of spices, opened one, pinched some, and added to the sauce, then stirred again.

"A list of things a person wants to do before they die."

Chef made a gesture of See? It's obvious. But it wasn't obvious to Katrina.

She pointed to his small leather book. "That's what your list is."

"No, my list is a list of things I want to do today or each day or any day. My living book. Things I want to do as I'm living."

"Before you die. It's the same thing."

"Not to me. I've lived my life with death looming over me. It's a constant battle to cast out fear and despair. Now I live without any regard for death. It will happen, but its' not my concern or my motivator any more. My list is now a list of things I do today. Today is all that matters."

"You said that in the news report."

He stirred the pasta, hooked a noodle on the spaghetti fork and ate it. "Are you ready to eat?"

"I don't like pasta al dente."

"It's fully cooked. When you make it fresh, it cooks extremely quick." He lifted the strainer up over the pot, water pouring from the holes. He dumped the pasta in a rectangular dish he'd brought with him, steam billowing from the pasta. He sprinkled olive oil over it, and then put the sauce in a tureen Katrina had supplied and took the food to the table.

Once they were sitting at the table with their food plated, Katrina returned to the subject she'd been curious about since she'd seen the internet video.

"Why do you have a picture of me in your food truck?"

He had raised his fork up to his mouth to eat, but he set it back down, a thoughtful expression settling on his face. "I think that day was one of the best days I've ever had in my food truck. Right up there with the first time I ever prepared a meal in it. Thank you, Katrina, for making my day. The picture reminds me of it, and it makes me happy when I look at it."

The compliment filled her with joy. She wasn't just a client to him or an obligation. He'd admitted he enjoyed her company.

"So, what kind of things do you have in your book?"

Chef smiled.

"World peace?" she guessed.

"Peace of mind." He twirled the pasta around his fork and placed it in his mouth. She waited for him to finish the bite before continuing.

"Is peace of mind in the book?"

Chef shrugged. "Not as a specific goal, but the list itself and my writing in it creates peace in my mind." He gazed into her eyes for a moment. "I'll read some of it to you, if you like."

"Okay."

He went into the other room and retrieved the book. The leather cover was scarred and worn in places, attesting to its age. A matching leather thong encircled the bound volume, holding it closed.

"Have you had it a long time?"

"About sixteen years." He unwound the thong and opened the book.

Katrina leaned forward to see the pages when he opened the cover.

"June 14th," he read. "Eat a red, white, and blue popsicle." Chef grinned at her, and turned the page.

Katrina saw more than that on the page, but couldn't read it from her vantage point. "What else does it say?"

"Oh." He turned back. "I usually write when and how I achieve the goal. I wrote on the same day, 'Dad brought me the popsicles. He calls them Rockets. He had to go to 2 gas stations and 1 grocery store before he found a box of them. I ate three. They were great', and great is in all caps." Chef turned the page, then a few more, reading a bit, then turned more pages. "A lot of the things are small, silly like that."

"Is getting a heart in there?"

"Yes. Achieved it, as you know. I could read it, but it's pretty intense." He gave her an apologetic glance.

He didn't want to upset her again, like when he'd been here the last time. That's why he didn't want to read it, Katrina guessed. He turned another page.

"Be in a parade, learn to surf, climb a tree, shave my head." He laughed. "Get my dad to shave his head, and he did, but only because he lost a bet to me. Go to culinary school. Done. Jump off the fifth street bridge."

"Goodness. That sounds dangerous."

"It is, and also illegal. I actually haven't achieved that goal, but I did get arrested trying it which was another goal of mine."

"Getting arrested?"

He arched an eyebrow at her. "Riding in the back of a police car."

"Ah. Riding in the back of a police car was a life goal for you?"

"Yeah. I'd never done it before. It seemed like an interesting experience if I could do it without doing anything horrible, or without actually asking a police officer if I could sit in the car just for the sake of doing it."

"I've never been in the back of a police car."

"I thought Eric was a policeman. He never let you ride in the back of his squad car?"

"The back is where the naughty people have to ride. I was always a good girl. The few times I was in the cruiser; I rode in the front."

"You've never broken the law?"

"This is about you. Not me."

He turned another page.

"March 13th. Own my own food truck."

"Which you've also done."

Chef shook his head. "I don't own it yet. The bank still does. I got a loan for it and bought it last year. It's a ten-year loan, but business is good, and I think I'm going to be able to pay it off in five years which is awesome. Meeting you is in here. Also doing something nice for you to thank you."

"Will you read it to me?"

"Umm. Okay."

Katrina wasn't sure, but it looked as if Chef was blushing. How sweet. He picked up the book, thumbed through it, and stopped. "I'll read this one. Three years ago, the goal was to meet Mrs. E.A. Then my entry from November first of this year, I achieved the goal. 'I met her today. Her name is Katrina, and she is beautiful. She's strong, but I already knew she would be. She doesn't want to be taken care of, and I think she's a little suspicious of who and what I am. It is so awesome to see her, listen to her voice, to be in the same room with her. She looks at me, really looks at me, and it's hard not to…." He cleared his throat. "To touch her. Hug her. Hold her. Tell her how much I appreciate the woman who said yes three years ago, so I could live, and how much I admire the quiet grace-filled woman I met today. She's trying to decide if I'm okay or not, likeable or not. I like her. I already like her so much, and I'm thankful."

He looked up at her. "That was the first day we met."

Chef's dark-fringed green gaze and the lovely sentiment he'd just shared caught Katrina's breath, captured it. Her.

No. I shouldn't. He's grateful. Deeply grateful. That's all it is.

Katrina dropped her gaze.

"What if you don't meet your goal? I mean, you're not going to keep trying to jump off the bridge, are you?"

"No." The sound of the chair creaking brought Katrina's attention back to him. He had set the book aside. His fork in his hand again. "It's my book, so I set the rules or break them. When you're young, you want to do some things that seem pretty dumb as you get older. If I have an insight on not meeting the goal, then I write it there, too. Like the bridge. I don't feel the need to jump it anymore. Now maybe when I've 80, I might decide to, but not now."

"You want to kill yourself at 80?"

He shook his head. "I own this body, but I don't own my life. I don't get to decide its beginning or ending. If I'm going to jump off a bridge, or do something really stupid like that, then I have decided I am willing to live with the consequences of surviving the jump. I love taking risks, but only if the adventure is worth the cost."

"You told me you've been skydiving in 11 states."

He raised his hands in a gesture of surrender. "With a parachute. It's relatively safe if your parachute is in good shape and folded well."

Katrina shook her head. "I'd never jump out of a plane."

"What's the riskiest thing you've done since Eric died?"

Katrina thought of what risks she'd taken in the last three years. None came to mind. She'd thought about selling the house, but someone had warned her about making any big decisions in the first six months. The advice was good. After six months, the pain of being in the same space she'd shared with Eric ceased to be painful and became a comfort.

She shook her head. "Nothing," she said softly. Her eyes burned. Stupid tears. She rarely cries her whole life and in the two weeks, that's all she had done. A tear escaped, and she angrily wiped it away.

"Texting me a picture of you and Ava was pretty

risky."

The unexpected comment elicited a chuckle from her. "I didn't mean to do that. In fact, I was thinking of deleting the picture that night."

"Why?" The word filled with disbelief and horror, as if deleting would be the worst thing she could have done.

"Because it's...." She sighed. "Because I don't like how I look."

"In the photograph, you mean?"

"Yes."

"Because it shows something." He paused. "About you."

She nodded, and another tear fell.

"I saw it, too."

Was it so obvious? Is that why her mother had picked up Katrina's phone and taken the picture? That Katrina wanted children of her own? A family to love and care for? A husband to be her life-long companion?

"You can still have it."

She took her napkin off her lap and set it beside her plate. "To get to that point would take more courage than I have, Trey."

"You're braver than you think. Just living is an act of courage."

"I haven't been living for a while. I realize that now."

"Well, okay. What are you going to do about it?"

"I am not willing to take any risks. Not on purpose. Not yet."

"You called me. Otherwise, I wouldn't be here. You called me on purpose, didn't you? I mean, it wasn't a pocket dial, was it?"

Finally, she met his gaze. His tone made her think her answer was important to him. For the first time since the emotional probing began, a small piece of happiness budded in the painful soil of loss and fear. Yes. Yes, she had called him. And it had been risky, but she'd done it anyway.

"Yes, it was on purpose."

His solemn expression softened, then a big grin shone on his face like a victory banner. The happy bud unfurled a bit, its petals opening to Trey's warmth. Katrina smiled in response.

Chapter Fifteen

The family gathered around the kitchen table. Tears ran down Melody's face, and Kyler looked as if he was close to crying as well.

"There's no way. No way, we can pull something together before the day after tomorrow," Melody said brokenly. "And we invited faculty from both schools. Two hundred people. What am I supposed to do, go to the grocery store and buy chips and salsa?"

The caterer they'd secured for the Saturday night party had cancelled on them. Barbara Sailors, the owner, and her assistant had been in a bad car wreck. Barbara was in ICU.

"And I can't even get mad about it because they're hurt!"

"Well." Dad patted his future daughter-in-law on the shoulder. "You can be mad about it, Melody. The woman can cook, but apparently she can't drive."

"It was not her fault, Charles, and even if it was, that's a horrible thing to say."

"I can say it here in the privacy of our house, sweetheart. I'm mad. We're all mad, probably, at the situation."

"This close to Christmas, no one is free to cater a party that big. We've already called eight places," Kyler said. He took Melody's hand in his. "It's no big deal, I guess. We can just do sandwiches and stuff. We'll figure it out."

"This is figuring it out, Ky," she snapped at him, snatching her hand out of his. "And I don't want to hear you say no big deal. This is a huge deal." She stood up. "This is my…." Her face crumpled and she ran out of the room. "Wedding!" the last word came to them from the stairs.

Mistress Penguin, Olivia's one-year-old Jack Russell mix, barked at her.

Kyler's mouth fell open in shock as he stared after his bride to be. He stood up. "It's my wedding, too," he yelled in her direction. "And I'm getting married if there's nothing at the party, but…."

"Bread and water," Keith supplied.

"If there's nothing but bread and water," Ky yelled. He stomped out of the room, heading to the front door.

Mistress Penguin continued to bark in excitement.

Olivia put her hands over her ears. "Inside voices, please. Inside voices."

"Mistress Penguin, shhh, girl." Mary-Kate looked at her husband with an arched eyebrow. "Did you purposely suggest to him a line about food known for being fed to prisoners?"

Keith smiled. "No. I was trying to think of something humble, but you make a good point, my love."

She looked down at baby Ava who was sucking on a pacifier watching her mommy. "Daddy thinks he's so funny, doesn't he?"

"I love being a prisoner of love,"

She glared at him. "Just be quiet before you dig that hole any deeper. Take the dog outside and go check on your brother." She stood up. "I'm going to see if Melody is all right."

"We could go simple. Do it ourselves. It's possible," Mom said. "I just hate for them not to have it nice if that's what they want. I hate for them to be disappointed."

"The important thing is the marriage. Not the reception or the party afterward," Dad said.

Chef would do it, and do a wonderful job, Katrina thought. But was he available? And would he be willing to do it with only two days' notice?

She pulled out her cell phone and discreetly texted him.

Are you busy Friday and Saturday? She texted.

Friday night, yes. Saturday, no. Came back his response.

Any way you could pull together a catered wedding reception for 200 people Saturday night?

Are you serious?

Yes.

Katrina's phone rang. She looked at the screen, ran her finger across it, and placed the phone to her ear. "Hello."

"You know I love a challenge," Chef said.

"Is it possible to cook for 200 people for a reception by Saturday at seven?"

"Anything is possible to those who believe," Chef said.

Katrina smiled at her parents. She gave them a thumbs up. "I just found a caterer," she told them.

The joyous and disbelieving voices drove Katrina out of the room as she attempted to hear Chef. Behind her the noise quieted immediately, and she saw Mom had followed her. Realizing she had an audience, she kept her comments professional as she told him the situation.

"I want to meet them."

"Can't you just talk to them on the phone?"

"I could, but I can get a better idea of the client if I'm face to face with them."

"We don't have much time, and I'm not at home. I'm in South Shore at my parents' house." She glanced back at Mom hoping she hadn't caught her comment. Seeing her mother's speculative gaze, Katrina cringed.

"That's good. I'm only 45 minutes away. I can be there by seven."

Katrina wanted to go out and greet him in the front yard. Warn him about her family, that her mom had the wrong idea, but then he might ask her what wrong idea she didn't want. And Katrina would have to say it.

She could just imagine Chef. He'd grin and say, "Your mom has the wrong idea about what?"

And Katrina would say, "About us."

Then Chef would say, "What about us?"

And Katrina would say, "That we're... you know...dating."

And Trey would look all shocked and say, "We're dating?"

Katrina laughed at the script she imagined. She had a book in her lap she'd attempted to read, but her mind wouldn't stay on the story. Instead, she went from her scripted conversation with Trey to what it would be like to have Trey and her family in the same room.

The only man they'd seen her with since she had been an adult was Eric. How would they react to Trey? Well, it should be a positive reaction since he'd agreed to help them with Ky and Melody's wedding.

Katrina looked at the clock on the wall. If he arrived when he promised, he'd be here in ten minutes. She caught a glimpse of her mother watching her.

"Is something wrong?" she asked Mom.

"Of course not. I'm just wondering how you know him."

"Remember I told you I took a vacation at a beach house in Florida? Chef cooked for me. That's why I'm having trouble buttoning my pants these days. He fed me so well I gained weight."

"What's he look like?" Mom asked.

"He looks like a chef, especially when he wears his ridiculous hat."

"How does he know where you live?"

Interesting. Mom had been eavesdropping on the conversation. "Because he came and cooked a meal at my house a couple of weeks ago. No big deal."

Katrina added those last three words hoping her mom

would agree.

The doorbell rang with five minutes to spare. She resisted the urge to jump up and run to the door. That's what Mom would expect her to do. And that's what she would do if they were dating and she couldn't wait to see him.

But they weren't dating, even if she really couldn't wait to see him.

Mom crossed her arms and gestured with a motion of her head that Katrina should answer the door. She set the book aside and went to answer the summons.

She didn't introduce him. She let him initiate the greetings. He stood on the porch and smiled at her, then past her to her mother and father.

"Hello," he said. "I'm Chef Trey Marshall."

Katrina opened the door wider and gestured for him to come inside.

"Hi, I'm Nancy Hendrickson, Katrina's mother. My husband Charles, and this is Ky and his fiancée Melody."

Melody leaned forward, reaching forward and grasping his hand. "I can't thank you enough. We were in a terrible predicament."

They gathered in the kitchen, sitting at the table. Chef set a notebook before him, and with pen in hand, he looked at Ky and Melody. "Tell me what you and the caterer planned," he asked.

Katrina watched him as he took notes, asking pertinent questions about the menu, and allowing Melody and Ky to express their anxiety over the circumstances which had brought him here.

Chef closed his notebook and stood up. "This is doable, and I will take care of everything, so don't worry, all right?"

"Thank you." Melody threw her arms around him, and hugged him. He returned the embrace. Immediately after

Melody stepped away from him, Kyler repeated the gesture.

He shook hands with Dad and Mom, then he nodded to Katrina.

"Nice to see you again. Thank you, Katrina," he said.

There was nothing inappropriate or suggestive in the words, the tone, or even his expression as he spoke. But there was something there. A hint in the last three words, especially when he spoke her name, that he and she shared a secret of something beautiful.

And he was gone. Katrina hoped he understood why she had been cool toward him and decided she would explain to him later in private why she'd done what she had done.

Her phone dinged, and she opened the screen to see the text. It was from Chef.

Meet me at the grocery store on Vine and Fifth, it said.

Her dad and Keith had left the farewells to the womenfolk and were watching television, so she stuck her head in the door. "Hey, Dad, I'm going out for a bit. I'll be back later."

"Okay, sweetheart. Be careful,"

She left and drove to the requested meeting place. Seeing Chef's food truck, she maneuvered her car beside it and parked. He stood next to it, and waved at her as he walked in front of her car, opened the passenger door, and got in.

Katrina's heart sped up at the clandestine meeting. What did he want?

"I'm sorry if I appeared unfriendly. I just...." The imagined scenario played through her mind, and she sighed. "I'm used to my privacy, and it's hard to do in a house full of people."

"It's all right." He reached forward and patted her hand in a quick gesture. "This Barbara Sailors. How did you all know she was in a car wreck?"

"Her assistant Lee called us from the emergency room. She said she was really sorry, but she didn't see how they were going to be able to do the food."

"So, no one actually talked to Barbara?"

"No."

"What hospital is she at?"

"Regional, I suppose. That's where all the traumas go."

"Okay. Let's go there." He did a search on his phone, then dialed a telephone number. "Hello, can you connect me to Barbara Sailors' room please?"

"What are you doing? Don't bother that poor woman at the hospital," Katrina said, horrified.

"Oh? Okay. What's her room number? Thank you." He ended the call.

"Why did you do that? She's injured from a car wreck. How could you try to call her?"

"She doesn't have a phone in her room, so we're going to visit her."

"No, we're not."

"Of course, we are. You think it's unkind to talk to her about the wedding? Katrina, she's a small business owner. If she's conscious, she's probably out of her mind with worry about what she's going to do and how she's letting Kyler and Melody down. So, we're going to go to the hospital, visit her, and if possible, put her mind at ease, and see if the food she's already purchased for this job is where we can get to it."

"But what if she's not conscious? Or what if she is and gets angry that we would bring up business when she's hurt?"

"If she's a good business owner, she will be glad to see us. I'll be diplomatic and very gentle. It will be all right, you'll see."

They arrived at the hospital and nervously, Katrina walked with Trey as they made their way through the hospital corridors up to the intensive care unit. At a glass partition which served as the patient room door, Trey knocked, waited, then heard a summons.

"Come in," a woman's voice called. "I said, come in."

Trey grinned at Katrina, opened the door wider, then stepped around the curtain. A woman with her leg in traction and a bandaged arm at her side. Lay in the bed. Her pale face was marred by bruises and a scrape across her cheek. A man about their age sat on a chair next to the wall. He straightened as they entered the room.

"Mrs. Sailors?" Trey asked.

"Yes," she said. "Come on in. You people can't leave a woman in peace. You have to come in here all hours of the day and night. I'm exhausted."

"Mama," the man said. "Please calm down."

"You calm down, Toby," she snapped. Her eyes shifted back to Trey. "What do you want? If it's more blood, then just leave. I feel like a pin cushion."

Trey approached the bed. "I am so sorry this happened. My name is Trey Marshall, and this is Katrina Aaron. She's Kyler Hendrickson's sister."

The woman's glare disappeared, and relief took its place. "Oh, thank God, you're here. No one has let me use a phone, and I need to get this mess straightened out for them."

"We're here now. If you have a plan for the wedding party for Saturday night, we're here to listen."

"All the food is bought. But I've been racking my brains to figure out what to do. I had three people lined up to serve, but they aren't cooks. Tell Kyler and Melody I'm sorry. If they want to postpone the party, then I can do it. I'll give them their deposit back, and the entire thing will be free of charge for the terrible inconvenience." She closed her eyes as if in pain. "That's the best I can do."

"I think we can help you, Mrs. Sailors. I'm a chef and a

good friend of the family. If you'll let me step in and use your food, I'll get it done. Kyler and Melody can have their party. You can lay aside your worry and get better, and everything will be okay."

"I can't allow you to do that. What if something goes wrong?"

"Something has gone wrong, Mama. You were almost killed in a car wreck." The man stood up. "Now, it seems to me this is what you've been praying for. A miracle."

"No offense, whatever you said your name was, but I don't know you, and I don't know how well you can cook. And I really don't want to put my business's reputation on the line by bringing a stranger in at the last minute."

Trey reached into his pocket and pulled out a card. He laid it on the bed tray. "This is my business card. You will find on the website testimonials of satisfied clients. I will not advertise this job as my own. I'm stepping in as a favor to Katrina. If you'll tell me what your vision is for the party, I swear to you I will do my best to make it as close as I can to what you would do." He held up his hand in promise. "Without any self-promotion."

Barbara studied him.

"Are you agreeable?"

"Well, I really don't have much choice." She sighed then grimaced. "But at least Kyler and Melody won't have to postpone the party. I've been sick with worry about it."

Pulling out his notebook and a pen, he opened the book and with his pen poised, he looked at the patient. "Tell me what you want me to do."

She shut her eyes, tightly. "Well, one thing that has me worried is their wedding cake. They wanted cake and punch at the wedding itself and a few salty items—pretzels, cheese straws, and so forth. Cheese straws are made and frozen. You know, they keep. Punch, also, is a no-brainer, but I was transporting the cake when we wrecked. I can't imagine what the inside of my van looks like. Probably like the inside of a bakery exploded.

"How big was the cake?" Trey asked.

"Three layers, but small. Eight on the bottom; four on the top."

He nodded.

"The punch is white grape juice based. Oh, Gosh." She shut her eyes. "My punch bowls were in the van, too."

"Mom has two punch bowls," Katrina said. "She could probably borrow more if needed."

"You won't need them for Friday night, but Saturday we'd planned on four total." She sighed. "What a mess."

"I'll borrow or rent what I need."

"I'd already arranged with Party Planners for plates, punch cups, utensils, table cloths, and napkins. They'll be at the school gym at nine Saturday morning."

"Who is decorating?"

"Melody has a group of her friends that are decorating as a gift. Eighties theme. I told her I didn't think you could make an eighties themed party in a gym elegant, but what do I know? I'm just the caterer. Or, was. Good luck."

"Eighties themed?"

"Not with the food. Just the decorations."

"So, no pizza or nachos?"

"No. She wanted elegant," Barbara said.

"Elegant in a middle school gymnasium." Trey wrote something in his notebook. "Okay."

"Toby can take you over to my kitchen, and you can get the food for the Saturday party. There's a folder there. Toby will get it for you with the menu, number of dishes. It's all in there."

"Great."

When Trey had the information he needed, they said their goodbyes, and exited the room. Toby, Barbara's son, left with them and led them into Barbara's bakery and catering business. Katrina drove back to the parking lot where Chef's truck waited. He was quiet as she drove, writing in his book.

"What are you writing?"

"Logistics." He shook his head. "Melody said there were 200 hundred people coming to the party Saturday, but Barbara only has 180 as an estimate. Usually you plan for more than the estimate. Especially if it's being held in the school gym, people will assume it's less formal and not feel the need to RSVP. I think we need to plan for more people, which means Barbara doesn't have enough food."

"What will you do?"

"Get more food. The menu she's set out is a good one overall, though I'm uneasy about serving shrimp."

"How come?"

"Because you're allergic."

"How do you know that?"

"You told me. Don't you remember?"

Katrina searched her memory, but couldn't recall. "Not really."

"For a venue this big, high allergen foods like peanuts and shrimp are potentials for problems. I avoid them unless the client specifically insists. I keep an epinephrine injector just in case, but having to use it will likely put a damper on the dinner party."

"We can call Melody and Ky and ask if they care whether they have shrimp or not."

"I'll call them later after I've worked up a plan. That way I can ask all of my questions in one call."

"Thank you for doing this, Trey."

He looked at her.

"What?"

"That's the first time you've called me by my name."

"Is it?" She snickered. "I only knew you as Chef at the beach. I'm terrible with names."

"How are you with baking?" he asked.

"What do you mean?"

"I can't come back until Saturday morning. That means we need to get the cupcakes done for the wedding tonight. Melody liked my idea for cupcakes since it will be a small number of people attending, and they want only a brief reception afterward. We can make three dozen, and I can ice them before I leave. Barbara has the ingredients for the punch. It's easy and you can do it."

"Okay."

"You think your mom will be okay with me using her kitchen?"

"She said make yourself at home. That means the kitchen, too."

"Great. Let's go make some wedding cupcakes."

Chapter Sixteen

Every last dish was washed. All of the food had been sent to the nearby homeless shelter or tossed. Chef had directed the workers to sweep and mop the floors and kitchen, clean all the surfaces, store the tables and chairs borrowed from the school, and place the napkins and tablecloths in laundry bags to be taken back to the rental place. It was nearly three in the morning. Katrina was tired and exhilarated. She'd been at his side, since he'd arrived early the morning of the wedding. Working with Chef had been the most fun she'd had in a really long time.

Maybe ever.

They carried boxes of unused supplies to his truck, parked at the service entrance of the cafeteria. At the last trip, Trey handed each of the workers, two women and one man, envelopes, she assumed was their payment.

They walked back into the cafeteria, looking bare now without the decorations and with the tables put away. Chef had hidden the folding tables behind a large storage partition for the party. Now the partition was against the wall and the school-issued tables and chairs were in neat stacks to be used again after the new year.

"Are we finished?" Katrina asked with her hand on the light switch ready to darken the room.

"Looks like it except for perhaps a small celebration of a job well done."

Katrina arched an eyebrow at him. "Do you have something in mind?"

A grin spread itself across his face. "Yes."

A tiny seed of uneasiness sprouted. "What?"

"There's a tree outside. A huge oak."

Yes. Katrina had seen it beyond the side patio.

"I was thinking of climbing it."

"Climbing a tree? Haven't you already met that goal in your life book?"

His eyes sparkled mischievously. "Yes, I've climbed a tree. That's not the goal I want to achieve tonight."

"What is it, trespassing on school property at three in the morning?"

"Howling at the full moon with a beautiful woman."

Katrina laughed at the unexpected and outrageous comment. "You're making that up."

He shook his head. "Full moon. I checked to be sure."

"You wrote in your life book that you want to howl at the full moon with a beautiful woman."

"Yes." Chef turned the key inside the security bar of the door to lock it then put it inside the holder inside the kitchen.

"You don't have to climb a tree to do that or… or be with me."

"Climbing the tree is part of the adventure. It's from a story I read as a boy."

"What's the story?"

"About the moon getting stuck in the branches of a massive tree. A coyote climbs the tree to free the moon, and as a reward the moon turns him into a man. So, the coyotes howl at the moon to entice it down to earth, hoping it will get stuck in another tree, so they can have their chance at becoming human."

She turned off the lights, and they exited the door, pausing at the patio staring up at the tree.

"How good of a climber are you? The lowest branch has to be at least ten feet off the ground," Katrina asked.

"I figure if I pull the truck up next to it, it would be just about right. Are you game?"

"Am I game?" Katrina laughed. "You're kidding, right?

First of all, I'm wearing flowy dress pants and flats, second of all, it's three o-clock in the morning, and third of all, this is school property."

"Yes, of course to all of those things, but how often do we have a full moon, a tree aching to be climbed, and no one around to tell us no?"

"Our consciences are telling us no. It's not a good idea."

Trey stared up at the tree. He nodded, and relief coursed through Katrina. They entered the truck, but instead of heading toward the driveway and exit, he turned toward the tree.

"You know what my conscious is saying?"

"That you should listen to me?"

"It's saying, Awoooooo!"

As he howled, he slowly drove the truck onto the grass and parked next to the tree.

She sighed. "You're going to do it, aren't you?"

In the dark, he smiled at her. "No. We are. Awoooo! Come on. Howl with me."

"I will do nothing of the sort.

Cutting the engine, he opened the driver door and standing on the seat, he climbed on top of the cab.

His hand appeared, his fingers curling in invitation. "Come on, Coyote Katrina, let's see if we can convince that moon to bounce down here and get caught."

She huffed. "I'm not dressed for tree climbing or moon catching."

"Awooo!"

She laughed. He was so crazy. This was crazy. She stepped onto the driver's seat, turned her body and put her hand behind her on the tree trunk. When she straightened, she could see over the truck. Trey was on his knees. He reached his arms down to help her.

"Use the trunk to hoist yourself up. It's easy," he said.

She followed his directions and with a little help from him, she was on the metal surface of his truck. His socks and shoes were off.

"What are you doing?"

"Those shoes." He shook his head. "Put my socks on. They will protect your feet and you'll be able to grip a lot better than in those things." He gestured to the flats.

"I can't believe we're doing this." She slipped them off and put on his socks, pulling them up and tucking her wide gauzy pants in the elastic of the bands.

She stood, and looking down at herself, she shook her head. "I look ridiculous."

"On the contrary. You look quite fetching. That moon will not be able to resist your high athletic socked charms." Trey held the lowest branch, tested it with his weight, then climbed on it, crouching. "Didn't even budge. This is going to be sweet. Can you do it?"

"Can I? Yes." She joined him, and he nudged her up to the next branch. "Should I? No."

"I disagree. I think absolutely, we should be doing this."

The branches were close together, and as she went up higher, there were several branches to choose with each higher level. The late season of the year, had most of the leaves missing, not that it mattered that much as close as they were to the trunk.

"How high up, Chef?" she asked.

"Just go as far up as you feel safe, then we'll stop."

"I stopped feeling safe when we climbed on the truck."

"You're doing great. Really great."

A bare spot on the trunk caused her to hesitate. "I'm not sure which way. To the left has bigger limbs, but it's kindof a reach. What should I do?"

Trey climbed up next to her, resting his hand on her back. The contact made her feel safer. They were close now, so close she felt the heat from his body in the crisp night air. But there was no tension. This was Chef. Trey. He was her friend, and she could trust him. He'd proven that many times.

"I think this is probably high enough. This branch is big enough for us to sit on." They settled on it, Katrina next to the trunk and Trey next to her. A small branch jutted out just above where she sat, and she used it as a handle to steady herself.

"I'm afraid to look down."

"Don't look down then. Look through the branches straight ahead. Oh, my gosh, it's gorgeous."

He was right. Katrina could see in the bright light of the moon, the blue, black, green, and grey tones of the landscape open before them. Christmas lights of decorated homes and businesses, rooftops, and trees, and ribbons of roads dotted with circles of street lights canopied the canvas for their pleasure.

"If you could do anything, what would it be?"

Katrina shrugged.

"Was there ever anything you and Eric meant to do, but didn't?"

"I always pictured us being old together. Sitting on the front porch in rocking chairs. We both were always working. He worked weekends, so we didn't have many days off together." A thought occurred to her. "The beach was something, too, I always thought we'd do." Katrina paused. "Huh."

"What?" Trey asked.

"It's just… when we met, at the beach, that was a trip I thought he and I would one day take. He worked so hard, I wish he could have made the trip, that he could have taken it."

"His heart made it."

Katrina waited for the ache of loss and loneliness

Trey's comment should elicit, but none came. Only the contentment of sitting high up in the tree with Trey. She reached over and took his hand.

"Would it be weird if I put my ear on your chest and listen to your heart?"

"No, it wouldn't be weird. We just need to be careful we don't fall." He patted her hand and let go, then he reached overhead and gripped a limb. Straddling the limb, he sat on the opposite side, then scooted closer to her. "See if this works."

Katrina shifted, but the angle was wrong. "No." She slipped a bit and gasped, but Trey's arm was already around her steadying her.

"It's all right." He moved his leg again over the limb so he faced her. "Yes, this is going to work."

Katrina leaned against him, moving her arm around his waist and listened to his heart beat and the breath moving in and out of his lungs. His arm was warm and heavy on her shoulders. She sighed contentedly, wishing she could bottle this moment.

"Thank you for letting me do this," she said.

"My heart is your heart. You're welcome to it anytime."

"For listening," Katrina clarified.

He gave a short chuckle and patted her shoulder. "Are you ready?"

She raised her head and looked at him. "For what? To climb down?"

"No. To howl. That moon's not going to come down here without a little encouragement."

Katrina shook her head and gave a long-suffering sigh. "I suppose, to climb all the way up here and not howl would be tragic since it's in your life book and all." She opened her mouth and let out a long howl. Trey joined her.

It was the dumbest and most fun thing she'd done in

years, maybe her whole life.

The noise of a car engine caught her attention. She looked down, and shuddered in fear. A police cruiser was driving through the parking lot toward the truck.

"Trey, look," she whispered.

He turned his head, his eyes narrowing as he tracked the movement of the car.

"It doesn't have its lights on. That's good. Maybe it's just making sure everything is okay."

"Everything isn't okay. We're up a tree, and your truck is down there with the door open."

"Yeah. Looks suspicious, doesn't it?" Trey said calmly.

The car stopped in front of the truck, the lights shone against the grill and illuminated the tree and the truck itself. The door opened, and a man in uniform stepped out, his hand on his holster. Another cruiser pulled into the parking lot as well and slowly drove around the other side of the building.

The policeman pulled a flashlight off his belt and turning it on, he shone it around.

"We're up here," Trey said.

Katrina looked at him with wide eyes, not believing he'd just given away their location.

The beam moved upward, searching the roof of the school.

"No, we're in the tree," Trey said.

"How many of you are there?" The officer called up to them.

"Just two of us. We're both up in the tree."

"There is no one else on the premises?"

"No, sir," he answered cheerfully, as if he wasn't about to get arrested.

The other car appeared around the corner of the building. The man spoke. "Subject is in the tree."

Katrina surmised he was talking into his collar radio.

The car stopped about thirty feet from the tree. The door opened, and a figure stepped out. The spotlight on the side of the windshield came on, and the beam moved upward, sweeping the branches until Trey and Katrina were illuminated.

"And just what in the sam hill are you doing up in that tree?"

"Howling at the moon," Trey informed them.

"Come on down then, and don't try to run."

Trey grinned at her. "Isn't this cool? Two police cars. Maybe they'll turn the sirens and lights on. Won't that be amazing?"

"No, it won't," Katrina said, carefully stepping down the branches.

What were her parents going to say when she had to call them to bail her out of jail? She'd never done anything this reckless before.

This is horrible.

Her foot slipped, and she clung to the trunk, righted herself and continued down, the light tracking their progress. She was somewhat thankful for the light from the distance made it easier to see how to get down. Finally, her feet were on the top of the truck, and with a clump, Trey jumped down beside her.

"Slowly, and keep your hands where I can see them," one of the policemen said.

"How am I supposed to get off the truck with my hands raised," Katrina complained.

The light shifted, and the men moved, their bodies tense as if they expected them to make a run for it. Finally, Trey and Katrina were on the ground, the flashlight blinding. She closed her eyes against the bright beam.

"Do you mind? You're going to blind us."

"Why are you climbing trees and disturbing the peace at four in the morning?"

"Disturbing the peace?" Trey asked.

"Yes. We've had two calls of coyotes howling on school grounds."

Katrina put her hands on her hips and glared at Trey. This was his fault. He looked at her and laughed. "Do you want to tell them, or should I?" he asked.

"I will. My brother got married last night, and tonight we had their reception here at the school."

"Who's your brother?"

"Kyler Hendrickson."

"Katrina?" One of the policeman said.

"Ummm."

"Katrina Hendrickson? It's me, Patrick Daniels. I graduated with your brother Keith."

"Oh. Hi, Patrick," she said.

"My wife Gail works with Melody. I would have been at the party, but...."

"You were working?" Trey supplied.

"Yes. Look, seriously, why were you in the tree?"

Katrina looked at Trey. Howling at the moon was the only answer she had.

"We were cleaning up after the party and just blowing off some steam," Trey said. "Sorry if we bothered anyone."

"Oh, it's okay, just you know, stop it."

"Okay."

"Have you two been drinking?" the other man asked.

"Of course not," Katrina said.

He stepped closer to them, Katrina assumed so he could see if he detected any fumes. Oh, this was so humiliating. And now, Kyler and Melody would find out.

"Are you okay to drive, or do you need a ride home?" Patrick asked.

"I'm okay to drive, but you might want to give Katrina a lift home," Trey said.

Her head snapped in his direction.

"She's never ridden in the back of a police car."

"That's because I've never broken the law," she snapped.

"Until tonight, anyway," Patrick said. "Disturbing the peace. Trespassing. Wanton endangerment."

"Wanton endangerment?" Katrina sputtered. "Climbing a tree is wanton endangerment?"

"To the tree, I would say," Patrick said. "Yeah. I guess I'll have to take you into custody, Katrina, and make sure you get back to your parents' house okay."

"Why don't you make him ride in the car? It was his dumb idea to climb the tree."

Trey shrugged. "Are you afraid to ride alone in the back of the car?"

"Yes. No. This is ridiculous," Katrina said. "Next you'll be wanting to handcuff me."

Patrick lifted his hat and scratched his forehead. "That's not necessary, is it? Are you going to resist?"

"Oh, for heaven's sake."

"Hahaha. I'm just kidding, Katrina." Patrick said. "I'll take you all home, though, if you want."

"Maybe you should. We've been up all night," Trey said.

"That doesn't make any sense. You'll have to come back to get your truck tomorrow, or today, rather."

"Sleepy driving is also impaired driving. Yeah. I think leaving the truck here is a good idea."

"Actually," Trey said. "I was going to bed down in the truck for a few hours, then take off."

"You're not going to sleep out here in the parking lot of the school. That's crazy."

Trey yawned. "I'll be in my bunk in the truck. I sleep there a lot."

"Well, you're not sleeping in that truck right now. You're coming to my parents' house and you can sleep on the couch."

Trey shrugged. "Okay. Let me get a few things, and we'll go."

His easy capitulation took Katrina by surprise. He must be really tired. Of course, he was. He'd cooked food for 240 people tonight after doing a meal course last night in Charleston. He was probably exhausted.

In a few minutes, they sat side by side in the back seat of the police cruiser.

Trey moved his hip up and removed his cell phone and opened the camera app.

"If you take a picture of us, I will kill you."

"Really? You'll kill me?" He grinned. "In the back of a police car? I would think murder in the back of a police car is going to be easy to prove."

"I concur," Patrick said. "No killing. That would make my job extra hard tonight, and I was just being nice by taking you home."

Katrina glared at the back of the policeman's head. "You said it was unsafe for him to drive, and that's why you're giving us a ride."

"Please smile. Don't you realize how cool this is? You're doing something you've never done before."

"I've never had cancer before, but you won't see me celebrating that if it happens."

"After you've had some sleep, you'll be glad I took a picture for posterity." He held up his hand. "Can I see your foot?"

Thinking he was going to take his sock back, she moved her legs up on the seat to remove the socks. Trey reached over and grasping her ankle, he moved his fingers over the bottom of one foot.

She laughed. "Stop." He took a picture, but didn't stop with her foot, so reflexively, she kicked, bringing her foot up in the vicinity of his face.

"Ooof." He stopped and put his hand up, covering his cheek.

"I'm sorry. Are you okay? I hate being tickled."

"Noted." He looked at his phone and chuckled. "But worth it."

He showed her the picture. A little blurry, but the image had captured them looking supremely happy.

"That picture misrepresents the situation."

"I think I'll call it. 'Trey learns Katrina doesn't like to be tickled.'"

She took the phone out of his hand, and took a selfie of them with her pointing at his cheek, a smile of satisfaction on her face. "There. That's the one you should call 'Trey learns Katrina doesn't like to be tickled.' Now, settle down....Chef."

He did, for about two minutes. Leaning toward her, he asked, "You want me to ask Patrick to turn on the siren?"

"No, I don't. We've awoken enough people tonight, don't you think?"

He kissed her cheek and hugged her briefly. "Thanks for asking me to do this. This is the most fun I've had doing a wedding reception in all the years I've been a chef." Leaning back in the seat, he covered his mouth and yawned.

Katrina touched her cheek in disbelief, her skin still tingling from his day and most of the night's growth of beard. Arriving at the house, Patrick waited until they entered the front door.

The lights were on downstairs, but everyone was upstairs asleep.

Katrina retrieved bed clothes for Trey and began to make the couch up for him. "That's okay. I can do it."

"You're dead on your feet," she said. "Go on, get ready for bed."

He nodded and with his duffel, he headed to the

bathroom. She arranged the sheet and blanket and placed the pillow at one end. As much as he'd done for them, she wished there was another bedroom to offer, but Keith and Mary-Kate had one bedroom, and the other spare was being used by the girls.

Chapter Seventeen

Some weird sound woke up Trey. Like the juicer he owned when he was juicing cantaloupe. He opened one eye.

Olivia, sat on the floor in front of the couch and stared at him. Her mouth was occluded by a pink pacifier.

"Good morning," Trey said, sitting up.

She reached up and took the pacifier out. "Good morning. What chu doing sleeping on the couch?"

"Aunt Katrina made me."

A look of shock settled on Olivia's face. "Are you sure? She's never been bossy to me." The little girl chewed on her pacifier, and it made a squeaking noise, just like his juicer. "So, what are you doing here?"

"Talking to you."

"Pop Pop says we can build a fort today."

"A fort? That sounds like fun."

"Yeah, he's not awake yet, though. Mom says I'm not 'llowed to wake anybody up 'cept her and Dad."

"Aha." Trey hadn't been around little kids much. What should he do? Kids eat. "Are you hungry?"

"Starving to death. Mom says get my fruit snacks out of the bag, but come on. What kind of breakfast is that?"

"I could probably help you out with breakfast."

They went together to the kitchen. He washed his hands and made coffee. Then looked through the cabinets and drawers for an apron. Tucking a towel in the waistband of his pants, he crafted another towel around his head since his hat was in the truck back at the school.

"Why are you putting a towel on your head?" the little

girl asked in astonishment as she watched him tie the ends at the nape of his neck.

"Covering it. That way there's less chance of my hair falling into the food."

"Oh, my word." The little girl's eyes got big, and she made a sound of disgust.

"I know, so the Chef covers his head."

"Will you cover my head too?" she asked.

"Sure." He pulled another towel out of the drawer and folded it, then tied it around her head.

"Is that how come you wore your dough boy hat all the time?" The child had seen him with his chef's hat on yesterday during the party.

"Any time I'm cooking." He looked in the refrigerator and the cabinets. Pulling out ingredients, he began to prepare French toast sticks and roasted apples with cinnamon and sugar, listening to Olivia chatter as he worked.

"If I ring the doorbell and Pop Pop wakes up because someone is at the door, do you think that counts?"

"Counts for what?"

"Me waking him up. I mean, it would be the doorbell waking him up. Not me."

"You want him awake because he promised to build you a fort?"

"Yes, and it's been a really long time. Forever plus a day."

Trey laughed. "Forever plus a day, huh? Tell me about this fort. Where is he going to build it?"

She made an I-don't-know sound with a shrug of her shoulders.

"What is a fort anyway?" Trey asked, attempting to ascertain her vision.

"Well, you can have a couch fort with cushions and blankets, or if it's outside, you can have it in the bushes, but

Mom will probably holler because it's cold." She dropped her voice to a whisper. "It's not that cold. I didn't even need a coat yesterday."

When he'd been looking for an apron, he'd found a stack of neatly folded tablecloths in the pantry. Retrieving two, he spread them crossways on the table, so that the length fell to the floor. He tucked the edge of one under, so as to make a doorway.

Olivia had offered to help him, so he sent her to get the covers off the couch he'd used to put on the floor under the table so the fort would be more comfortable. When she came through the door, she had gotten a couch cushion.

"Is your Granny Nan going to be okay with you using the couch cushion?"

"She'll say 'No problem.'" The little girl poked her head through the draped entrance. "This is going to be so awesome. We'll need all of the cushions though."

Trey walked around the table to help her with the wide cushion.

"I think one more will be enough."

She retrieved the second cushion then got the blanket, sheet, and pillow he'd used the night before and disappeared under the table.

"When somebody comes in, don't tell them where I am," her voice came through loud and clear from the fort. "Can I eat breakfast under here?"

"It's okay with me, but I'm not really in charge."

Nancy, Katrina's mother, walked in as he spoke. Dressed in grey slacks and a soft white sweater, she surveyed the cloth covered table and Trey at the stove. Trey realized as he looked at her, he had a glimpse of what Katrina would look like in about twenty-five years. He hoped he would still be in her life by then.

"Well," Nan said, smiling. "What have we here?"

"I thought I'd fix some breakfast. I hope your offer of making myself at home in your kitchen carries over to today."

"Oh, Trey darling. Haven't you cooked enough this weekend? You poor thing, you didn't have to feed us again this morning."

Trey pulled the pan out of the oven, and spooned up several apple slices for Olivia. Setting them on a plate along with the French toast sticks, he set them in the freezer for a quick-cool.

Olivia's head appeared at the fort entrance. "Speak for yourself, Granny Nan. I'm starving."

"Well, my goodness, what are you doing under the table?"

"This is my fort."

Nan smiled at her granddaughter. "I see." Her gaze graduated to Trey. She graced him with a warm expression of approval.

"Would you like some coffee?" he asked.

"Yes."

He poured her a cup and placed the sugar and half and half next to it on the table where she sat. Soon, Charles, Mary-Kate and the baby joined them. Trey served food on plates as each person came in the room. He didn't realize Olivia had left until she came back in again, leading Katrina by the hand, as if the woman was sleep walking. She wore a long cotton candy blue flannel gown, and her hair mussed from sleep fell in big waves around her face.

Had she looked more beautiful? He didn't think so. He retrieved a mug from the cabinet.

"You'll have to crawl inside, Aunt Kat."

"Okay." Obediently, she bent on hands and knees and went under the table followed by Olivia. "Would someone be kind enough to pour me a cup of coffee?" Her arm appeared with her fingers outstretched.

Trey put his hand on the outside of hers to guide her as he placed the coffee cup in her waiting hand. Carefully, she lowered the cup until it disappeared. "Thank you."

"Where's Keith at?" Charles asked his daughter-in-law.

"He took the Mistress Penguin for a walk," she answered him.

Charles leaned back in the chair. "That name's bigger than the dog is."

"Who made this coffee?" Katrina asked from under the table.

"Your—" Charles began, but a hand on his arm from his wife stopped him.

"Trey did. He cooked breakfast too," Nan said.

Trey fixed a plate of breakfast food. When he turned around, Olivia was leaving the room. He knocked lightly on top of the table. "Katrina?"

"Yes?"

"Here's something to eat." He bent and handed the plate into the opening of the table cloth. The plate disappeared from his hand.

"Do you want more coffee?"

Her cup appeared, handle out so he hooked his finger through it and filled the mug. Olivia came back in the room. "Granny Nan, will you help me find Aunt Kat's make-up bag? She needs it because she looks like a hag."

Charles chuckled.

Standing up, Nan nodded. "Yes, sweetheart." They walked out of the room, and the front door opened. Men's voices carried from the front foyer.

Trey crouched down and lifted the cloth flap. In the shadowy interior of Olivia's fort, he saw Katrina sitting cross-legged on the floor. He handed her the cup of coffee.

"Hi."

She sipped from the mug. "Hello. Thanks for the coffee and breakfast."

"You're welcome."

Some of the food was missing from the plate. Good. He resisted the urge to crawl in there with her. Was building a fort and hanging out with Katrina in it life-book worthy? Sure, it was. In fact, in the last month or so, he'd written her name in his book several times.

He recognized Keith's voice coming into the kitchen. "Dang. I guess that's what I get for coming back here and going to sleep. I missed all the trespassing, tree-climbing, getting arrested fun."

Katrina's mouth opened in an expression of dismay. She'd heard her brother's comment and concluded it had something to do with them.

She was right.

Trey stood up and saw Patrick, still in his police uniform walking into the kitchen.

"Morning, want some coffee, Patrick?" he asked the officer.

He shook his head. "No, thanks though. I stopped by to see if you wanted a ride over to get your van."

"And to check on your eye," Keith said. "Patrick said Katrina kicked you in the face when y'all were riding in the back of the police cruiser."

Olivia and Nan came back in the kitchen. Olivia held a small black bag, and without a word, she went into the table fort.

Every person's attention was on him now, searching for the mark of Katrina's foot. "I'm fine."

"Huh," Patrick said. "Well, it hardly bruised at all. So, you want a lift over to the school? I'm about to go off-shift, so I don't mind taking you."

Trey took off his do-rag and pulled the towel-apron out of his waistband. "That'd be great. Thanks." He folded the towels and put them on the counter. "Excuse me, everyone." He headed out the door with Patrick.

"Chef...err...uhh, Trey?" Katrina called.

He turned around. Katrina crawled out from the table and raised up on her knees.

"Are you coming back?"

As if he had the choice to refuse her. Absolutely, he was coming back even if it meant he had to forge rivers or scale mountains. If Katrina wanted him to come back, his task was to do her bidding. Joyfully. Of course, he toned down his answer.

He grinned. "Sure. K.P. is part of the job, you know." Turning around, he followed Patrick out the door.

****

"What's that mean?" Keith asked, giving Katrina a hand up off the floor.

"It means he thinks he's cleaning up the kitchen," Katrina said. "Of course, he's not."

"Of course not," Mom said going over to the stove and picking up the casserole dish.

"Mmm, what's that?" Keith said picking up a plate from the counter.

"Wash your hands first," Mary-Kate directed.

With her make-up bag tucked under her arm, Katrina hurried out of the kitchen toward the bedroom to change clothes. Hopefully, she'd have time to do something about her haggard appearance before Trey returned.

She couldn't believe he'd seen her in her flannel gown, literally rolled out of bed by her niece. Catching sight of herself in the mirror as she entered her room, she groaned at her bed-mussed hair and the bags under her eyes. How had he not run in terror when he'd seen her?

In ten minutes, she'd covered the ravages of too-little sleep to her face, brushed her hair, placing it in a high knot on her head. With jeans and a black cashmere sweater, she sprinted out of the room, downstairs, and to the front door in answer of the knock.

Trey stood there. He smiled in greeting. "Good morning. Have you had enough coffee to talk yet?"

"Yes."

"Oh, good."

She led him into the kitchen. "Did you even eat yet?" She asked the question already knowing the answer. He was in work mode, but this was her parents' home. Didn't he know he didn't have to cook for them? He acted as if he were a servant.

He wasn't.

Katrina noticed the drying rack next to the sink was full. Good. Mom had been busy while she'd been in her room.

Keith sat at the table eating. Mom and Dad had cups of coffee in front of them.

"Hello, Trey," Nan said. "Can I get you some coffee?" She rose, anticipating an affirmative from him.

"Thank you, no."

"We cleaned up so you wouldn't feel as if you had to," Charles said.

"Of course, we wouldn't expect you to do that," Mom added, pouring coffee in Katrina's mug and handing it to her.

"Thank you," Trey said again. "I should go. It's been a pleasure meeting all of you."

Disappointment ballooned inside Katrina. She didn't want him to leave. But she didn't have the right to ask him to stay either. He'd come here to help with the wedding and the party. That was done. Why would he stay?

Charles stood. "Okay, then." He walked over and shook Trey's hand. "Appreciate all you did."

Trey turned to leave with Charles following. What was Dad doing? Katrina trailed after them, wanting a moment of Trey to herself before he left.

"Ky wanted me to be sure we settled up with paying

you. Do you have an invoice or something, or will you just bill us later?"

They had arrived at the front door. Trey opened it. "There's no charge." He smiled at Dad, then at Katrina. "Thanks so much for asking me. I'll see you later."

He'd see her later?

Dad paused, as Trey went out the door, but Katrina continued outside. "What do you mean no charge?"

On the front porch, Trey turned. "I assume Kyler and Melody paid the caterer already. This was her job. Not mine. I was just helping out."

Katrina shook her head. "But you paid for the roast beef. You paid for the fruit. You made the cake for the wedding. You cooked. You served, and you supervised the other workers. What about all of that?"

Trey shrugged. "I did it as a favor to a friend."

Anger and frustration bubbled at the surface of Katrina's mind. She crossed her arms over her chest. "That's too much, and you know it."

He gave a brief chuckle, his gaze roving over her face affectionately. "No, it's not."

This was about Eric's heart. Still. When was Trey ever going to be over this debt that he thought he owed her.

"You don't owe me anything."

He stared at her for a few seconds. Then he stepped forward and kissed her cheek. He whispered in her ear. "Sweet Katrina."

He drew back, and for a moment, Katrina thought he'd kiss her on the lips. He squeezed her upper arm in a warm gesture, then stepped away, breaking contact.

"Trey," she said with all of the unresolved emotions she couldn't even name in her tone.

He walked on to his truck. "Call me, Katrina, if you need me," he said over his shoulder.

Shaking, she watched him go, then turned to go in the

house. Mom and Dad stood in the foyer.

"Darling," Mom said. "What is going on?"

"Trey is… was the recipient of Eric's heart. He thinks he owes me his life. But he doesn't, and I wish he'd get over it."

Brushing past them, she went to her room to brood.

She lay on her bed thinking about Trey and what he was to her. She wanted to be friends. She wanted to keep a connection to him. She wanted more, even, but how could she? He obviously felt gratitude to her, and she understood that. But she didn't want his gratitude. She wanted…him. Sometime during their time at the beach, or her house, or here, she'd fallen in love with him. If she wanted him she was sure he'd say yes. But his yes would only be about gratitude.

She hated gratitude.

She wanted his love.

Chapter Eighteen

A knock sounded on the door.

She sat up. "Come in."

The door opened, and Mom entered the room. A look passed between them, and her mom arched an eyebrow at her. "You think you can drop a bomb like that and then come in here and expect me not to follow?"

Katrina sighed. "Pretty unbelievable, huh?"

She sat on the edge of the bed, placing her hand on her daughter's leg in a gesture of affection. "How did you two meet?"

"You know the two weeks in Florida? He arranged it. I didn't know who he was at first. I thought he had been hired to cook for me. Well, that's what he said. But he told me—later—who he was."

"Oh, my dear."

"He's so good, so amazing, Mom. But everything he does, it's out of the stupid sense of appreciation. Okay, I get it, he's glad he has a new heart. I made a decision when Eric died to do a small thing because what did it matter for Eric? He was dead. I barely remember even saying yes. I don't want Trey to spend the rest of his life thanking me."

"What do you want from him?"

Katrina shook her head. "It doesn't matter what I want from him. Our connection will always be about him trying to repay me for Eric's heart. That's all I'll ever be to him. A debt."

"How do you know? Have you asked him?"

"No. I can't, because he'd do whatever I asked, he'd be whatever I asked, no matter what it was. He's told me, he thinks he owes me his life."

Nan patted her daughter, then leaned over and kissed her. "Relationships have been built on much less noble foundations."

Katrina snorted. "You're kidding."

She smiled at her daughter with a twinkle in her eye. "Do you know why I went out with your dad? Because he had the most beautiful eyes I'd ever seen in a man. His eyes, Katrina. That's why I said yes."

"Okay, but your whole relationship wasn't based on his blue eyes, Mom."

"No." She crooked her head at her daughter. "But it was a start. And can you really tell me that there is nothing between you and Trey but his gratitude to you?"

Katrina sighed. She didn't know. Really, she didn't.

"On his side, yes, I think so."

"And on your side?"

Katrina felt her throat close up with emotion. "Oh, Mom. Of all the men in the world, why him?"

Nan reached forward and pulled her daughter close in a hug. "Oh, my dear, he's so wonderful. How could you not?"

****

Trey sat in beautifully furnished Victorian house which had been converted to the law offices of Hendrickson and Westing.

He had been summoned by Nancy Hendrickson, Katrina's mother. He hadn't known she was an attorney when he'd made himself at home in her kitchen at her request. When she'd sent an appointment request through his website to cater her holiday meal Christmas day, he'd called her thinking this was a mother's way of getting him and Katrina in the same room again.

He'd be willing to bet Katrina didn't know about it. He hadn't heard from her since the morning he'd refused to be paid for helping out with her brother's wedding. She'd been angry, but he'd stood his ground. He wasn't going to be paid for it. And it wasn't just because he owed Katrina. He'd told Barbara this was her gig, her job, and he wasn't going to take it away from her. That meant he'd stay out of the business of it. She'd owe him, and that was always a good thing in small business. Because if she ever got in another bind, she'd probably call him.

That's what he hoped anyway.

A mahogany pocket door slid open, and Nan stood there looking very lawyer-like in a tailored suit.

She smiled. "Hello, Trey. Come in, why don't you?"

He stood and entered a room with a table and leather backed chairs, obviously used for meetings though decades ago, families perhaps ate formal dinners here.

She gestured for him to sit as she settled into the chair at the head of the table. He sat to her right and pulled his notebook out. "So, you want me to cook your Christmas dinner?"

"Yes, and eat with us."

Aha. He'd been right. Nan had intentions for him and Katrina.

He shook his head. "The chef doesn't eat with the clients."

A folder lay on the table. She opened it. "Yes. I saw that in the contract you emailed me. Which is why I've rewritten it with a few changes."

Trey laughed. He took the paper she pushed toward him on the table.

"The changes are in red. If you are in agreement, I will reprint it, and we'll both sign."

He read it, red and black script just in case Granny Nan was trying to pull a fast one, more so than attempting to contract her daughter a boyfriend for Christmas dinner.

But, no, nothing was different except for the red, as she'd stated. But, oh boy, the red. He looked up at the woman across the table. "Does Katrina know you want me to enter a legal agreement with you to stay overnight in the house?"

"She enjoys your cooking, as you probably know. I thought this could be a… Christmas present, of sorts, for her. I didn't want to tell her until I knew for sure you could come."

"I'm a Christmas present?"

"Your cooking, of course. It wouldn't be ethical to make a person a Christmas present, now would it?"

"As a chef, I adhere to an ethical code, too. I cook for my clients, but I don't fraternize with them."

"What about in your in-home cooking course? Your website states you do cooking lessons. Don't you eat with your clients when you're teaching them to cook?"

"No. Eating is social, personable. Sitting down at a table with people tends to blur the lines of professional service and expectation. You understand that, don't you, Nan?"

She smiled and nodded. "Yes, I do."

"And anyway, Christmas dinner tends to be pretty traditional fare—ham or turkey, cranberry sauce, casseroles, and such. The food is easy to prepare usually, and not something that needs to be taught unless someone has special dietary needs or desires, like paleo or vegan."

"Trey, perhaps I've gone about this the wrong way, then. Because I want you to join me and my family for Christmas, and I want to be able to compensate you for all of the time, work, and money you spent on food for Ky and Melody's wedding. We—Katrina included—feel we took advantage of you, and I really want to correct that."

He moved the papers toward her. "You didn't take advantage of me. I did it as a favor to Katrina."

"Your time, maybe, but she told me you paid a couple hundred dollars for food and ingredients. I wish, at the least, you'd let me reimburse you for that."

"When I talked with Barbara, I told her that the job was hers, that I would not take any credit for it. I was only stepping in for a friend."

"Yes, you helped us out, and we appreciate it. We owe you for that. Let me at least pay for the cost of the food and ingredients you bought. If you'll let me do that, I will also contract with you for a Chamber of Commerce lunch and the Lions' breakfast in January. Those are some of our top business people in the area and if you do a good job, which I know you will, it may lead to some more work for you."

"And if I say no, you'll contract those jobs to another caterer?"

She watched him steadily. "Probably not, but play along with me, won't you? I want to be able to tell Katrina you let me compensate you. It's important to her that you didn't have to pay out for helping us."

If it was important to Katrina, then he'd do it. He hadn't meant to make her feel bad about the party. He'd wanted to help, and if she felt he'd done too much, she might not ask him again.

He nodded. "All right. I'll get my receipts together and email them to you."

She smiled, and he was struck again by how much Katrina favored her. "Wonderful. Now, what about Christmas?"

He shrugged and held his hands up in an I-don't-know gesture.

"Will you come eat with us?"

"I usually spend that day with my own family."

"In Louiston? What time do you all eat?"

"Around noon."

"Lovely. Join us for supper then. We'll eat at eight, and you'll stay with us the night. All right?"

"I appreciate your invitation, Nan. I do, but I think it would be better coming from Katrina."

Nan's eyes dropped for a second. "Katrina hasn't spent Christmas with us since Eric died."

"What does she do for Christmas?"

"She stays at home alone. I think. We went to her house that first Christmas eve. It was less than two months after he died. She had no decorations. Nothing. When I insisted we get a tree, she went to her bedroom, went to bed, and stayed there." She shook her head. "You can't imagine how difficult it is to see your child hurting like that and to not be able to do anything about it. Last year, I thought she'd come to our house, but at the last minute she called and said she just couldn't come." Nan's pained gaze pinned Trey. "After Ky and Melody's wedding, I've been very hopeful that I could convince her to come for Christmas, especially if you are there."

Trey chose his words carefully. "You've known Katrina a lot longer than I have. I could be wrong, but she seems the kind of person that too much pushing causes her to withdraw instead of jumping in."

Nan nodded slowly.

"So, you telling her I am coming to your house and cooking Christmas dinner or even just showing up, it wouldn't necessarily mean she'd come at all. It might even compel her to stay home again."

Nan sighed. "It seems, then, I've wasted your time, Trey." She rose.

"Wait a minute. Maybe not. Let me see what I can do. I'm not promising I can get her to your house, but maybe I can help her have a happier Christmas this year. I want to do that for her."

The woman's posture relaxed, and she gifted him with a warm motherly grin.

****

Trey texted Katrina Christmas eve.

Are you free tomorrow?

No, she texted back. She didn't want to see him on Christmas day. Or anyone else for that matter. She'd go into work. She'd bypass the office Christmas tree and continue to ignore the wrapped gifts from Brenda and her co-workers. She'd pleaded a headache during the office party instead of enduring the pitying looks and good cheer. Glad to be free from the Christmas music Beth had been playing for three weeks in the outer office, Katrina had gone home and sat on the couch flipping through channels searching for anything non-holiday related.

Gee whiz, was there any network that understood some people hated Christmas?

Tomorrow she'd go to her office, and she'd pretend it was like any other day.

It wouldn't feel like any other day since no one else would be there. But that was okay. She'd just pretend it was a Saturday. She sometimes went in on Saturdays when she was really busy.

Need help.

She stared at the message. Help? What kind of help did he need on Christmas? And why from her?

Sorry, she texted back.

Thanks, Katrina.

She rolled her eyes. Again with the thanks. She'd said she wouldn't help him, and he still thanks her.

She scrolled through her contacts and called him.

"This is Chef," he answered.

He sounded tired.

"Are you okay?" she asked.

"Sure. Been a little busy is all."

His voice had brightened a bit, but Katrina wondered if it was an attempt on his part to distract her from being concerned about his wellbeing.

"How busy?"

"Twenty holiday parties in three states. I don't think I've slept more than four hours straight the whole month. Oh, wait. Maybe it's twenty-one. Did I say three states?"

"Chef, go take a nap."

"I can't. I'm cleaning up from my noon gig, then dropping off hor d'oeuvres for a four o'clock party before a catered meal at seven."

"It sounds exhausting. You sound exhausting."

"I'll be able to rest after tomorrow's meal, but we need people to take food to shut-ins. One of our drivers canceled on us at the last minute. Sure you can't come over and help?"

The urge to come to Trey's rescue pushed at her like the undercurrent in a tide. She'd called him for Melody and Ky's wedding, and he hadn't hesitated. He'd come over. He'd given them a beautiful party. He'd done it all.

"Where are you?"

"Louiston. Well, I'm not there yet, but that's where I'll be in the morning."

"What are you doing exactly? Just providing food to shut-ins?"

"The Blue River Restaurant cooks a holiday meal and serves it every Christmas free of charge. About ten years ago, they started taking meals to people who couldn't get out to come eat. Last year, we fed fifty-two people in house and sixty-one shut-ins. So far, we've had seventy-nine orders for shut-ins. But that was two days ago. I haven't heard the latest count. So, are you in?"

"I'm not...." Katrina sighed. "I don't do Christmas, Chef."

"What does that mean? You don't celebrate it?"

"Yes, that's what I mean."

"Okay, don't celebrate it, but do you think you could drive around Louiston and take meals to about twenty old people? You can pretend it's their birthday, or something."

Katrina sighed in resignation. "I suppose I could do that."

"Great. I'll send you the address. I know it's asking a lot. I know it's a two-hour drive to get here. I owe you."

"Oh, no you don't. And if you start acting like you do, I'm not even going to come."

"Fine. I don't owe you. Can you be here by nine?"

"I will not wish anyone a Merry Christmas."

"Understood. Just try not to glare if anyone wishes one to you. See you in the morning."

He ended the call. Katrina turned around caught sight of herself in the mirror—the big goofy smile on her face held her attention.

"Okay, so I like him," she said to her image. "I can like him, can't I?"

Yes, she could.

Katrina smiled again. She was going to see Chef tomorrow.

By the time the sun had peeked above the horizon, she was on the road to Louiston. With fifteen minutes to spare, she pulled her car into the parking lot of the Blue River Restaurant. Butterflies feeling more like bats flapping around in her stomach. Why had she agreed to do this? Because Chef had asked for her help.

She left the warmth of her car, walking in the brisk morning to the building.

Garland and lights hung from the front windows, and two wreaths graced the front doors.

Ugh. More Christmas decorations.

That was all she needed.

Wishing home was closer so she could turn around and go there without the two-hour drive, she opened the door and entered.

"Because I said there would be fourteen hams and

twelve turkeys, that's why!" an angry woman's voice carried across the room.

"If we had just stuck with hams like we've done every other year, this wouldn't be an issue," a man yelled back.

"Not everyone eats ham for Christmas, Bill."

Katrina spotted the owners of the voices. A man and a woman argued as they carried a long banquet table—completely set—next to the far wall.

"It was good enough before."

"For you, yes. But people ought to have a choice. Including me."

"You never complained before."

"I have wanted turkey every single year we've been married, and I have complained about it every single year."

"Excuse me if I have given up sorting out your valid complaints from the invalid ones."

Katrina saw a man near the back and hurried toward him hoping it was Chef. He entered a doorway, and Katrina was about to follow him when she saw a movement out of the corner of her eye.

Chef stood in front of a computer with his cell phone up to his ear. She approached him.

"Don't worry about it, Sharla. Really," he said. "I know. I know you didn't."

He caught a glimpse of Katrina, and the somber expression on his face lightened. He stepped back and held up his arm, pulling Katrina to his side in an embrace.

Automatically, she put her arm around his body for a second, then two. When she would have stepped away, instead Chef held onto her.

How long was a greeting hug supposed to last anyway?

"We have it covered."

As close as Katrina was, she could hear the distress in the woman's voice on Chef's phone. The man and woman's argument about turkey and ham continued as they walked by and disappeared into the door the other man had gone through. Katrina assumed it was the kitchen. She resigned herself to the close contact with this man. Then realized she could hear the intake of his breath and the beating of his heart.

Eric's heart.

How amazing.

"I am standing here with your replacement. I called her yesterday, so Merry Christmas, and stop worrying. It's fine. Goodbye, Sharla."

His hand left her shoulder, and he pressed the screen on his phone. "Hi. Sorry about that." He stepped away, and looked down into her face. "It's a little hectic."

Raised voices reached them.

"Did you meet the owners of The Blue River?"

"Umm. No. Was it the couple who came by a few minutes ago?"

"Yes. I probably should have warned you they argue a lot."

"Are they married?"

He laughed. "Yes, though some of us have wondered why. I have something for you." He picked up a small pearly gray box with the Chef@Home sticker on the top.

She shook her head. "I don't do Christmas presents."

"Who said anything about Christmas? This is required for the kitchen."

With a skeptical glance at him, she took the box and opened the lid. Pulling at the tissue paper, she unfolded what she thought was a white linen napkin at first, but it wasn't. Instead, it was a cotton cooking cap with…. Katrina gasped in delight…. her name embroidered in blue on the front.

She smiled up at him and put it on. "I love it."

Folding his arms, he took a few steps backward. "Come on." He led her into the kitchen where five people in various stations worked—the couple she'd already seen, an elderly woman, and a younger couple. "Everyone, this is Katrina Aaron. She has agreed to take Sharla's place." Trey pointed. "Over there is Bill and Maria, the owners of the restaurant." He pointed to the two young people in turn. "That's Gretel at the chopping block. Raesh with the hams." With a wink, he indicated the older woman. "And MiMi on roll patrol."

Maria came forward with a hard look in her eyes. Katrina thought the woman might have in mind to punch her. Instead, she grabbed Katrina and hugged her tightly. "Well, aren't you a sight for sore eyes? I am telling you, what, we sure appreciate your willingness to help us out." She stood back holding onto Katrina by the shoulders. "You do have a license, don't you?"

"At this point, who cares if she's got a license?" Bill said, coming forward and embracing her as well.

His hug was brief, and he put her away from him. She watched as Maria scowled at her husband.

"Because she isn't going to drive Horace around without a license. Can you imagine if she gets stopped with twenty-five meals in the car from the restaurant and Horace blabbing his mouth? They'd both end up in jail, for sure," Maria said.

Chapter Nineteen

"Don't you let these two scare you," Mimi said. She held up floury hands and kissed Katrina on the cheek. "They're both as high strung as the power lines outside."

"Now, Mama. Don't you start with me. Every year, I swear this is the last time. The last time I do this because everything just falls completely apart." Maria strode to an oven and opened it. "Trey, some of the turkeys on the right look a little too brown."

"Close the oven, Maria. All that hot air from your mouth is going to burn the turkeys for sure. Why in the world you pick this year to go turkey is beyond me. Seventy-five-degree difference in the temp, and don't even get me started on cooking times." Bill moved next to his wife and closed the oven door.

She glared at him and opened the door again, standing next to it as if daring Bill to say something more.

Mimi smiled at Katrina. "High strung." She winked, then called over her shoulder. "Maria, I'm out of flour, and I still have three more batches of rolls."

Maria closed the door. "Three more batches? You should have been done with the last one half an hour ago. Three more batches don't have time to rise." She jogged away from the group. "And we better not be out of flour. If someone has used the last of the flour, and not put it on the list, heads are going to roll. I mean you, Mama. You never put things on the list."

Trey ambled over to the oven. He turned a switch and peered into the window, then came over to where Katrina stood attempting to overcome her shock.

Gretel, a woman who appeared to be in her early

twenties, waved a knife in greeting. "Welcome to the nuthouse, Katrina."

"Yeah, welcome to the nuthouse." Raesh picked up a cutting board with slices of ham on it. He carried it over to a long counter covered with open Styrofoam containers.

Two women and a man came from the back with Maria at the helm informing MiMi that there was a forty-gallon bag of flour which hadn't even been opened yet, finishing her tirade with, "This is the last year I'm doing this. I mean it."

"Promises. Promises," Raesh said as he deftly placed two ham slices in each square plate.

"You watch your mouth, boy," Maria said. "If I stop Christmas, that means you won't eat either."

Katrina's startled gaze fell on Trey. He leaned down and whispered in her ear. "You see? You're not the only one who isn't a fan of Christmas." He straightened. "James, Daphne, and Savannah, this is Katrina. She'll be on the drive crew. Do you all want to go out front and strategize?"

"Not even you can stop Christmas," Bill said. "Though you've been threatening it long enough."

Maria fisted her hands at her hips. "Watch and see."

"Where's Horace?" Daphne, a coal-black haired woman who looked to be in her sixties asked.

"Tim is picking him up. But Tim can't stay. He's on call at the hospital," MiMi had found her way back to the industrial sized mixer with the roll dough.

A bell dinged. Trey moved, as if we were Pavlov's dog, opened an oven door and with a mitt, removed a massive pan of perfect rolls. Without glancing at him, MiMi moved an empty pan, placed two hot pads on the counter, in just the second that Trey set it down.

Wow. They have the choreography down.

"Potatoes, Maria," Bill said.

"I know what I'm doing," she groused, heading to the

stove.

"Katrina?" Daphne said. "It's nice to meet you. Thanks for helping."

Katrina followed them to the dining room, and they sat at a table. Daphne passed papers to each person with the delivery routes on each. "We'll leave at ten for the first round. Come back and leave again at 11:15, and we should finish up by noon."

Katrina looked at her paper. "I only have five deliveries? Chef said I'd have twenty."

"I think you were going to be with me, but when Sharla called off, we needed someone with Horace. He'll be with you. He will actually be doing the getting out and taking the meal in. He tends to talk, so…." She shrugged her shoulders.

"And his knees," Savannah, a silver haired woman with glasses said.

"His knees?" Katrina wondered what had she gotten herself into.

"He's eighty-two. If anyone had good knees at eighty-two, they haven't been living, in my opinion," James supplied.

"You expect an eighty-two-year-old man to deliver meals to shut-ins?"

"He does it every other day, except Sharla is usually with him. She can get him to… errr…curb his conversations long enough to get twenty meals to the shut-ins."

"Does she actually go in with him to each house?"

"House or apartment, yes."

"I could go in with him. I could hurry him up."

Daphne tapped her fingernail on the table top. "We could try it." She pulled a paperclip off from her own sheaf and slid the paper to Katrina. "Here are six more. If by nine-thirty, you haven't gotten through the five on your first sheet, call me. We'll meet you and get the list and meals. I'll give you my number."

Katrina nodded, appreciating the fact that though Daphne didn't know her, she was willing to take a chance on her.

"All right. Katrina? If you haven't done so already, move your car to the back door, and we'll load up. Horace should be here any minute."

Katrina did as she was told. Carefully maneuvering her car to the back entrance of the restaurant. Another car idled in the parking lot. Daphne, in coat and scarf stood at the driver's side, the window down. She leaned down and kissed the man briefly on the cheek and handed him a covered plate. The passenger side opened, and an elderly man stood, walking with purposeful steps to her car. He raised his hand in greeting.

Reaching the car, he opened the passenger door and leaned in. "Name's Horatio Barker, but everyone calls me Horace. Hear you and me are going to be riding together this morning."

"I heard the same thing. Have a seat."

"Don't mind if I do."

He settled himself in the vehicle and directed her to pull forward. Next to the rear entrance, James opened the back door and spread a pad over the backseat. "This will protect your car from any spills."

Raesch and Gretel came next with five containers each and laid them across the backseat. Horace looked at the list and told Katrina how to get to the first address, and they were on their way.

"You a chef?" He asked.

"No. I'm an accountant."

"Huh. An accountant. How'd you get roped in to doing this?"

"Chef… that is, Trey… asked me."

That earned her a once over by the gentleman. "He did, did he? Been wondering what his type was."

Katrina laughed. "Oh, nothing like me, I'm sure. He just needed some help, and I was available."

"Ooo, you're available? Don't you have a family to be with today?"

Katrina tried to figure out a way to answer his question without being rude or sharing more of her story than she wanted to.

"Excuse me, young lady. It really isn't any of my business. Whatever your situation, you are welcome here. Christmas can be a lonely time for some folks. That's why Maria and Bill have this meal, so that anyone who wants to can come eat with us. Make it a little less lonely."

"I don't mind being alone. Not really."

"There's a difference between being alone and lonely. Here we are. Just pull up into the driveway now. That's a girl." He opened the door. "Oh, my knees." He lifted his arm and held the frame of the door as he hoisted himself into a standing position, grunting in pain. Katrina left the car and handed him the sealed plate. "What chu doing?"

"Hurrying you along. If we don't have the first five meals delivered by half after, Daphne is going to come and take the other six meals. I want to be able to deliver all of them."

"Me, too. Well, come on then. We can't let Daphne take away our route."

They went up the walkway, and Horace rang the bell before entering the house. "Always let them know you're here. You walk in unannounced, you're liable to catch someone unawares." He shot her a wicked grin. "Either give them a heart attack, or they'll give you one. Anavieve? It's Horace," he raised his voice for the greeting, then lowered it again. "Got to holler loud for this one. Deaf as a post."

Katrina followed him into a sitting room where an elderly woman sat in a recliner, her television set on, the volume blasting. Horace walked over to her, set the plate on a tv tray next to her chair, leaned down and kissed her cheek.

"How's my girl today?"

"Just fine, Horace, and Merry Christmas to you."

"Merry Christmas to you. You doing okay?"

"Just fine. Who's this with you? You're not cheating on me, are you?"

He chuckled. "Of course not. This is Katrina. She's my driver today. Sharla's kids came in unexpected, and she said she'd drive anyway, but Trey said he'd find someone, and so he did."

"Hello."

"Merry Christmas, Katrina." She reached up her hand, and Katrina took it, unsure what else to do. The woman's skin felt soft next to hers. She squeezed Katrina's fingers.

"Thanks."

"Would you like to kiss the cheek of a hundred year old woman?"

"A hundred years old?"

"That's right, and still living by myself. I told them that nursing home will cave in before I'll agree to go live there."

Katrina obediently bent down and kissed her, the smell of White Shoulders enveloping her.

"We can't stay, Anavieve. Daphne's got us on a tight schedule today."

"What?"

"We have to go," he said louder.

"Merry Christmas then, and be careful."

They left, and on the way to the car, Horace patted her back. "Good job."

"I didn't do anything."

"You gave her the gift of your touch. Very important

to someone who spends most of their time alone."

Horace and Katrina made their delivery quota and beat Daphne and James who arrived a couple of minutes later. Loading the car again, they left for the second set of deliveries and arrived back at the restaurant at noon. With perhaps twenty cars in the parking lot, when they entered the dining room, it was teeming with adults and children. Katrina noticed each table had platters of food and place settings.

Trey appeared next to her. "Want to sit next to me?"

"We're eating?" She expected the dread of forced Christmas gathering to blanket her, but it didn't.

"Yes. Aren't you hungry?"

"Actually, yes."

He led her to a table where most of the staff and shut in deliverers were gathered. Horace was taking the chair next to Mimi. "The meal is served family style," Chef said. "That means each table has its own food. Once it's all served, then we all eat instead of having to wait on the different tables."

"What about seconds?"

"We pile the platters high so there is plenty of food at each table. Unless it's the Folsom family," He indicated a table nearby with three young men looking like football linebackers and a woman who Katrina assumed was their mother. "No one runs out of leftovers. Tiny has been trained to get their own second helpings."

"Who's Tiny? Their mother?"

"No. The smallest and youngest of the three."

Katrina chuckled. "Are you serious?"

"As a heart attack."

She narrowed her eyes at him, not liking the sentiment. But the feelings of loss for Eric didn't surface. Only concern for Trey and the potential of him having problems with the obtained heart. "Don't say things like that."

He thumped his chest. "You know he had a good heart, right? Good enough for both of us."

"This is weird."

"Let's eat. I'm starving."

Katrina counted twenty-one people at their table. Though Trey was the only person she knew well, the easy manner and comradery apparent put her at ease. Both Trey and Daphne, who sat on the other side of Katrina, included her in their conversations. As the meal drew to a close, Maria came to stand behind them.

"Trey." She made a shooing motion.

He looked up at her. "K.P. is part of the job."

She glared at him. "Don't give me that. You need to get going. We've got plenty of hands here for K.P."

He gave her an unrepentant look.

"I'm serious....Chef."

Katrina giggled, realizing the woman had just used his title exactly how Katrina herself had when she wanted to make a point with him. Trey looked at Katrina and winked.

"Now, stand up and give me a hug, then get going."

Trey pushed his chair back and rose. "Has anyone ever told you how bossy you are?"

"That's because I'm the boss."

He said something to her, but Katrina didn't catch it since he was embracing the woman. Her face broke in a smile and she patted him on the back. She then whispered something to him, and stepped back gazing down at Katrina.

"It was very nice to meet you, Katrina. You are welcome back any time, and we won't put you to work. Will we, Chef?"

"Not unless she wants to."

Katrina stood, and Maria enfolded her in an embrace. Katrina smiled as she sniffed the aroma of pumpkin pie concluding it was because she'd spent the morning cooking the pies they'd just enjoyed.

"There is going to be a lot of hugging. If you want to avoid it, we should make a run for it now," Trey advised.

Katrina nodded. "Okay."

They turned, and Horace stood in front of them. "You weren't going to leave without hugging your delivery partner, were you?"

"Umm."

His white bushy eyebrows rose high on his forehead. "My knees got up to say goodbye."

"It seems to me the getting up wasn't the problem, but the sitting back down, if you don't mind me saying," Katrina said.

"And what do you think I'm going to do when you leave?"

"Point taken." She embraced the elderly man who grunted when she tightened her arms around him.

He moved away from her, and put his arm around Chef. "That gal's got arms like vices."

"You asked for it," Chef said.

The brief exchange had been enough for most of the table to stand. A gauntlet of hugs occurred between them and the doorway. When they entered the parking lot, Chef stretched. "Will you give me a few more hours of today?"

"Doing what? Is there an orphanage somewhere you want to visit?"

He indicated his truck in the parking lot. "I'll bring you back when we're done."

She followed him and watched him open the passenger door for her. "The fact that you won't tell me what we're doing means I should say 'no'."

He shut the door, walked around the front of the truck, and sat on the driver's seat. "Your job, if you choose to take it, is keep me awake during the 45 minute drive." He started the engine.

"45-minute drive?"

Trey looked at her and waited. What was 45 minutes away?

Oh.

Her parents.

She sighed. "I don't want to."

"How come?"

"How come? Because being with them is difficult. Christmas was a big deal to Eric, and I don't want to spend it at home without him." Katrina shook her head. "I don't think you have any right to ask me to. You just spent your Christmas with people you work with. Why don't you spend Christmas with your family?"

A smile broke out on his face. "I did."

"What?"

He nodded. "Every one except my other sister who is in Spain presently."

"Maria and Bill?"

"Mom and Dad. Horace is my granddad. Mimi is my granny. Raesch is my brother. Gretel is my sister. Aunt Daphne and Uncle James. Savannah is my other aunt."

"How come nobody said anything?"

He shrugged.

"What did you tell them. Do they know...." She pointed to his chest.

"No. No way. If they knew about that, the little hug fest back there would have been nothing compared to the smothering you would have gotten. I wouldn't have done that to you."

"That's your family?"

"It didn't occur to you?"

"No. My gosh. Maria is your mother? I can't believe it."

"Yep, so we're going, right?"

"No. I.... can't. It's too hard."

"It's not too hard, and I'll come with you. It would mean a lot to your mom. She wanted to hire me to cook Christmas dinner, you know, because she was hoping to get you over there."

"Please, don't ask me to do this."

"Let Eric's heart go back and spend Christmas with your family. Won't that be something?"

The sweet and sad sentiment nearly broke her. She covered her face with her hands. Yes, it was something. It was a big something.

"I'm just not ready for this. It won't be the same."

"Of course not. Nothing ever stays the same. Kyler is married, and Olivia is older. Ava will be there. Her first Christmas. But just like the clouds in the sky and the sand sculptures, change is constant, and that's okay."

"It's not okay. It's not!"

"You didn't die that night," Trey said in that calm manner he had. He had nailed the unspoken pain: Eric had died and had left her alone.

"But I wanted to. I wished I had. Many times." Her eyes burned with unshed tears.

"Would Eric have wanted you to? Would he have wished that you had died too? Let me ask you something. If it had been you, what would your wish have been for him? Would you have wished for him to spend the rest of his life shutting himself off from the world, too sad to celebrate Christmas and go to the beach and laugh and live again, to…love again?

"You don't know what it's like," Katrina said vehemently.

"No. I don't know what it's like to lose someone close to me to death. But I do know what it's like to think each day is my last. To see my parents pray over me each night not sure whether I'd live to see another day. Don't you see, Katrina? You've got today. You won't ever have this day again. Please, can't you find some joy in it? Can't you find something to be thankful for?"

Chapter Twenty

She took a shuddering breath. "Okay. I'll try."

Trey reached over, took her hand, and kissed it. "Thank you."

"Stop thanking me. I am so tired of hearing you say that." She snatched her hand back.

Trey turned the key, and the engine started. "Then you say it."

"Say thank you?" She barked a sarcastic laugh. "All right. Thanks, Trey, for having me in a room full of your family without telling me."

"You're welcome. Say thank you again." He drove out of the parking lot and headed to the highway.

"Thanks for guilting me into going to see my family."

"Just hold that thanks for later when you really mean it. What is something you are really thankful for. Something that happened today?"

Katrina thought through the events of the day. "The food was very good, so thank you for a delicious meal."

"And?"

"Thank you for pairing me up with Horace. He is such a sweetie."

"And?"

"You were never this bossy in Florida."

"So, you're thanking me for being bossy now?"

"No. I suppose I'm thanking you for not being so bossy in Florida. I wouldn't have liked you as much."

"So, thank you for...."

"Thank you for not being so bossy in Florida."

He yawned, and shook his head a bit.

"Should you be driving?"

"I'm okay, as long as you keep me awake by thanking me."

"I wish I could drive us. If you turn around and go back to the restaurant, we could take my car."

"I wish you could drive us, too, but I might need my truck. You never know when you're going to have to carpe diem with a food truck. What else do you want to thank me for?"

"I am thankful for your food truck. Do you still have my picture up?"

"Yes."

"Why?"

"I am thankful for…."

"I am thankful that you didn't tell your family about me having a connection to your heart, and I am thankful you didn't tell me about them. I would have been very nervous."

He smiled and graced her with a warm glance. "I don't think you would have come if you had known your help was going to include sitting down to eat Christmas dinner with my family."

"No, I wouldn't have. Since Eric died, being around families at Christmas time makes me sad."

"What about this morning? Were you sad?"

No, she hadn't been. She looked at Trey, and he glanced at her with a knowing smile. He raised one hand and made a keep going gesture.

"I am thankful that being with your family was enjoyable. It's odd, though, no one told me they were your family."

"I may have asked them to back off on the family endearment so as not to overwhelm you."

They drove for a while until Trey pulled into a gas station.

"What are you doing? It looks closed."

He parked and unbuckled his seatbelt. "I'm just going to go in the back and get something to drink. You want something?"

She shook her head, and he bent down until he was out of the cab. She freed herself from her own restraint and turned to watch him. He opened the freezer and pulled out a small blue bag. Holding it to the back of his neck, he opened the refrigerator and retrieved a bottle of water.

He swigged it then came back into the cab. "Do you want to call your mom and tell her we are on our way?"

"No. If I call her, I can't back out."

Trey snickered. He shifted gears and returned to the road. "What would backing out look like to you?"

"I would say, 'Trey, I can't do it. Please take me back to my car,' and I think you would."

"Yes, I would."

"Even if we were ten minutes away from my parents' house?"

"With some cajoling, yes, I would still take you back."

The knowledge made her feel better, as if she still had the safety net.

"Thank you."

"That's what I'm talking about."

When they arrived, Trey maneuvered the truck into the driveway and parked. He exited the vehicle, came over to her side, and opened the door. They gazed at each other.

Even now, he'd take her back. She knew it. She took a deep breath for courage and stepped out of the car. With her heart thundering in her chest, she walked to the front door. Eric had always been with her. He'd loved Christmas, loved being with her family. They'd always have a pile of presents when they'd entered the house. *Ho, ho, ho*, he'd say as he came in, and Mom would say, *Oh, my, Santa, I always pictured you as much older*. Fear and dread engulfed her, and she stumbled and paused.

She couldn't. No, she couldn't do it.

"I have your back, Katrina."

She realized she was holding her breath.

"Do you want to take my hand?"

She took a deep breath, then another. Reaching her hand behind her, she felt Trey grasp it, his fingers curling around hers.

Okay. Okay. Just walk in.

Katrina stepped forward, then took another step.

The door opened, and Dad stood there. His face lit up. "Katrina! I thought I heard somebody out here. I can't believe it, Sweetheart." He called over his shoulder. "Nan, hey Nan! Got a Christmas present for you at the door!"

"What is it?" Olivia's voice got louder as she ran toward the front. She screamed in glee when she saw her aunt and launched herself at her. Katrina caught her, but would have fallen backward if Trey hadn't been there to steady her.

"Told you," he murmured.

He had her back. Yes. She believed him. It's the only way she could have gotten this far.

They came into the house, and Nan—with apron on— appeared. She blinked a few times, then ran forward and enfolded her daughter in a tight hug.

"Oww. Oww, Granny Nan, you're crushing me," Olivia said between them.

Nan stepped back, her eyes suspiciously watery. "I'm so glad to see you. Have you eaten?"

"Yes. A huge meal."

"Well, that's good, because I'm in the middle of cooking. Ky and Melody won't be here until just before seven. Mary-Kate is trying to help, but Ava is clingy, and it's hard to do anything with a baby in your arms."

"Where'd you get that cool hat, Aunt Kat?" Olivia asked.

"Trey gave it to me. He makes me wear it if I go in the kitchen."

"Looks much better than the towels we were wearing," Olivia said.

Nan went to Trey. She kissed him on the cheek. "Thank you." Putting her arm around his shoulders, she guided him toward the kitchen. "Now, since you're here...."

"No, Mom. Let him sit down and let someone else do the cooking," Katrina said firmly extracting her mother's hands and directing Trey to the living room. "Keith, find something decent for him to watch."

"Hey, sis, and Merry Christmas to you too."

"Aunt Kat, don't you want to see my toys?"

"I suppose, but it sounds like Granny Nan needs some help in the kitchen."

"Hi, Katrina." Mary-Kate greeted her sister-in-law. "I'm so glad you made it. I didn't know you were coming."

"Neither did I." Ava snagged her attention. Already she'd grown and changed since she'd seen her less than two weeks ago.

"Do you want to hold her?"

Yes. Absolutely, she did.

"Oh, come on. Aunt Kat. Can't you give her to someone else and play with me first?" Livie said in a belligerent tone.

"Keith, take the baby," Mary-Kate said.

"She doesn't want me. She cries every time I hold her."

"Why don't you go take a shower and shave? She probably can't stand your horrible whiskers," Mary-Kate snapped.

"It's not my fault I had to stay up half the night and was too tired to shave or shower."

"What'd you stay up half the night for, Daddy?"

Keith looked down at his daughter. Mary-Kate huffed.

"Umm. I was making sure Santa didn't get confused since we were here instead of home."

"Boy, that was dumb. He doesn't come if you're awake."

Keith pursed his lips for a second then opened his mouth to speak.

Mary-Kate elbowed him. "I'm sure what your daddy means is that he was so excited about Santa coming that he had trouble going to sleep." She placed Ava in Keith's arms. "Don't snuggle her to your face, and she won't cry."

"Katrina, after Livie has shown you her toys, come on to the kitchen, okay?" Nan said as she and Mary-Kate left the room.

Katrina sat on the floor with Olivia in front of an elaborate pink plastic doll castle. The little girl chattered as she rearranged the furniture and moved the dolls from room to room. Katrina glanced up at Trey who had settled on the end of the couch. He lifted his hand in a wave, and she smiled in response.

He had her back.

When Olivia decided to play a video game with her Granddad, Katrina headed into the kitchen and was given the task of peeling and shredding potatoes for the casserole. Keith came in and picked up a can of peanuts from the counter. He opened them, flicked the nuts into his hand, then emptied them in his mouth.

"Where's the baby?" Mary-Kate asked.

"I decided to wash up, so I gave her to Trey."

"Trey?"

Katrina had never heard Trey mention his feelings for infants. Had he even ever held a baby before? She strode out of the kitchen and stopped short.

Hunkered down in the corner of the couch, Trey's head was bowed in sleep with baby Eva, also asleep, nestled in the crook of his arms. Reaching into her pocket, Katrina pulled out her cell phone and took several pictures of the sweet scene thinking now she had a picture of her own to cherish.

"Ohhh," Mary Kate whispered next to her. Katrina looked at her sister-in-law. "He's going to be a good daddy."

Katrina pivoted and returned to the kitchen with the other woman at her heels. "Don't get any ideas," she said. Hoping her heart would listen to the advice as well.

With an hour yet to the meal, Ky and Melody still hadn't arrived. Katrina, finished with kitchen duties and conversation, had gone to check on the sleeping beauties and found them exactly as she'd left them. Her heart turned over in her chest as Mary-Kate's words played through her mind. She sat down next to Trey, and he stirred. Katrina reached over to take Ava before Trey inadvertently dropped her. The motion awoke Trey. His eyes opened and grew big as he saw Ava.

Katrina suppressed a chuckle, settling the baby next to her.

Oh, Ava, I hardly know you, and I adore you already.

She glanced up at Trey who was watching her.

"Thank you for bringing me here today." Because Katrina couldn't resist it, she bent and kissed the baby's delicate forehead. "Isn't she the most beautiful thing you've ever seen?"

"Yes," Trey sleep-husky voice agreed.

"Have you ever held a baby before?"

"Not while sleeping." Trey shifted, and Katrina realized he'd slid his arm around her.

It felt cozy, good, comfortable. This was Trey, and she trusted him to be this close to her, to share this moment with her niece.

Mary-Kate strode in the room. "I should feed her. She'll be hungry soon."

When Mary-Kate held her arms out, Katrina leaned away from her. "Why don't you let her eat when she wakes up?"

"Because that will probably be about the time we sit down to eat. Now, come on. Give her up."

Reluctantly, Katrina did so. Thinking Trey would probably wonder why she was still sitting so close, she moved a little further away from the couch.

"Did you have a nice nap?"

He smiled, and Katrina felt something tickle her neck. She glanced behind her and realized Trey had a lock of her hair wound around his finger.

"I didn't mean to fall asleep."

"You said you were tired."

"Want to do something fun before supper?"

"What did you have in mind?"

He shrugged. "We already climbed a tree. Got any ideas?"

Actually, yes, she did. "Would you let me drive your truck?"

"You're supposed to have a Class B license to drive it in this state."

"We could drive it in the mall parking lot. There will be plenty of room there today."

"I love it." Trey stood up. The warmth and joy on his face arrested her breathing. He held his hand out to her. "Let's go."

So, she did.

In the parking lot, she and Trey changed seats, and she drove wide arcs in the parking lot. "This is a breeze. Why do you need a special license to drive?"

Trey cast her a smug look. "Because it's a food truck. You have to be able to park."

"I can park just fine."

"Parallel park."

"I am very good at judging distances. I don't think parallel parking will be that hard."

His smug expression morphed into a cunning one. "Want to have a friendly wager on that?"

"Sure. What's the winner get?"

"If I win, you have to…spend next Christmas with my family again."

Katrina laughed. "Deal, and if I win, you have to deliver a jar of butter peanut butter to me every month for a year."

"Agreed."

Trey went in the back of the truck and retrieved a bag of flour in which he marked the curb of the parking lot delineating the space Katrina had to enter and leave without disturbing the flour. She pulled in, and they examined the area.

Perfect.

She entered the truck again and maneuvered out of the space. When she exited the vehicle to see how she did, a line of flour led from the rear tire to the parking boundary.

She put her hands on her hips and looked at Trey and the bag of flour in the crook of his arm.

"You put that flour there," she accused.

His overly innocent expression didn't convince her.

"You cheater." She strode to him, stuck her hand in the still open bag, stepped back, and flung it at him.

He chuckled. "Oh, you're going to pay for that, Mrs. Aaron." He reached his hand in the bag, and Katrina took off running, screaming for him not to do it.

When her cell phone rang, she called for a time out so she could answer it. Trey used the opportunity to empty the bag of flour on her head.

The call was a summons from her dad for them to come eat as Ky and Melody had arrived.

"Oh, my gosh. What are we going to do? We look like

a couple of ghosts."

Trey shook his body like a dog. "Shake off what you can, then we walk in, and act like nothing's weird."

"You're kidding."

He attempted to brush the flour off his shirt. "I don't think they'll notice if we don't say anything."

"Of course, they're going to notice. Look at us!"

"Well, so what? They're your family. They will still love you. I'm the one who should be worried. I don't have any family ties to fall back on."

"They won't decide they don't like you just because you're covered in flour."

"My point, exactly."

"They might decide they don't like you because you've covered *me* in flour."

He pursed his floury pale lips. "I'll take the chance. Come on. Let's go eat."

Nearing bedtime that evening, Katrina sat on her parents' bed as they looked through family photo albums, including Katrina's wedding album. Looking at pictures of her and Eric didn't hurt as much as it used to. Keith and his family had left to go back home, and Ky and Melody had left as well. When Nan had asked Katrina and Trey to stay the night, they had accepted. Trey had stated he'd sleep in the truck, but he'd been outvoted by Katrina and her parents who had relegated him to the guestroom which had been Ky and Keith's room when they'd lived at home.

"Why don't you take this and show it to Trey? I think he'd really like seeing what Eric looked like."

"Yes, I think you're right."

"I think Trey has been very good for you, and you're good for him."

"We're just friends. Eric's heart. That's our connection."

"You enjoy each other. The trail of flour from the

driveway to the dining room tells me so."

"We were just horsing around. It doesn't mean anything."

"Your horsing around didn't have anything to do with Eric's heart in Trey's chest, Katrina."

"Mom, please don't make this into a...."

"A what?"

"A romance. It's not. It can't be."

"Why not?"

Katrina looked up from the book. "Everything he does for me is because he appreciates that I gave permission for someone to have Eric's organs. He got his heart, so everything he does is about showing me his gratitude."

"I see something in him, Katrina. Something much deeper than gratitude. More powerful and poignant. Don't you see it too?"

"I'm not...." Katrina closed the book and pushed it away from her. "It's hard to be objective. There's so much emotion and feelings. Not just with Trey, but Eric, too. I mean, Mom, I feel like.... I mean, I think I could love him, and maybe I do love him, but what if what I feel is me still loving Eric?"

"A part of you will probably always love Eric, sweetheart. But don't overthink it. If you want to be with Trey, then do it."

"It's not that simple."

"Why isn't it that simple?"

"I can never be sure that Trey would love me for me. I think he would always feel like he owes me, that he'd even love me as an obligation."

"Oh, honey." She reached over and took Katrina in her arms. "How can you not know how beautiful and wonderful you are? That any man would love you for you, including Trey?"

Chapter Twenty-One

She was right next door.

Trey lay on his back with his hands behind his head and stared at the ceiling. Yep, just a thin wall between him and her.

Was she asleep yet? After he'd fallen asleep on the couch and slept for who knows how long, he'd awoken with Katrina sitting next to him and reaching over to take Ava who, to his amazement was tucked in his arms. He didn't even remember picking up the child. Katrina had smiled at the baby, then had looked up at him, the maternal light so bright in her gaze, that it had crossed his mind to propose marriage right then so they could have a baby of their own. Just so he could see her looking at him with the love and joy he'd seen in her.

"Thank you for bringing me here today," she'd said softly, then she'd bent down and kissed baby Ava's forehead. "Isn't she the most beautiful thing you've ever seen?"

He'd wanted to say that her holding Ava was the most beautiful thing he'd ever seen, but he hadn't clarified his affirmative answer.

A light tap sounded on the door. Trey rose from the bed and opened it.

As if he'd conjured her from his thoughts, there stood Katrina, looking all soft and happy. Yes, happy. "Hi."

"Hi." He opened the door wider and stepped back. "Want to come in?"

"No." A crease formed between her eyebrows. "My dad." She shook her head. "He's old fashioned." She gestured for him to come out. "Let's go downstairs. I want to show you something."

Interesting. Her dad would jump to conclusions. Did that mean her dad, at least, thought he and Katrina were more than friends?

Trey followed her downstairs, and she led him to the couch they'd occupied earlier. When they were settled, she placed a large book in their laps with the words "Us" on the front.

"I thought you'd like to see Eric, get to know him a little bit."

She opened the book, and there was a teenage boy and girl in the pictures—posed photographs at a homecoming dance. "He was fifteen. I was fourteen. He and Keith played football together, and Eric didn't have a date, and Keith's girlfriend's father wouldn't let them go alone, so he got Eric to ask me."

"And you said yes?"

"Oh, gosh, yes. I had had a crush on Eric for years." She turned the page. "Here we are at the amusement park. He loved roller coasters. As you can see by my pale face, I did not."

The pictures documented them as they grew older. A picture of them in front of a Christmas tree laughing. Eric had his arm raised above them.

"He's holding Mistletoe. It was the first time he kissed me though we'd been going out since September. I was so nervous, I couldn't quit laughing, and then he started laughing."

He watched her as she smiled at the pictures. Finally, she looked at Trey. "Does he look like you thought he would?"

Trey looked at the book. He'd been so intrigued by seeing Katrina as a young teenager, he hadn't paid much attention.

"I don't know. I never thought about what he might

look like. Since you told me he was a police officer, I guess I mostly pictured him in his uniform."

Katrina turned several pages. "Here he is. This was about a year before we got married. He'd just graduated from the academy." She sighed, but it seemed to be a happy sigh. "He was so handsome in his uniform."

She turned another couple of pages to their wedding pictures. Trey's heart skittered, and he rubbed his chest above his heart wondering if it was him or Eric making his heart palpitate as he gazed at Katrina in a long ivory silk strapless dress dotted with pearls along the bodice. Her hair was curled and pulled up under her veil.

"Katrina, you're the most beautiful bride I've ever seen."

"Thanks."

Eric had worn his dress blues, and they smiled at each other as the minister stood behind them in the church. Other posed pictures showed the wedding party with them at the reception. A series of pictures were taken at Christmas time with Katrina's family.

"This was when Olivia was born. Her first Christmas. Eric insisted he would dress up like Santa even though she was too little to know anything." She traced the picture of Eric in the Santa suit holding baby Olivia. "He said, 'Next year, she'll be big enough to know what's going on, and I'll ho, ho, ho, and I'll tell her what I'm bringing her for Christmas. It'll be so much fun.' He never got to though. He died before the next Christmas."

Trey put his arm around her shoulders and squeezed. "Thank you for introducing me to Eric. I'm glad to see him and know something about him."

"You're welcome. It makes me happy that I can do this."

"Really?"

"Yes."

"Do you mind me saying I'm proud of you coming back here and being with your family today?"

"You didn't give me much choice."

"I would totally have turned around if you'd asked me."

She laid her head on his arm. "I'm glad I didn't. It hasn't been as bad as I thought it would be. I still miss Eric, but, Trey, having you with me, it's made it easier. And I don't think it's because you have his heart."

Trey didn't trust himself to speak.

She was so close. He wanted to kiss her, but should he? What did she need from him? Would it freak her out if he did kiss her?

He wanted to, and for most of his life, he'd grabbed any moment when it presented itself, because he knew another opportunity might never occur. But he loved this woman beside him, and he still had to take her back to her car tomorrow. If she didn't feel the same way he did, he didn't want to make the ride uncomfortable for her.

He'd wait until she gave him a clue she liked him more than a friend, or until another opportunity arose in which he could let her know his feelings without causing her embarrassment or harm.

****

The new year arrived, and with it a resolution to be near Katrina. Trey stood in a downtown storefront with a newly renovated vacant apartment on the second floor. The space was perfect for him if he decided to run his catering business out of a building instead of his truck and the tiny office his parents had provided him at the restaurant in Louiston.

Andy, the realtor, rocked back on his heels. "What do you think?"

"I love it, but the rent is too high."

"You'd be getting the business space and the

residential upstairs."

"I know, but I'm still paying on my truck. I can't do both."

"Get rid of the truck. With the fully furnished kitchen, you have everything here you need."

"Twenty percent of my business is selling food out of that truck. I need it. And part of the attraction of this place, is I've got a garage off the alley big enough to park it securely. So, my question to you is how firm is the rental price?"

Andy shook his head. "I can ask, or we can go look at the Weimer building."

"Ask and—" Trey's cell phone rang. He unclipped it from his holder and looked at the screen.

It was Katrina.

"Excuse me. I need to take this." He ran his finger across the screen, and answered.

"Did I just see your truck downtown?" Her astounded voice greeted him.

"Yes, you did."

"What are you doing here without letting me know? I ate Spaghettios last night."

"If you wanted me to cook for you, why didn't you call me?"

"If I had known you were in town, I would have."

"If you just drove by and you've got a few minutes, turn around and park. I want to show you this building I'm looking at."

In five minutes, Katrina stood beside him. Andy had called the owner who had promised to call back. At Trey's request, Andy took Katrina on a tour of the first and second floors of the building. When Andy's phone rang, he excused himself and walked out of the loft apartment into the small hallway connected to the stairwell.

Katrina folded her arms as she gazed out of the

window. "Gorgeous view. You can see the river from here."

Trey walked up behind her as if he needed to see. He didn't. He'd seen the view before, but he hadn't gotten stand this close to Katrina the last time.

"Are you really thinking about moving here?"

"Yes."

"Why?"

"Three reasons. Location. Location. Location."

She huffed, and moved away from him. "Be serious."

"What makes you think I'm not?"

Her troubled gaze skirted to his then dropped. "It's not because I live here, is it?"

"Would that bother you?"

"Yes, because I think you think you owe me, and you don't. I was hoping we could get beyond this sense of obligation you have."

"Okay. No more obligation. I've been thinking of a permanent place for my business. It's convenient to the business ties I've already made in the tristate area. The chamber of commerce has some sweet incentives for attracting downtown businesses, and I wouldn't have to pay extra for living space. If I can negotiate a reasonable rent, I think this is it. Won't that be great? We'd be neighbors."

As he'd talked, the worried crease between her eyebrows had disappeared. "Do you promise this isn't because you think you owe me?"

He held up his hand as a promise. "It is absolutely not because I think you owe me."

"No. You owe me."

"That's what I said. You owe me."

"I owe you."

"You do? What do you owe me? Spending time with my family next Christmas because you can't park?"

Her eyes narrowed in irritation. "Stop trying to change

the subject. This isn't trying to pay me back, because if there ever was a debt, it's been paid."

"This isn't about your decision to donate Eric's heart. I promise, Katrina."

Her gaze searched his face, as if she weren't sure she could believe him, but he was telling her the truth. He wasn't moving here because he felt obligated to help her for the rest of his life. He was moving here because he loved her, and he was going to see if he could get her to love him back.

He'd recorded it in his life book.

Goal: To get Katrina Aaron to marry him.

Location was important for that goal.

"All right." She smiled at him. "If it works out, it means I can drive your truck."

"Not without a Class B License unless we're in the mall parking lot."

She opened her purse and pulled out a sheet of paper. "You mean, like this?"

Trey peered at the paper, then looked at her happy expression beyond it. "Wow. I just obtained a driver for my food truck."

He stepped toward her to kiss her, but the door opened, and Andy entered. Probably a good thing. Trey had sprung the news on her that they were going to be living within 8 miles of each other. Throwing in a neighborly kiss might be asking too much.

Andy smiled. "The owner is willing to come down $550 a month."

"Six hundred, and I'll sign today."

****

Katrina stared at herself in the foyer mirror. The woman looking back at her wore a dark blue velvet dress with tiny sequins lining the waist. The last time she'd worn it, Eric had taken her to the Christmas ball the department sponsored for needy children. The cost of attending was a new toy valued at $50.

She'd always felt good in the dress, beautiful.

She needed that confidence tonight because she'd asked Trey to take her to the Celebration of Life dinner.

If he'd cajoled her into going, she wouldn't have. But he hadn't even mentioned it. She knew though, he was attending. She'd noticed his calendar on the wall in his new office. He'd exed out the date as unavailable for catering jobs.

When Dinah had dropped off two complimentary tickets for the dinner as she had done the last two years, Katrina had looked at the date. It matched the date on Trey's calendar.

"Do I need to RSVP?" Katrina asked.

Dinah shook her head, her gaze burning into Katrina's.

"Don't get too excited. I'm just thinking about it."

"You do not need to RSVP."

"If I come, I don't want anyone to know who I am."

"It will be your choice if you decide to tell. The donor families and recipients have the same badges."

Trey had invited her over that night to try out some bison he'd bought. They'd sat at the only table in the room. At least fifty candles flickered around the room, and jazz played from the speakers overhead.

"Hope you have fire insurance," she'd said.

"I would have thought the atmosphere would appeal to the romantic in you."

"You know what appeals to me? That you were willing to sit at the same table with me. I need to ask you something."

"All right."

"Are you going by yourself to the Celebration of Life dinner?"

Trey had been about to take a bite of the steak. At her

Jennifer Johnson

question, he carefully laid the fork down, watching his progress as he did it. "No," he said quietly.

Disappointment slammed against her. He was taking a date? Who? He'd only lived here two weeks. Who had he met in that time, and why hadn't he told her?

"My parents are going with me."

"Oh." Relief replaced her anguish. "I was thinking I'd like to go. With you. I have two tickets already. Me, plus one."

"I'll be your plus one, Katrina."

The tender tone in his voice caused her throat to tighten. She swallowed a few times in an attempt to clear it.

"I might change my mind, but right now, I think I want to go."

"It's a date."

The unexpected word jarred her. "It is?"

He sat back, a lazy smile on his face. "Do you want it to be?"

Was he flirting or teasing her? She didn't know. "Umm. Yes, I guess that would be all right."

"Great. The candles weren't wasted then."

The doorbell rang bringing Katrina back to the present. She looked at the image of herself in the mirror. "You can do this," she whispered to herself. "Trey has your back."

Turning around, she opened the door and gasped. "Is that a kilt?"

Trey looked down at himself with a proud grin. "It certainly is. The Marshall Tartan."

"You're wearing a kilt to the dinner?"

"It's a celebration of life. I always wear my kilt to it." He ran his fingers along his matching sash.

"Well, that actually solves a problem for me. Will you put my lipstick, keys, and phone in your purse?"

"What purse?"

Katrina pointed to the pouch hanging below his waist with a merry expression.

"That's not a purse. It's a sporran, and yes I'll carry your stuff."

"What else you got in there?"

"A ring. In case I decide to kidnap you and carry you off to my kin and force you to marry me like my ancestors used to do."

They walked out of the house toward the driveway. "So, your ancestors were so ugly they had to kidnap their brides?"

"Yeah, something like that. Too bad you didn't bring your license. I was going to let you drive."

Katrina held out her hand. "It's taped along with my regular license, a credit card, and a folded fifty-dollar bill to the inside of my phone case. Keys, please."

He placed them in her hand.

"Where are your parents?"

"They're meeting us there. Not enough seats in the truck."

"We could have taken their car or mine."

Trey opened the door for her and held her hand, assisting her as she stepped up into the truck. "We both know you wanted to drive the truck, so don't act like anything else was acceptable."

"I'm going to parallel park, too," Katrina informed him as he joined her in the cab.

"There is a parking lot there."

"I'm going to park at the curb."

"You're a show off."

She graced him with a smile as she cranked the engine. They arrived at the Celebration, held at a hotel and conference center near the airport. Her chest tightened, as they walked down the corridor, directed by the signs. Reaching toward Trey, she took his hand, and he enfolded her fingers within his.

"Still want to go through with this?"

She nodded.

"Not too late to back out."

"You make me think you do have a date already here."

"Just you." He paused and turned to her. Placing his hands on her arms, gazed into her face. "Katrina, if you start feeling like… you need to leave, just tell me, and we'll go immediately. No questions asked."

"Even if we're in the middle of dinner?"

"Even then."

Gratitude filled her. "Thank you, Trey. You're so good to me."

Dinah and another woman sat at a white cloth-covered table inside the door. When she saw them, she rose and walked around the table. She hugged Katrina.

"Welcome. You all are at table one."

"Table one," Katrina said as they traversed the banquet hall. "I don't like the sound of that."

"My dad's speaking, and since we're sitting with them, we get to be up front."

Her startled glance met his calm one.

"No, they don't know, so unless you spill the beans, they won't know."

"Do you want me to tell them?"

"Do or don't, but my mom and dad will make a scene. So, if you want a scene, go for it."

"I'll keep that in mind."

They approached the table, and Bill and Maria were already there, seated with several other people Katrina didn't know. They greeted each other with Maria and Bill hugging Katrina.

"Trey didn't tell us he was bringing you," Maria said, smiling at her.

"I think his other date canceled on him," Katrina

replied.

Bill laughed. "Yeah, right. As if he'd even look—oof." Maria had elbowed him, and he glared at his wife briefly. "Well, anyway, good to see you again, dear."

The other couple stood, and Trey shook hands with the man and hugged the woman. "Katrina Aaron, this is Joe Chambers, his daughter Leslie Buchannan and her husband Perry."

Leslie Buchannan. Where had Katrina heard that name before? She smiled at her, then an image popped in her mind of a small figure made out of a potato.

Oh, my gosh. Leslie had Eric's kidney. One of them anyway.

Trey put his arm around Katrina's waist. She glanced up at him, thankful for the support.

"Let's sit," he said, and with his other hand, he pulled out the chair.

In a daze, she sat through the meal, remembering to eat, remembering to breathe, and aware that Trey carried the conversation with Leslie and the other people at the table. Dinah, who also sat at their table, stood, walked to the podium, and spoke. Katrina attempted to concentrate on her words, but it was as if a haze surrounded her brain. Everyone clapped, and then Bill arose.

Katrina looked down and saw her hands were shaking. She couldn't do this. She needed to leave. Her stomach roiled uneasily. What if she threw up in front of everyone? That would be a way to break up the Celebration of Life, wouldn't it?

Trey leaned toward her until his lips touched her ear. "Are you okay?"

She nodded.

"Are you sure?"

She shook her head.

He moved away, and the coolness of the room made

goose bumps rise on her skin. Trey gazed at her. The kindness in his eyes, the knowing expression there told her he understood, and he had her back.

He gripped her hand, and they stood, moving to the side of the room. He put his arms around her shoulders, and she realized her whole body shook. He opened a door, and Katrina sighed in relief to be out of the room.

"I'm sorry. I'm sorry." She felt tears sting her eyes.

"Don't be. Please. Just being here is a huge thing. You know that, right?"

She shook her head. "I... I need to find a bathroom."

"There's one right here." He indicated a sign beside them.

The door to the banquet hall opened, and Dinah appeared, her face full of concern. "Is everything okay?"

"Yes, she just needed some air."

"I can stay with you, Katrina."

"No. I'll be all right."

Dinah's attention turned to Trey. "Do you think you could go back in there? Your dad wants you at the podium with him."

Trey's eyes never left Katrina's.

"Go on. I'll meet you out here," she said.

He didn't move.

"Do you really want your mom coming after you? Go on... Chef."

He smiled, took the two steps to her, cupped her face, and kissed her sweetly. He disappeared inside the conference room door, and Dinah and Katrina stared at each other. Recovering first, Katrina went into the bathroom and collapsed on a vanity chair.

"Oh, here he comes. Trey, what took you so long?" Bill's voice said.

Katrina looked up at the speaker in the ceiling. The PA system was piped into the bathroom, perhaps so no one would miss anything during a trip to the lavatory.

Chapter Twenty-Two

Bill laughed.

"Now, what was so important that you had to have me come back in here?" Trey said, obviously at the podium next to his dad.

"I wanted everyone to see you, to see this life that someone gave you so that you'd have the chance to live, really live and love and grow old." The older man's voice cracked. "Say something, why don't you, about what the donated heart means to you."

The door opened, and Dinah appeared. By her expression, Katrina knew she had heard the remarks.

I shouldn't be hearing this, should I?

"Hi. My name is William Marshall, but most everyone calls me Trey or Chef. A little over three years ago, I received a heart. I was no longer restrained by the limits of my health. I had told myself if I lived long enough to get a new heart, I'd make each day count, doing all the things I dreamed of doing and even some things I never dreamed of doing so that I could honor the person who let me live by giving me his heart. Each day I would dedicate to that man. Recently, I met someone, and my heart... this heart...showed me a new trick. That I could fall in love and, in a figurative way, give that heart away to someone very special. I have to restrain myself when I'm with her because I want to grab her and say, 'Let's get married. Let's have a bunch of kids. Let's live our lives to honor this guy who let me live long enough to meet you and love you. Now. Right now' But she's had different experiences than I have. She's lost a lot, and some of you know that when you lose a lot, it's very difficult to risk living again. So, my hope is that by this time next year, she'll decide I'm worth risking her heart for, because she's already got this one which was donated to me."

Dinah's hand covered her mouth, and tears fell from her eyes.

"Do you think he's talking about me?" Katrina asked.

"Of course, he is."

Katrina stood, hope falling on her like snow in a blizzard.

"Are you sure?"

"Of course, I'm sure. Don't you see how he looks at you?"

Katrina pushed against the door in an effort to open it. Dinah moved her out of the way and pulled the handle. Katrina ran across the hall to the conference room, entered, and walked toward the front of the room. She knew the second Trey spotted her because a look of unease crossed his face, the first time she'd ever seen the emotion from him.

She strode to the podium. "Excuse me," she said, nudging him out of the way. "My name is Katrina Aaron, and my husband Eric who was a police officer, was killed in the line of duty three years ago. He was." Katrina took a few breaths. "He was a really amazing man, good-hearted, kind, and so loyal. I am sure many of you know Dinah Windingham. I don't remember much about those awful days, but I do remember Dinah's kindness. It seemed a rather simple decision to say yes to donating my husband's organs since the doctor had declared him brain dead. For several years, I felt dead, too, so covered up in my pain and grief. Each year, Dinah would invite me to this, the Celebration of Life, but I couldn't understand anything to celebrate because all I could focus on was what I had lost and what Eric had lost. What we no longer had, and I wanted so bad to hold on to what was gone, to make time stop and cherish those moments when he was alive. And then, someone, an anonymous someone, gave me a gift of time in a beach house. While there, I met Trey, this silly and gifted chef who cooked for me. I didn't know it at the time, but the gift he really gave me was an invitation to live again. To appreciate each day, maybe even each moment as it is before it changes into something new, something different. To live a life of gratitude for what is, and to take risks on the new because it might be fun. It might be pretty wonderful."

She glanced sideways at him.

"Trey, did you know the bathroom is wired with speakers?"

He shook his head.

"I heard every word you said."

His eyes grew round.

"I thought you were joking about having a ring in your purse."

"It's a sporran."

"Is there a ring in there?"

He nodded slowly.

"Is the ring for me?"

He nodded again.

"Just for clarity's sake. You were talking about me, right? You love me?" She gave a brief laugh. "You really love me?"

"I think I've loved you from the first moment I saw you asleep on the couch, but when I knew. When I really knew for sure was when you said you'd seize the day with me and make lunches for the homeless people at Harmony House."

"I will marry you. I would love to have a bunch of kids with you, and I would love to spend the rest of our lives honoring Eric's life by loving each other and sharing his heart that beats in your chest."

Trey grasped her hand and led her a few steps away from the podium. His gaze searched hers. "Are you sure? Katrina, are you sure?"

She nodded her head, a tear of happiness falling down her cheek. "Carpe diem… Chef."

Trey lowered his head and kissed her then embraced her. "I love you. Thank you for loving me back."

"No, I'm thanking you and loving you."

Turning back to the podium, Trey spoke into the microphone. "Is there a minister here?"

"No! No!" Maria joined them, gripping each of them by the arm, tears streaming down her face. "You are not getting married here tonight and deprive me of a real wedding for my eldest son." Pushing Trey aside, she peered at Katrina. "Oh, my darling, my darling Katrina. What you did for us. You saved our child, and now you're going to be my daughter-in-law, but not tonight."

"Carpe diem," Katrina said.

"Oh. What am I going to do with you two?" She grabbed both of them and hugged them. "Bill? Talk some sense into them. Bill?" She looked at her husband. "What are you doing?"

"I'm going to call Reverend Clarence and see if he knows anyone in town who can do it."

"Don't you dare."

"Katrina! Trey!" Dinah sprinted to them, her face alight with joy. "Melanie Glen is here. She's a minister, and her husband is the county clerk. She said she'd marry you right now, and her husband is emailing a marriage license to the front desk of the hotel for them to print out. If you really want to get married tonight, we can make it happen."

Epilogue

Katrina sat back on her haunches and surveyed her work.

"Hey, where'd you go?" Trey called to her from the back patio of the beach house where they'd first met. "Lunch is ready."

"Come here. I want to show you something," she called back.

He stepped off the wooden stair and traversed the sand. "You're sand sculpting? Why didn't you wait? I want to help." He came to stand near her, giving her a hand up then catching her in his arm, pulling her next to him.

"Can you tell what it is?" She asked.

"Yeah, it's a bird."

"What kind?"

He crooked his head studying her creation. "Egret."

"No, it's a stork. See the bundle hanging from his beak?"

Trey shook his head. "Storks have deeper beaks, so they can carry fish in them."

"Or babies."

"Yeah."

"Or a baby, Trey. Or a baby Trey."

He turned to her with a hopeful expression. "Are you?"

She laughed and nodded.

He picked her up and swung her around in his arms. "This is so awesome." Setting her down, he kept his arms around her. "We're going to have a baby. When?"

"October, I think. We will really have something to celebrate at the Celebration of Life next year: our one-year anniversary and a new baby."

"I love you so much. Thank you for making me a dad."

Katrina smiled up at her husband. "You're welcome."

The End

About Jennifer Johnson

The Greatest Love Story.... Has been and continues to be God's amazing love. This story continues to be written every day of my life. I hope that in my books and in my work that I demonstrate my deep gratitude for that love. I write romantic fiction and Inspirational Romance. Find out more at **www.booksbyjenniferjohnson.com**.